Blessed

KD Fraser

Dawn of the Zodiacs

Libra Blessed

(A Dawn of the Zodiacs Novel)

KD Fraser

Copyright © 2024

KD Fraser All rights reserved

This work of fiction is intended for mature audiences only.

The characters and events portrayed in this book are fictitious. Any similarity to real persons, living or dead are entirely coincidental.

KD Fraser asserts the moral right to be identified as the author of this work.

No part of this book may be reproduced, or stored in a retrieval system, or transmitted in any form or by any means, electronic, mechanical, photocopying, recording, or otherwise, without express written permission of the author. No part of this book may be used to create, feed, or refine artificial intelligence models, for any purpose, without express written permission from the author.

It is illegal to copy this book, post it to a website or distribute it by any other means without permission.

Cover design: Mythical Worlds Publications

For anyone who accidentally made a baby after reading this.

Preface

This book is a dark paranormal why choose romance with male/male intimacy. There are several TWs listed on the next page. If there is anything on that list that makes you uncomfortable, I ask that you refrain from reading.

Your mental health is more important than this book. I promise.

If you read the TWs and decide that this book is for you, I hope you enjoy it. And if you enjoy it, I hope you leave a review.

KD

Content Notice

- Breath play

- Breeding contract

- Bullying (by one of the MMCs as well as by other people)

- Death of a loved one (on page)

- Foster care

- Graphic violence

- Gun violence

- Impact play

- Kidnapping

- Knife play

- Light Stalking

- Masochism

- Mind control for the purpose of killing, and sex

- MM relationships Insta lust/love

- Noncon somnophelia (By an MMC)

- Parental drug use (mentioned briefly)

- Parental death (not on page)

- Pregnancy (epilogue)

- Primal Play

- SA (on page and off)

- Sex work

- Talk and attempts of breeding

- Withholding of birth control as a method of controlling the FMC

If you find one that I missed, please feel free to reach out and let me know on: authorkdfraser@gmail.com

Prologue

A long time ago, when the universe was first born, so were the Constellations, beings of great power who watched over the universe. The Dark Ages brought around the time of the supernaturals and unleashed magic across the universe.

The Constellations watched as Earth's inhabitants abused their newfound power, causing a rift to open many light years away–a speck at first that grew larger until it consumed the very stars around it. The Constellations knew if Earth's inhabitants didn't stop their misuse, the rift would consume everything.

A prophecy was released telling those on Earth that if they did not change, then twelve Zodiacs would be born to make the change for them. But those with power were greedy. They refused the prophecy and instead twisted it for their own nefarious purpose, pushing it on the masses in its' bastardized form to suit their version of the future and secure their power.

No one, not even the Constellations would take what was theirs, and thus the true prophecy was lost to all but a few, leaving only the twisted version in its place:

At the dawn of an era
Twelve Zodiacs will rise
Swiftly and fiercely
They will change the tides

The divines have bestowed
The daughters with power
They come for your children
To destroy and devour

Hear the call of their magic
Hear them cry and decree
The dawn of the Zodiacs is here
No one is safe, no one is free

Chapter One

Jinx

Thud! Thud! Thud! Thud! My knee-high black combat boots hit the pavement. I'm going as fast as I can, slowing only as I round the corner of the building. My long green hair whips behind me, and the chill of the autumn air stings my face. The footsteps behind me are gaining. *I'll be damned if that fucking pig catches me tonight.*

"Keep up, Linnie!" I hiss at Elolyn, my familiar.

Her wings beat at an impossible speed to keep up, much like a hummingbird. "I'm doing my best!" she chirps.

"Stop running!" the cop behind me commands.

"Over my dead body!" I murmur.

Ahead there is a chain link fence—about twelve feet high—blocking my escape. That won't be a problem for me though. I break into a sprint, and bring my elemental powers to the surface. I'm closing in-twenty feet, fifteen, ten, five. Air energy erupts from my hands, pushing me off the ground, and allowing me to glide over the fence.

I land, superhero-style, on the other side and hang a left. The fence will slow the cop down but it won't stop him entirely. Linnie cackles in celebration of my success. I spare a smug glance over my shoulder. The cop is staring back at me through the fence with his arms crossed over his chest. The smug look on his face mirrors my own. *Why did he stop?* And then I collide with something hard, and bounce backward onto my ass.

"What the hell!" I shriek.

A man—a second cop—lunges on top of me and forces me face down on the ground. His heavy weight is sitting on top of my ass as he holds the side of my face down against the pavement of the filthy alleyway, gravel digging into my cheek.

"Geroffme!" I slur out.

It's too late.

The cold metal handcuffs encircle my wrists followed by the telltale clicking of them being locked into place. The unobtainium alloy in the cuffs renders my powers useless. He pulls my ID out of my small cross body bag, not bothering to remove his weight from my back. My knees and face sting from the mild brush burn I have from being tackled. I squirm beneath him, trying to free myself.

He chuckles. "You'll have to do better than that if you wanna escape. Jinx Monroe, you're under arrest for prostitution. Anything you say can and will be used against you. You have the right to an attorney. If you cannot afford one, one will be provided to you. Do you understand your rights as I have read them to you?"

"Yes, I understand, now get off of me, pig!"

He stands and aggressively hauls me off the ground, then spins me around to face him. My breath hitches. He's got at least six inches on my five foot eight frame. His expression is stoic, but he has laugh lines decorating the corners of his sparkling blue eyes. He has blonde hair in a crew cut, and a neatly trimmed beard that perfectly accentuates his full lips.

A tattoo of bright colorful swirls cascades down his right arm forming a galaxy. My gaze roams over the corded muscles of his arms, then back up to his eyes. *Of course I would get arrested by officer hottie while I was pimping myself out to some weasley tax accountant.*

"Why did you have run?" he asks with a raised brow as if I've inconvenienced him in some way.

"Because officer—" I glance at his name plate "Campbell, I don't relish the idea of spending the night in a cell."

"It'll be more than a night," he says as he grabs me by the bicep and spins me away from him. "Let's go."

"Yes, sir," I sass.

His grip on my arm tightens, making me hiss in pain, but I don't complain. Linnie is following nearby, invisible. She's a Sylph–an air spirit–when she's not invisible, she's blue, and her skin shimmers. She has pure white eyes, and white hair. Her wings are fragile and thin like a dragonfly's. I'm the only one who can see her when she's like this; when she's camouflaged with the air. She's been with me for ages, and I don't know where I would be without her.

"Does this get-up work for you?" Officer Hottie asks a hint of condescension in his tone.

Even without looking, I can feel his gaze roaming down my body, and I purr, "I don't know. Does it work for *you*?"

"Shut up," he says, but his words lack any bite.

It would seem that my knee high combat boots, pleated black mini skirt, black bra, mesh shirt, and cropped leather jacket *do* work for him. I don't hide my smirk.

Guys like him always act like they want a pretty little blonde to take home to mommy and daddy, but most of them would give their left nut for a night with me. Which is how I make all my money. I toss my long green hair over my shoulder as best as I can without access to my hands, and give him a seductive grin.

His partner finally catches up to us, having taken the long way around rather than scale the fence. "You're in better shape than I expected," he says, catching his breath at the end of the alleyway.

His name plate reads Sullivan. He's handsome too, in a very boy next door kind of way. He has black hair, and lightly tanned skin. I chew my lip, taking in his brilliant smile.

"I promise that my stamina is the least surprising thing about me," I say with a wink.

"Stop it!" Campbell hisses in my ear.

"You're no fun." I stick out my bottom lip.

He flicks my lip with his middle finger—hard. "I'm not supposed to be. Now move."

"Ow! Fucker!" I growl. "I would break your fingers if my hands were free."

He chuckles and a dark look settles over his face, "I'd like to see you try, Buttercup."

The promise in his voice is enough to make me squirm. But I get the feeling he's all bark and no bite. Something about him is screaming that he's a softie at heart.

They flank me on the way back to the car, but Campbell is the only one who puts his hands on me. I consider several times if I can maneuver out of his grasp. This is my first offense, and I might get off light if I don't mess around. The risk isn't worth it. Besides, I kind of like having his hands on me.

Campbell shoves me into the backseat with unnecessary aggression, and reaches over me to buckle the seat belt.

"You smell good," I say with a sultry voice.

"Stop talking."

"Make me," I challenge.

He grabs my chin and stares into my eyes as if he's considering *making me*. He abruptly releases me and slams the door before he takes the driver's seat. Sullivan slides into the passenger seat and radios in that they've got me in custody and they're bringing me to the station for processing.

"You look clean for a pro," Sullivan says, casually.

"Personal hygiene has always been important to me," I mutter.

"You also look familiar. Where do I know you from?"

I shrug. Not that he can see me. I don't want to tell them that he's likely seen me shaking my naked titties on the stage at The Naughty Nebula. I'm not embarrassed about my job, but men look at me differently if they know about my jobs.

"Just one of those faces," I say dismissively.

They escort me into the jail and straight to booking.

Fingerprints.

Photos.

Paperwork.

"Murph, you got time to get this one set up in a cell?" Campbell asks another officer once the basic stuff is handled. "I'll be back to finish her booking paperwork, but we've gotta get back on the beat."

"I always have time for the pretty ones," he says, flashing a predatory smile that makes my hair stand on end.

"Thanks, man. I owe you," Campbell says, clapping 'Murph' on the back.

The new officer's name plate reads 'Murphy'. He's a big dude with a bald head and a goatee. He places a jumpsuit on top of my cuffed hands and escorts me down a long hall to a private room. There's a large table and two chairs across from each other. It looks like an interrogation room.

"Strip search," Murphy says.

"What?" I gasp.

"Protocol." He smirks, crossing his arms over his chest.

"This is a first time offense, and a female officer should be conducting the search," I argue.

He moves into my space. "Are you resisting?"

"I'm telling you that if you make me do this, I will ruin you."

"Oh, come on. You get naked out there all the time. I've seen you down at the club shaking your ass for money. You can take your clothes off for me."

"No. There's a difference. At the club, I'm getting paid."

He grabs the back of my neck and squeezes. "Just another whore."

He grabs the hem of my skirt and yanks it down, exposing my caged bikini underwear. He spins me around and forces me face down on the desk, bending me over, and ripping my underwear down.

"Stop!" I scream.

"All you hookers are the same. You act like you don't like it, but you do it for money. Meanwhile men like me are out here making a decent living that could easily provide for you, and you don't pay us any attention."

The sound of a zipper has me flailing beneath him. I feel him at my entrance. Tears are spilling down my cheeks when the door clicks open.

"Hey Murph—what the fuck?!" It's Campbell.

"Close the fucking door!" Murphy says, but he doesn't move away from me.

Campbell lunges across the room and punches Murphy in the face, sending the big bald man to the floor. He approaches me, and without asking, pulls my underwear and my skirt back up and puts himself between me and Murphy who's now back on his feet.

"Get out of here, Murphy," Campbell says.

"The fucking skank wanted it," Murphy roars, advancing on Campbell and pulling his gun from his holster.

Lucky for us, Campbell is faster.

Pop!

Loud ringing takes up residence in my ears thanks to the gun going off in an enclosed space. Murphy drops to the floor, a bullet in his head. Within seconds three more officers are swarming into the room. They pull their guns on Campbell who holds his hands up in the air before putting his gun on the floor gently.

He locks eyes with his partner and says, "Midnight came too soon, Sully."

"What the fuck does that mean?" A female officer says.

Time seems to slow as a male officer grabs me by the shoulders and escorts me out of the room. My eyes land on Campbell's. His jaw is clenched tight as his gaze falls on where the officer's hands lay on my skin. *Is he mad at me?*

My stomach churns, and I fight the urge to vomit on the shiny black shoes of the female officer as I'm pulled out of the room. My life has not been sunshine and roses by any stretch of the imagination. There have been long nights on park benches, and days where I went without food. I am no stranger to death. The streets take people from you all the time when you live like I do. But this is the first time someone was shot in front of me. It was so much more violent than I expected, but what I wasn't prepared for was the peaceful quiet that followed.

The officer guides me down the hall a little ways and positions me with my back against a wall before returning to the interrogation room. I vaguely heard him say 'stay here' when he left, but that wasn't necessary. I am in no shape mentally to try to leave. I lean my back against the wall and slide down to the floor. Linnie's weight plops down on my lap. Her presence is comforting while I process what I just saw.

"Monroe!" someone shouts, but they sound so far away–like they're underwater.

"Monroe!" the distorted voice calls one more time as black boots appear in front of me.

I lift my eyes to find Sullivan standing in front of me. He grabs me by the arm and hauls me to my feet. His gaze darts up and down the hall before landing back on me.

"Come on. We need to get out of here."

"What?" My brow furrows.

"We need to go. I'm getting you out of here."

"Why? Where are you taking me?"

The shock gives way to fear. *Is this guy kidnapping me?*

He leans in and whispers. "I don't have time to explain, but I know what you are. Now hurry. We need to go before the captain gets here and you end up stuck here behind a bunch of red tape."

I nod.

He grabs my hand and pulls me further away from the room—away from Campbell. I only hope that I'm not making a terrible mistake.

Finally, Sullivan is dragging me out a side door, back into the crisp autumn air. The last bit of shock clears my head as he leads me into a parking garage.

"Where are we going?" I ask. The cool air hits my sweat-slicked skin and makes me shiver.

Sullivan pulls his jacket off and drapes it around my shoulders as he says, "We're going to a safe house. We need to do whatever we can to make sure we can't be found."

He keeps a constant watch around the garage as we make our way to a vehicle that's parked in the deep shadows of a dark corner of the garage. He unlocks a black sedan with windows tinted far beyond the legal amount. I reach for the back door, but he places his hand on mine and stops me. My eyes drift up to his handsome face. My confusion is probably written all over my face.

"You're not a prisoner anymore, Jinx, you can ride up front."

I hop in the passenger seat, and buckle up. Within a minute we're out of the parking garage and flying through the city at unsafe speeds. Sullivan weaves in and out of what little traffic there is on a Tuesday at two a.m. and twenty minutes later the lights and sounds of the city give way to trees and stars.

My nerves get the best of me. "Won't you get in trouble for taking me?"

"I've been preparing for this day for a long time. I always knew it would come to this."

"Come to what?"

"We'll explain more later, once we're all together."

"Who's we?" My stomach is doing somersaults.

"Well, me and Camp, and a handful of others."

"You're being really vague, and I'm freaking out. What is going on?" I put my hand on the door handle and prepare to jump out of the car—moving or not.

"We need to protect you at all costs."

"Why?" I snort. "Because I'm a witch? Supes get arrested all the time and you don't go through these lengths for them."

Sullivan angles the car off the road and slams on the brakes, stopping so hard that I lurch forward in my seat. He inhales deeply and faces me.

"Do you know what you are?"

"Yes. A witch. I *just* said that."

"What else?"

My head cocks to the side. "A...mid range call girl? A stripper? Did you finally remember why I looked familiar?"

"You're safe with me. You don't have to play dumb."

"I'm not dumb but I'm also not playing. I have no idea what you're talking about."

"You're The Zodiac—the Libra specifically."

Chapter Two

Campbell

My hands are held high in the air in faux surrender. If this goes south, I can get myself out, but I don't want it to come to that. I've grown to like these people. Using my foot, I slide my gun across the floor to my fellow officers. My gaze meets Jinx's, and then falls to where Blake has his hands on her. I grind my teeth so I don't do anything stupid. No one should be touching the Zodiac; especially after she was just attacked.

The second my eyes landed on her in the alleyway, I knew there was something special about her—and not just the fact that she's smoking hot. I could sense her power before I even made physical contact with her. I should have checked her before we brought her in. But I probably wouldn't have found her Libra mark. I wouldn't have violated her like that. It had to happen this way.

"What the fuck happened Campbell?" Redd demands. She's a scary woman, and one of my best friends. Although...she won't be for much longer. I've been lying to her for years.

My gaze drops to where Murphy lies dead on the floor, his cock still hanging–now limp–out of his pants.

"He tried to rape the girl and when I threatened to tell the captain, he pulled his gun on me. I shot to stop the action."

"Jesus H tap dancing Christ," Vick says. "I told him he was going to get in trouble for that one day."

Redd and I both turn our attention to Vick, and Redd holsters her gun.

"What the fuck do you mean by that? This wasn't the first time?" I demand.

Vick pales.

"You *knew?* You knew he raped female inmates and you didn't do anything to stop him?" Red roars, advancing on him.

"I thought it was common knowledge. I thought that's why you asked him to take the girl back to her cell. Neither of you knew about it?" he sputters out.

"No we didn't fucking know about it!" Redd shouts and punches the steel door.

"Hey, calm down," I say, stepping toward her, and placing a gentle hand on her shoulder.

"I had inmates tell me that he assaulted them and I didn't believe them, Camp!"

"There's nothing that can be done about it now, except to learn from it and move forward," I say. I know exactly how she's feeling, but we don't have time to dwell on it.

Redd nods and sighs. "It's just going to be a lot of paperwork. And probably a sizable lawsuit against the city."

"If it doesn't get swept under the rug," I mutter. "How far out is the captain? I want to give him my statement and go home."

"I'll check with Blake. He was going to call the captain after he got the girl out of the room."

Redd ducks out of the room, leaving me alone with Vick. *Weaselly little shit.*

"You're not going to tell the captain that I knew, are you?"

"You gonna shoot me if I say I'm going to? I still have my taser, just so you know."

"Please don't tell him. I don't need another write up right now."

Tense silence fills the air between us for several minutes before Redd steps back into the room.

"We have a problem," she says.

"Aside from the fact that I shot one of our coworkers for being a sleazeball?"

"The girl is gone. So is Sullivan."

"*What?!*" I roar in feigned surprise. "How did this happen?"

"Blake left her in the hall to go call the captain, and when he came back they were gone."

"Why would he leave her unattended?"

I try to shift the focus of the conversation onto someone other than my partner. But it doesn't matter. He's gone; so is she. Even if he was able to scramble the camera feed, they'll have to connect the dots eventually.

"He's green. Thought she was 'too in shock to go anywhere'. So he just left her there."

"Idiot," I mutter.

"Why would Sullivan take her?"

So much for taking the heat off of him. "I have no idea. He had a soft spot for her in the car. Maybe he felt bad after what happened, and he decided to take her home."

"That's against procedure."

I shrug. "You know he's not a bad guy."

He's not. Sully's one of the most outstanding guys I know. He's smart, and kind, and wouldn't hurt anyone who didn't earn it. And he did exactly what he needed to.

The captain strolls into the room."Fucking stars above, Camp. What the hell? Get out of the room. CSU is on their way. We have to do this by the books. My office. Now!"

I follow him out of the room and to his large office. He shuts the solid oak door behind me and gestures for me to sit across from him.

"What happened?"

Starting from when we arrested Jinx during the sting operation, I fill him in on all the details, ending with, "And Vick knew about it!"

The captain scrubs his hand down his face and sits back in his high backed office chair. "These dirty fucking cops are ruining everything. Whatever happened to protect and serve? This force is a farce." He pauses before groaning and saying, "I'm going to have to do so much paperwork. There's going to be an IA investigation. I can't believe this was happening right under my nose, and I didn't know about it. As far as I'm concerned this is a clean kill. Go home and get some rest. We'll handle the rest in the morning. Expect a suspension until the thing is handled. And don't leave town, Camp"

"Yes, sir!" *No sir.* He doesn't know that Sully took Jinx, yet. And I need to get out of here before he finds out.

Moving as fast as I can without drawing attention, and avoiding eye contact with any of my fellow officers, I head for the exit. I need to get out to the safe house immediately. I *need* to make sure that Jinx is okay. From the second I laid eyes on her I felt an overwhelming need to protect her, but I talked myself out of it. I told myself that it was just because I thought she was cute. But now I know that my urge to protect her was because of our link through the Zodiac.

Letting Sully drive her feels like a mistake. Not because I don't trust him, but because I won't be there in case something happens. She's *our* responsibility, not just his. And now I'm behind them, and he's going to have to handle any potential threats alone. But this was the plan we put into place. We discussed every possible scenario. If either of us was unable to go with her, the other would have to take her alone.

Sliding into the driver's seat of my car, I speed out of the city, hopeful that I can get to the safehouse shortly after them. I begin making the calls to the rest of The Believers. We need to make sure that we have someone with her at all times.

The phone rings three times. "Hello?" Layna's sultry voice filters through the car's speakers.

"We found her."

Chapter Three

Jinx

"I think I would know if I were some evil daughter of mayhem. What are you even doing with me then? Are you going to kill me?" I snap at Sully and reach for the door handle. Again.

"No!" he shouts and slams on the locks. "You're not evil. Let me explain. Please. The prophecy that the Council has pushed all these years is wrong. You're *not* evil. All of that 'destroy and devour your children' crap isn't in the real prophecy. The real one is:

At the dawn of an era

Twelve Zodiacs will rise

Swiftly and fiercely

They must change the tides

The divines have bestowed

The daughters with power

To right that which is wrong

To destroy all who devour

Hear the call of our magic

Awaken in our time of need

The dawn of the Zodiacs is here

To undo the faults of your greed

After a long pause he continues, "You're meant to save the world. The Council are the evil ones. They're siphoning the magic and creating a tear in the universe that's going to destroy all of us if you don't accomplish your ascension by the end of the Winter Solstice."

"So you're a looney tune. Got it. Please let me out."

"Please just come to the safehouse with me. Camp can explain all of this so much better than I can. He should be the one taking you. Not me. I know this must sound insane, but it's the truth. And if we found you, so can they. If they get their hands on you, they'll kill you."

When I don't respond, he sighs and says, "Look, it's either come with me or go back to the jail, and I tell them you ran off so I had to go catch you."

"You wouldn't," I say, narrowing my eyes. But I can see in his eyes that he means it. I do *not* want to go back there. I hate being caged. A shiver runs through me, and images of Murphy's brains splattering across the wall make me cringe. I especially don't want to be caged *there*.

"Fine." I pout.

"Good girl. Stay right here. I gotta change the license plate, and get out of this fucking uniform."

"Are you sure? It kinda works for you," I say with a smirk.

He snorts. "Well maybe I'll wear it for you later, but for now, it's gotta go."

He pops the trunk and steps into the crisp clear night. He darts around the back of the car, and rifles around back there for a minute. The trunk slams shut. When he doesn't come back right away, I shift the rear-view mirror so I can see what's going on.

The moon reflects off of the tattooed skin of his muscular chest and abdomen. He's not as ripped as Campbell, but he's still in great shape. He tugs his pants on first, then pulls his shirt over his head. His dark hair glints in the moonlight.

He's a fine specimen, Linnie says.

He's certainly something, I mutter back. *Shit, he's coming back.*

I try to put the mirror back to where it was, but I wasn't paying attention when I moved it. I can already feel the heat rushing to my cheeks. *Why am I embarrassed?* I never get worked up over this kind of stuff.

He gets back into the driver's side. My face remains stoic, pointing out the windshield. In my periphery, I see him frown as he glances at the mirror, and adjusts it. He gives me a curious look, but doesn't say anything.

I lean my head against the window and watch the shadows of the trees pass us by. Linnie's weight settles onto my shoulder, and she lays her head against my neck, the cool calm of her connection spreading through me. She hates when I'm distressed.

Forty five minutes into our drive, we come up on an exit with all the usual amenities. There's a Denny's, and a couple of gas stations, and a truck stop.

"You hungry?" Sullivan asks.

"A little," I say, and that's an understatement.

I haven't eaten since breakfast around one p.m. I worked a slow afternoon at the club, then was out on the street immediately after. My stomach growls at the thought of a burger.

Sully raises an eyebrow and glances at me.

"Okay, I'm starving."

With a chuckle he puts on his turn signal and heads off the exit. We opt for the truck stop since it looks less busy. We pull into a parking space toward the back of the diner portion of the building.

"I don't have any clothes for you. I wish we had some way to make you less...conspicuous," he says, gaze traveling down my body.

I snort in amusement and pull my magic to the surface. My hair goes from green to brown, my goth makeup disappears, and my clothes shift to jeans and T-shirt. Or at least that's how they appear to Sullivan.

His eyes widen. "Okay. That's useful."

"Witch, remember? It's just an illusion so if anyone touches me they'll know that this isn't what I'm actually wearing, but I generally don't let people get close enough to touch me unless I'm working."

He gives me a crooked grin and slides out of his side of the car. I tug on the handle but it's still locked. I roll my eyes as he opens my door for me.

"Scared I'll run?" I ask.

"No. I just wanted to be a gentleman," he says, holding his hand out and waiting for me to take it.

Call girls like me don't really ever provide the girlfriend experience unless a guy is trying to piss off his family. And in those situations they're very rarely a gentleman. Guys like Sullivan, and Campbell would fuck me and then never give me another look.

"I've got it," I grumble and elbow him out of the way as I stand up out of the car.

"Of course you do," he mutters and slams the door behind me.

He doesn't bother to open the door to the building for me, and I appreciate him not making me feel awkward again. It's late enough that there is no hostess, so we seat ourselves at a booth in the corner.

A chipper blonde waitress practically skips to our table within seconds of us being seated. Since it's so late, the only other patrons are a couple of truckers sitting at a bar.

"Hi! I'm Marcella. What can I get you folks to drink?" the waitress asks with a blinding smile of straight white teeth. She doesn't even look up from her notepad as she takes our orders.

"I'll have a cola," I say.

"Water for me," Sully says.

"I'll be right back," she says and struts away.

Shifter, Linnie links to me, telepathically as if I didn't already pick up on that.

She may look like a normal twenty something waitress, but she's not. She's some type of shifter. Probably a wolf.

Once she's back in the kitchen, I lean in toward Sully. "I'm not the only supe here."

"I know," he says casually.

My brows furrow. "How?"

"First of all, I can see your familiar–a Sylph, right? Second, I'm not human—not strictly speaking anyway. And third, I can sense other supes just like you can."

I blink slowly, processing all of that. The waitress returns to the table, puts our drinks down, and pulls her notepad out of her apron pocket.

"What can I get ya?" she asks.

"Burger, medium, swiss cheese, lettuce and tomato, hold the pickle. For sides, I'll have fries, and coleslaw."

"You got it. And for you?"

Her gaze settles on Sully, and her eyes widen as if she's just seeing him for the first time. She made him—whatever he is. I'm annoyed that I didn't pick up on his magic. It makes me even more curious about him.

"Chicken tenders and french fries," he says with a smile as if he doesn't have a care in the world. She bounces away to the computer to put the order in.

"Should I be worried?"

"About Marcella? No. She's harmless."

"No, I mean about you. What are you?"

"An Icarast."

"A what? And how did she know?"

"She doesn't know *what* I am, but shifters can smell the sweet scent of my blood. She knows I'm a supe. My turn to ask questions. Why are you out there turning tricks?" he asks bluntly, completely ignoring my first question.

I sit back in my seat to put some distance between us. "That's not really your business."

"Come on. You're pretty and smart. You sound well educated. Why are you out there selling yourself."

"That's a very personal story for when we know each other better."

"*When?*" His voice drops to a sultry tone. "You want to get to know me better, little witch?"

A blush creeps up my neck. "I just meant...we're going to be spending a decent amount of time together so maybe in the future..."

"Mhmm," he says skeptically, sipping on his water.

"So an Icarast?"

"Half angel."

My mouth pops open and a laugh escapes me. I knew the term sounded familiar. They're just extremely rare. "Seriously?"

"Yup," he says with a smirk. "I'll show you my wings sometime if you'd like."

My knowledge of the angel race is limited to the small section that was dedicated to it in school. There was something about them being descendants of Hera, but I don't remember the rest.

"Yeah, maybe." Is all I can think to say in response to him 'showing me his wings'.

Marcella drops off our food and leaves us to eat. I close my eyes and a groan escapes me when I bite into it. When I open my eyes again, Sully is staring at me, french fry halfway to his mouth, green eyes wide.

"Do I have something on my face?" I reach for my napkin.

"No. Not at all," he mutters and continues eating.

We eat in relative silence, Sully stealing glances at me from time to time over his plate of food. After the fourth or fifth time my curiosity gets the better of me.

"Why do you keep looking at me like that?" I ask with a raised eyebrow.

"It's nothing," he says, and waves his hand dismissively.

When the check comes, he puts forty dollars down on the table, stands, and offers me his hand to help me out of the booth. This time I accept. I expect him to let go, but instead he laces his fingers with mine and leads me out of the building. I don't fight him. It's been ages since a man wanted to just hold hands with me.

We round the corner, walking back to where his car is parked, and he pins me to the wall, stealing the breath from my lungs. He stares into my eyes, a silent question. I don't push him away. When I let my magic drop to reveal my true self to him, a growl erupts from his throat and his mouth lands on mine.

His hand creeps up to cup my jaw, his thumb stroking my chin, as he seeks entrance to my mouth with his tongue. After long seconds, he slows the kiss and pulls back.

"I'm sorry. I shouldn't have...you've been through a lot today," he says.

"Don't apologize." I say. "Welcomed physical contact is just what I needed."

He gives me a sad smile.

"Don't pity me," I say, anger flaring in me.

"I don't. I just feel guilty. We shouldn't have sent you with Murphy. It was lazy, and it almost got you..."

A car pulls into the parking right next to where we stand, and we break contact. Campbell steps out of the car when it's barely stopped moving. He rushes over and grabs me by the chin and begins looking me over.

"Are you okay? I'm so sorry. I'm so fucking sorry." He pulls me into his arms and rests his chin on my forehead. "I didn't know..."

I push him away gently. "I'm fine. Or I will be. I need to get some sleep."

He takes stock of how close Sullivan is. "What were you two doing?"

"Uh..."

"Just making out a little," Sullivan deadpans with a challenge in his eye.

A muscle feathers in Campbell's jaw. The two silently stand off with one another, Campbell's arm still wrapped firmly around me; a little *too* firmly.

"You're kind of squishing me," I say.

"You're with me, Buttercup. Hop in and buckle up. I'll be right there." He tosses me the keys.

I step away from him and glance at Sullivan with a questioning look. He gives a small jerk of his head, telling me to go ahead. I step over to the car and glance at the guys one last time before getting inside.

Campbell advances toward Sullivan, and pokes a finger into his chest. Sullivan snaps back and they both begin gesturing wildly, shouting at each other.

Causing trouble already, Linnie laughs in my head. *You've always had quite the effect on men, but this is impressive even for you.*

Shut up, I link back. *Do you trust them?*

I can't get a read on them, but I think they're okay. Then again I didn't peg the short one as a supe.

Me either.

Which one do you like better?

I don't answer her. I just watch their argument continue. Eventually, Sullivan rubs the back of his head and throws his hands up in the air before stalking away to his car and getting inside. I watch him drive away and hope he's not mad at me.

Campbell scrubs both hands over his face and stares at the sky before he finally returns to his car. He turns the car on and whips out of his parking spot and pulls out onto the road.

"Everything okay?"

"Fine."

"It doesn't feel fine."

He grinds his teeth. "You were just doing what you do best."

The comment catches me off-guard. I close my eyes and take a deep breath. "You don't need to attack me and my profession because you got your ego bruised or whatever."

"You're the Daughter of Libra. You're not supposed to be—"

"To be what? Doing whatever I can to survive with the hand I was dealt? You know nothing about me. And as far as your weird culty 'Daughter of the Zodiac Savior of the Universe' bullshit, you can shove it up your ass. I want to go home."

"It's not a cult. And going back is no longer an option."

"What do you mean?"

"With Sully and I going off grid, it'll spark an investigation into why we both went AWOL from the force following the death of an officer, and absconding with a prisoner. They have your name, your address, your phone number...Soon they'll know where you work and who all of your friends are. There will be cops swarming your apartment, and someone will connect the dots. I'm sorry, but you're stuck with us—at least until your ascension is over.

"The good news is that you have never been safer than you are with us. You'll have round the clock protection. You will have food, shelter, and pretty much anything else you could need while in our care."

"No."

"You don't have a choice."

"You didn't think to *ask* me before you wrapped me up in this weird 'true believer' shit?"

"We thought you *knew*! The daughters are supposed to know that they're blessed by their Zodiacs. Your parents should have...How could you not know!?"

"My parents..." I trail off. I don't need him to pity me. "How did *you* know what I was?"

He chews his lip in contemplation. "You bear the Mark of the Zodiac."

"*What*? Where?"

He heaves a sigh. "It was on your left ass cheek. I saw it when I walked in on you and Murphy..."

"My what?!"

I rotate in my seat, and lift my skirt in an attempt to get a look. Campbell does a double take and his jaw goes slack. He takes his eyes off the road for too long and has to swerve to correct course.

"Keep your eyes on the road!" I shout.

"Would you please cover yourself?" he asks in exasperation.

"How did I not know?"

Linnie, how did I not know?

You never asked, silly.

"Your parents should have told you. I'm sorry that it had to be me—well, Sullivan."

"How did no one else ever notice? Surely one of the men I had been with saw it; or one of the patrons at the club..."

"It looks kind of like a small tattoo. If you're not looking for it, you don't really notice it. What club did you work at?"

"The Naughty Nebula."

"That's a fairly upscale place."

"Yeah, well, I worked my way up."

"You're a fairly pricey call girl, too." He's fishing for something.

"Ask me whatever it is that you're dying to ask me."

"I just want to know why."

I shake my head before resting it on my hand and staring out the window. "Yeah, all you pretty boys do. You wanna know what makes me so special that you've gotta pay for it. To know what kind of daddy issues or mental illnesses I have that make me do this. Am I an addict? Do I have a pimp?

"I have abandonment issues, sure. But the rest is just because I was given a shit lot in life and I've had to claw my way out. And wouldn't you know, I just got accepted into college and got a scholarship and now I'm on the run."

"College?" he asks, shocked.

"Big building. Classrooms. People teaching things. You get a piece of paper at the end that says you are worth more money."

"I'm just surprised."

"Can't take my clothes off for money forever. I need to draw the line somewhere. No one wants to see a fifty year old stripper."

"Wanna settle down with a man and have a family? Retire from sex work?" he asks with a chuckle.

"Or woman, but they would have to be one hell of a person. I don't really believe in monogamy."

"Have you ever tried it?"

"I never saw the point. From a biological standpoint, it doesn't make a ton of sense. And from an emotional standpoint...well let's just say I don't like to get too attached."

He doesn't seem to know how to respond. Which is fine with me. We can drive in silence. After the harrowing events of the day, my body has had enough, and I lean my head against the window and doze off.

Chapter Four

Sully

Kissing Jinx may have been a mistake, but it's one I'll likely keep making. She tastes like heaven. And stars above, those titties. Campbell's my best friend, but he can get bent. He thought he had some sort of claim on her, but he doesn't.

I pull up to the safe house and do a perimeter check to make sure it's still uncompromised before I can do anything else. I have to turn on the generator. My internal check includes a bug sweep, and a full check of the inside of the house to make sure no one is stowed away somewhere.

There are no bugs, and no squatters, we're good.

I set to work putting sheets on the bed that Jinx will be staying in. It's a king size bed. There's plenty of room for her, me *and* Campbell if she wants us to share.

The others will be able to come and go, but Campbell and I will be just as stuck here as she is since the police will be looking for us.

My mind whirls from the kiss. I swear I can still taste her on my tongue. Her energy is magnetic, and I'm desperate to hold her again. I hope that she is interested in sharing her room with me, but I might be getting ahead of myself.

Around the time I finish with the master bedroom, the security camera app on my phone alerts me to their arrival. I step out onto the porch and wait, hands on my hips.

She gets out of the car and approaches me, sleep shadowing her eyes. "Hey you," she says in a sultry tired voice.

"Hey back," I say with a smirk. "You wanna get some more rest? I got the bed made up for you."

"Yeah, I'm wiped. I don't have anything to change into for sleeping, though."

"You can borrow one of my shirts to sleep in," Campbell says, meeting us on the steps with his duffel bag slung over his shoulder. He scowls at me which I return with a sarcastic look.

I slide my hand to the small of her back and lead her inside. "Well, welcome to your new home for the foreseeable future."

We step into the small entryway where there's a coat and shoe rack combo. She immediately takes off her combat boots and hangs her leather jacket on the coat hanger. Her crop top exposes the soft pale skin of her stomach, decorated by the mesh of her undershirt.

"This is the living room," I say, gesturing to our right. "The dining room and kitchen," I say gesturing to our left. "And over here..." I say directing her further into the house, "is the master bedroom. You also have your own bathroom attached to it. I know the house is small, but we didn't want to draw a lot of attention by constructing something huge."

She takes in the room where she'll be staying then spins to face me. "Where will you two sleep?"

"There's a room next door with a few sets of bunks specifically for this type of situation. We'll be close by if you need us."

Campbell is digging in his bag for some clothes for her to sleep in. He pulls out a black T-shirt and a pair of PJ pants and hands them to her.

"Thanks," she says softly, taking them from him.

"No problem. Here's a toothbrush and toothpaste. There's shampoo and stuff in the bathroom. If you need anything, just come knock on the door."

We leave her on her own in the bedroom and go to the kitchen to make a plan. I pull a bottle of water out of the fridge, and offer one to Campbell, who is staring me down like he wants my head on a stick. When he doesn't take the water, I set it on the counter.

I raise an eyebrow, take a sip of my water, then smirk. "So you wanna know how it was?"

"I want you to keep your hands off of her," he says in a loud whisper.

"If she's into me, that's not gonna happen."

"What happened to the bro code?"

"Doesn't apply to the Zodiac, dude," I say with a shrug. "When do the others get here?"

"Few hours. Except Colt. He'll be here tomorrow. And don't change the subject; I saw her first."

"This isn't 'finders keepers'. She's not an object. Besides, none of this is as important as making sure she completes her ascension."

Campbell looks away from me for a long moment with his jaw clenched. "You're right. We'll make a plan when the others get here. We'll start without Colt though. We can't wait that long."

The door to the master clicks open and Jinx shuffles out of the room wearing nothing but Campbell's shirt and a pair of black panties. Her hair is tied up in a bun on top of her head, and all her makeup is gone. Stripper Jinx is hot. Natural Jinx is beautiful.

"I thought you guys would be getting ready for bed. I just needed a drink."

I hand her the bottle of water that Campbell refused. Our fingers touch and she gives me a shy smile that immediately turns to a frown.

"What's wrong?"

"Um...my birth control and my cellphone were in my stuff at the precinct. Were you able to grab that?" She's looking at Campbell.

"Do you really think you're going to need it," Campbell snaps.

Her cheeks turn pink. "What if I do and I don't have it?"

"We have a guy with...pharmaceutical connections in our group. I'm sure we can get you a new script," I offer. "As far as your cell phone, it's better that we left it. The guys at the precinct would be able to track it if you had it. We'll get you another one."

"Thank you," she says to me and gives Campbell a snarky look.

Campbell storms off into the bunk room and slams the door like a child.

"What's his deal?" she asks.

I step into her space and wrap my arms around her waist, letting my hands rest just above the swell of her ass.

"He's just jealous," I say.

She brings a hand up between us, places it on my chest and pushes me back an inch, but doesn't break the contact I've made with her.

"Jealous of what? That we kissed a little? That doesn't make us a *thing*."

Her words sting, but I play it off. "No I know, but I think he wanted to be the one kissing you."

She considers me for a moment before a devious smile spreads across her face. "Let's find out."

She pulls away from me and walks over to the bunk room door. I follow her. She throws the door open, and steps inside. Campbell whirls around, standing in nothing but his underwear and is about to protest when Jinx takes his face in her hands and kisses him.

Her reaching up makes her shirt lift just enough that I can see ass cheeks sticking out of her black panties, and I stifle a groan. Campbell freezes at first, but then gives in, sliding one hand down and toying with the hem of her shirt, and placing the other on the back of her head. *Fuck. That is so hot.*

She pulls away from the kiss, and tosses a look my way. "I think you were right."

"I told you," I say, leaning against the door frame.

Chapter Five

Jinx

"Right about what?" Campbell asks.

"That you wanted to kiss her," Sully says with a smirk.

"I think he wants to do more than that," I tease, rubbing my hand up Campbell's hard length.

Sully steps up behind me, and hesitantly places his hands on my waist. Campbell makes eye contact with him and a silent conversation passes between them.

Things are getting spicy, Linnie teases

Get out! I tell my familiar, and she flits out of the room, cackling as she goes.

Sully places soft kisses down my neck, and slides his hand around to cup the apex of my thighs, outside of my panties. A small gasp escapes me, and I grind into him. Campbell's mouth crashes back onto mine, and both men press themselves against me. Sully moves his hand to make way for Campbell's impressive erection.

Campbell presses himself into me, desperate for more contact, and Sully nips at my neck while he slides his hand up under my shirt and pinches my nipple. I've been with two guys at once before, but never this fevered and passionate. I've also never been with two guys who I was innately attracted to at the same time.

Their hands are roaming all over, leaving a trail of goosebumps in their wake. Campbell's right hand slides around and down the back of my underwear, cupping my ass cheek and giving it a squeeze.

I push away from Campbell's bruising kiss. "We should take this into the other room." I grab both of their hands and lead them into the master bedroom and shut the door. They said others were coming, and I really don't want anyone interrupting us.

Campbell sits on the end of the bed and leans back on the palms of his hands. I prowl over to where Sully is standing and reach for his belt.

"You're wearing an unfair amount of clothes," I say and kiss him while I remove his pants.

"Tit for tat," he says with a smile and pulls the T-shirt over my head, leaving me nearly bare to them.

"Fuck," Campbell whispers, and palms his erection in his boxers.

He pats his lap, and I can see the feral need in his eyes. I pull Sully along behind me. I hook my thumbs into my underwear and bend over, sliding them off, giving Sully a great view of my ass when I do. He moans and slaps my ass with a stinging blow that makes me jump. Campbell chuckles, and bites down on his bottom lip.

I reach for Campbell's underwear and he lifts his hips to let me slide them off, his cock springing free when I do. The bulbous head is already leaking drops of precum. I bend over and lick the tip of it, cleaning it off.

Campbell gasps, and sully slaps my other ass cheek. The sound of his clothes hitting the floor quickly follows. I take the head of Campbell's cock into my mouth and present myself to Sully. Then responsibility kicks in.

I pull my mouth off of Campbell with a *pop!* "Condoms," I pant.

Campbell lays back on the bed and groans. "I don't have any."

"Me either," Sully says in frustration. "I'm clean though. I was tested a couple months ago, and I haven't been with anyone since."

"I always use protection, and get tested regularly," I say.

Sully and I both look to Campbell, whose face is bright red.

"I...fucking hell—"

"You're not a virgin, are you?" I ask, slightly horrified.

"*No!*" he shouts. "But you don't need to worry about me. It's been well over a year since I was with anyone. I don't just go around falling into bed with people."

"Dude, I knew you needed to get laid, but I didn't realize how dire the situation was," Sully says with a laugh.

I give Sully a 'shut up' look and place my hand on Campbell's cheek. All of the experience I've gained dealing with awkward and insecure men rises to the surface. "There's no reason to be embarrassed. If you don't want to do this, we can stop."

Campbell wraps his hands around the backs of my thighs and pulls me onto his lap, his hard length pressing against my core.

"The only thing I want right now, is to be buried so deep inside of you that you forget your own name." He swiftly maneuvers himself so he can slide inside of me with one aggressive thrust of his hips. He growls into my shoulder then says, "You are so wet for me...for us," he adds and tosses a glance to Sully.

Campbell takes my nipple into his mouth. I begin bouncing on his hard length, and I toss a 'come and get me' look back at Sully who advances. He grabs my hair tie and pulls my hair loose, letting it cascade around my shoulders, before wrapping it around his fist and kissing me hard.

He releases me, then pushes me forward, forcing Campbell to lay back on the bed. I pause my movements, waiting for Sully's instruction as his dominant energy fills the room. He shoves his thumb in my mouth.

"Suck on it," he demands.

I whimper around his thick digit before he pulls it out of my mouth and slides it inside of my ass. I moan softly as he works his thumb in and out of me, getting me ready for him. Campbell is underneath me with a pained expression, waiting as patiently as he can for me to start moving again. I give him a coy smile, and bounce gently, giving him a fraction of what he needs.

"Spit for me, both of you," Sully commands, and offers his hand.

I spit into his palm with no hesitation. Camp leans up and looks between the two of us, finally he spits into Sully's hand. Sully adds his own saliva to it before smearing it over the head of his cock. He lines up with my ass and pushes at the entrance. A needy whimper escapes me at the fullness.

"Fuck," Campbell and Sully whisper in unison.

They both begin tentatively moving in and out of me, warming me up for what's to come. Campbell picks up the pace first, grabbing my hips and slamming up into me over and over, hitting that perfect spot deep inside. I close my eyes and tip my head back, but he grabs my chin.

"Eyes on me, Buttercup."

He brings his other hand up and cups my breast, then pinches my nipple and twists it. Blissful pain winds its way through me, making me moan and clamp down around him. His eyes light up at this revelation.

"You like that?" he grunts, and he makes eye contact with Sully. They both pause their movements, making me whine. "Tell us what you need."

"Pain," I gasp as Sully grabs my hair and jerks my head back.

"Tell us if you need to stop," he says, eyes threatening if I don't do what he says.

I nod.

"Use your words, Little Witch."

"Yes, sir."

Sully's eyes roll back in his head at the use of the word 'sir'. He pulls out of me and I whine at the loss. He yanks his belt loose from his pants and doubles it over.

"Move into the center of the bed and fuck my partner. Don't stop until I tell you to."

Campbell and I follow Sully's orders and shift into the middle of the bed. I straddle him once more, and slide him effortlessly inside of me. It's like he was made for me. His heated gaze finds mine, and I lean down and kiss him. I sit back upright and start sliding up and down his thick cock as he absently plays with my nipples.

"Lean forward," Sully says, and I do as he says, not slowing the movement of my hips. "Good girl," he praises.

I want him to call me a 'good girl' again and again.

The belt comes down on my ass with a loud *crack*! I let out an embarrassing sound. Campbell looks like he's seconds away from exploding inside of me. Another *crack* of the belt pushes me closer to the edge.

"One more, and then you're going to come on my partner's dick and milk him for everything he has while you're screaming my name. Do you understand me?"

I nod in agreement.

Sully grabs my hair and growls, "Use your words. I will not tell you again."

"Yes, sir! Please."

Crack! That's all it takes, and I'm coming undone. "Fuck! Sully!" I scream.

Campbell lets loose rope after rope of hot cum inside of me, roaring his release. Sully doesn't give me any time to recover. He pulls me off of Campbell and throws me back onto the bed. He settles with his head between my legs and spreads my pussy open. He gives me a devious grin before lapping up the cum leaking out from between my legs.

Fuck! Why is that so hot?

He crawls up my body and grabs my cheeks, forcing my mouth open, and spits Campbell's cum into my mouth. "Swallow."

I writhe beneath him as I follow his instructions, desperate for more—desperate to have him inside of me. But he doesn't give me what I want. He moves off of the bed and says, "I'll be right back. Touch yourself while I'm gone."

I obey. Something about Sully makes me *want* to obey. Campbell stares at where my hand meets my flesh like he's trying to memorize the movements. Finally, Sully returns and tosses the hand towel he was using to dry his hand to the side. Without a word he stalks to the bed, he flips me on to my stomach, and pulls my ass up in the air. He notches himself at my entrance and slides into me, slowly; with intent.

Campbell is laying with his back against the headboard, watching with hooded eyes, not breaking eye contact with me. He begins stroking his cock as it hardens once more. I reach for him and he moves onto his knees and shifts toward me.

"Neither of you can get enough, can you?" Sully says with a smile in his voice as he continues moving in and out of me at a painfully slow pace. "I think she needs her face fucked, Camp. What do you think?"

I look up at Campbell and bat my eyes, begging him to take an ounce of the control that Sully has over us.

"Is that what you want?" he asks me.

"Don't ask for permission," Sully says, "Just take it. Our sweet Little Witch wants to please us."

The last shred of self restraint Campbell had snaps. He grabs the back of my head and forces the head of his hard length past my lips, all the way to the back of my throat. It catches me off guard and I gag a little, but that seems to only spur him on. He pistons his hips back and forth, hitting the back of my throat over and over.

Sully fucks me harder and harder until I feel like I might split in two, then reaches around and rubs my clit sending sparks of pleasure through me. Tears start streaming down my face as I struggle to breathe around Campbell's cock in my mouth.

"Come for us, pretty girl."

I moan around Campbell. He grabs the back of my head with both hands, shoving me all the way down on his dick, and groans out his release for the second time.

My pussy clamps down on Sully as he leaves his own mark inside of me, coming with one last forceful thrust. Campbell slides himself out from my lips, and we collapse in a sweaty mass of limbs.

Sully doesn't pull out right away. He peppers kisses down the back of my neck and whispers, "If we didn't have to worry about the world ending, I wouldn't let you have your birth control. We would just keep filling you up until you gave us a little angel baby."

"Or a blood hunter," Campbell adds, kissing my forehead. "Or a witch I suppose."

"Absolutely not. Neither of you will be putting any babies in me," I say with a laugh. "Don't even joke about it."

"Not even if we manage to save the world?" Sully says, wrapping me in his arms and running his fingers through my hair.

"What, and you would both help me raise a baby?" I say with a laugh. "This is fun and everything, but I don't expect either of you to stick around after this is done. I'll have to go back to work, and hope that I can actually start college."

"What if we want to stick around though?" Sully asks.

I raise an eyebrow at him. "That would be a first. No one has ever wanted to stick around me longer than a few months."

"Well either way, we've got plenty of time to figure it out after everything is over. Let's just enjoy this for now," Sully says, and kisses me, slipping his tongue inside of my mouth.

When he pulls away, I glance at Campbell who looks uncomfortable.

"What's wrong with you?" I ask, confused.

Chapter Six

Campbell

I'm staring at Jinx and Sully wrapped up together on the bed. Jinx has a mixture of his cum and mine leaking out of her on the bed, and I've never felt so sated in my life. But she's already planning an escape after the ritual.

"You want to go back to stripping and hooking after this?" I ask in surprise.

She shoots daggers at me with her eyes. "Don't do that. Don't act like you were saving me from a horrible situation like I'm some damsel in distress. I am capable of slaying my own dragons, and I always have been.

"Just because it's not the life you would have chosen, doesn't mean it wasn't working for me. I worked my ass off to be able to afford a nice place in the quiet part of the city. It wasn't much, but it was mine."

"I just don't understand why you'd want to sell yourself like that," I whisper. "You're worth more than that."

"You think my job makes me worthless?"

"No. I just–"

"I like what I do, and I want to go back." she says, definitively. "Honestly, I'm not sure how long I can even stay here without going insane. I've been on the move my whole life."

"We'll keep you plenty busy," Sully says with a suggestive smirk.

She scowls at him, but it lacks any real anger. I, however, start to spiral. It was stupid of us to have sex with her; especially the first day here. Now what? We share her for the foreseeable future? We both have to live here. *What the fuck were we thinking?*

Sully takes her hand in his and laces their fingers together. A ball of jealousy expands inside of me, my lip raises in a sneer. Jinx notices before I can get it under control.

"What's your deal?" she asks in frustration.

"Nothing. I'm going to get dressed."

I slide off the bed and pull my boxers on. I storm out of the room not bothering to look back before I leave.

I plop down on the bottom bunk and press my palms to my eyes. I had one job. Find the Zodiac and protect her. Fucking her senseless and getting attached to her was stupid. I'm not even sure how it happened. I never sleep with women I've just met.

I'm not sure how long I'm wallowing before Sully unlocks the door and lets himself in. He shuts the door with a soft click, and leans against it, arms crossed. I don't look at him, but I can feel his expectant eyes boring into me, waiting for an explanation.

When I don't give him one he finally says, "She thinks you hate her."

"That's ridiculous. I don't hate her. I don't even know her." Then I add bitterly, "I fucked her, but I don't *know* her."

"Well you'll have to explain that to her later when she's awake. She took a quick shower and passed out."

"Yeah, well two orgasms and two partners will do that to you." There's a level of jealous rage in my voice that I don't expect.

"I don't see you passing out," he says with a smirk. When I don't return his amusement he asks, "Why are you being weird?"

"Because I don't want to fucking share her."

His eyebrows go up, and a dry laugh escapes him. "You should have thought about that before you helped me double stuff her."

I whip a pillow at his head, and it finds its mark. Sully laughs deeply. He's still in his boxers, clearly not worried about appearing decent around me. I find myself comparing my appearance to his. Objectively, I can see why Jinx is attracted to him. He's got a good body, and he's handsome. Not to mention the way he took control in the bedroom. It's no wonder she wants him, too. It's possible she even wants him more.

"We fucked up," I say. "Lanya is going to kill us."

"The succubus is going to kill us for indulging in a little sex?"

"With the *Zodiac*."

"You're too high strung. Lanya is always harping on you about getting laid. As long as we don't let it affect the mission, she will not care. Besides, I don't know about you, but I don't care what anyone thinks. If I died right now, I would die a very happy man." He spaces out like he's replaying our rendezvous with Jinx in his mind, then shakes his head. "I'm gonna grab some sleep before the others get here. I recommend you do the same. You're welcome to join us in the master bedroom if you want."

"You're going to sleep in the bed with her?" I saw it coming, but the jealousy wells up inside again.

"Yeah," he says with a shrug like it's a completely normal thing for him to do.

Sully never sleeps over with women. It's something he practically brags about. He grabs his bag and leaves me alone in the bunk room. I sit and wallow for another couple of minutes.

"Fuck it," I mutter, and grab my own bag and head into Jinx's room.

Sully is already cuddled up behind her. He lifts his head and holds a finger to his lips, urging me to be quiet. Jinx's pouty lips are parted slightly in her slumber. I want to kiss them for the rest of eternity. If things don't go as planned—if the other Zodiacs don't complete their missions—eternity may not be very long. The realization dawns on me that I'm not going to waste any time worrying about the after. I'm just going to focus on the now, and spend as much time with her, and my best friend as I can until her ascension.

I slide under the blanket, taking in a glimpse of her perfect, naked form. Facing her, I lay my head on the pillow, and watch her peaceful breathing. Until the ritual is done, I will take whatever piece of her she's willing to give me. We can handle everything else after the end of the world.

Chapter Seven

Jinx

"Oh it smells just *delicious* in here," a sultry feminine voice rouses me from my sleep. "Breaking in the bed already, I see. Archer will be pleased that his money is going to good use."

I sit upright, holding the sheet to me. Even more startling than the gorgeous brunette standing at the foot of the bed, is the fact that Sully and Campbell are both in my bed with me.

"Who the fuck are you?" I snap at the intruder.

"Jinx!" Campbell hisses at me, and I stick my tongue out at him. He turns back to the other woman. "Lanya, some warning would have been nice."

He slides out of the bed wearing nothing but his boxers. A large bloody skull tattoo covers most of his back. It has a rose for one eye, and a moon for the other. I hadn't noticed it in our frenzied fucking earlier.

"And miss all this gooey fun? Nonsense. I smelled sex and I needed to see what all the fuss was about. Aren't you just spectacular?" the woman says, advancing to the side of the bed that Campbell just vacated.

She's wearing a red bodycon dress with strappy cutouts at the hips. It accentuates every curve in her body, making her absolutely mouthwatering. Her hair is done up in victory rolls. Her makeup is perfect. Not an eyelash is out of place.

"I hope these two were able to keep you *properly* entertained. Come dear, lots to discuss."

She offers me her hand and I just stare at it. "I'm naked under this sheet. Can I have some privacy to get dressed?"

She clicks her tongue and says, "Humans. The modesty thing is so bizarre. Especially for a girl as beautiful as you, who takes her clothes off for a living. But if you must. I'll be in the kitchen."

She leaves the room and Campbell closes the door behind her. He pulls a henley over his head and slides his legs into a pair of faded blue jeans that perfectly conform to his thick, muscular thighs. I bite my lip and his eyes catch mine.

"You gonna get out of bed, or will I have to make you?" he asks with a raised eyebrow and a smile.

"I'd like to see you try," I say and pull the cover back and step onto the soft carpet.

Campbell's eyes rake over me with a hunger, and I want to pretend that Lanie or whatever the fuck her name is isn't out in the kitchen waiting for us.

Sully climbs out of the bed, and steps up behind me, pressing the hard planes of his chest into my back. "Campbell said he didn't want to share you, but he looks pretty eager right now, don't you think?"

Sully's erection is pressing into my back, and there's an obvious tent in Campbell's jeans. My skin is buzzing and a deep craving worms its way into my core. I step forward and press my body to Campbell's, and Sully sandwiches me between them.

"Kiss him," Sully whispers in my ear.

I'm about to comply when Campbell shakes his head clear and mutters, "Fucking succubus." He yells, "Stop it Lanya!"

A cackle comes from the kitchen. *What the fuck.* Campbell rolls his eyes and hands me the clothes he had loaned me earlier. I pull them on and follow him out to the kitchen with a half dressed Sully in tow.

"You never lighten up and have any fun. Sue me for trying to take the edge off," Lanya pouts. "I'm surprised you fell into bed with her so quickly. I didn't even have to influence you."

Campbell's ears turn red. Apparently he always has a stick up his ass, and it's not just with me. Which is a relief.

"Don't act like you were trying to play matchmaker. You just wanted to feed off of us."

Lanya gives him a bright smile. "The match is already made, darling. I'm just trying to cash in."

This isn't the first succubus I've ever encountered, but it is the first that's tried to feed directly from me. Being influenced by the desires of someone else makes my skin crawl.

"Where are the others?" Lanya asks.

"They shouldn't be too far behind," Campbell says and pulls up a stool at the counter. "Trixie is bringing supplies, and Dalton is bringing weaponry and traps to secure the perimeter."

"Some coffee while we wait?" Sully asks.

He pulls a tin and some filters out of his duffle bag, still shirtless. He has a large tattoo across his chest of a set of scales. The beam is a sword stuck into the base. The weights on the scales are an anatomically correct heart and a skull. I was too wrapped up in our activities to really take it in.

"You're a saint," I mutter, drinking in his abs and arms. *A very hot saint.*

"Angel. I'm an angel."

A giggle escapes me. *A giggle! I don't giggle; not for real anyway. Must be the succubus. Focus!*

"A set of scales?" I ask, trailing my finger down the center of his chest.

"I've been waiting for you for a long time," he whispers in my ear, then kisses me on the nose.

Without another word, he steps around me and sets up the coffee pot and turns it on, then pulls up the other stool on Campbell's side of the bar. I lean on my elbows against the bar next to him. He grabs my hand and pulls me between his legs facing away from him. I don't hate the contact, but we're going to have to discuss the clinginess.

"When do Colt and Niall get here?" Lanya asks.

"Not until tomorrow."

"We'll have a plan in place by then. You'll call and fill them in?"

"Yes."

"I feel very in the dark about everything that's happening," I say.

"All in due time," Lanya says cryptically, and gently caresses my cheek sending a shiver through me.

Where Sully's fingers are grazing my skin, it warms, and I once again feel his hardness press into me.

"Stop that!" I say and bat her hand away.

She makes a sound of mock disgust. "None of you are any fun."

Campbell sets a cup of coffee and a container of powdered creamer and a couple packets of sugar in front of me. I look up at him through my lashes and give him a smile.

"Thank you," I say.

"You're gonna need your energy, Buttercup." He kisses me on the forehead then exchanges a look with Sully.

The second I place the cup to my lips, the front door swings open and in walks a slight fairy girl with silvery powder blue hair that's done up in space buns with straight bangs. She has dark purple makeup, and is wearing a black skater dress and converse.

"Hey guys!" she calls, carrying several heavy looking bags of groceries looped over her arms.

No one makes a move to help her except for me. Sully reluctantly lets me go.

"Let me help you," I say and take half of the load from her arms.

"Oh thank you! Dalton's getting the rest before he brings in the heavy artillery. I'm Trixie, by the way! You must be Jinx! I would give you a hug, but..."

We carry the food to the kitchen and drop it on the floor. Campbell busies himself by putting it away. When I try to help he shoos me away because 'I don't know where things go'.

I take up residence back at the bar, and Sully immediately pulls me back to him like he needs to stake some sort of claim. Trixie eyes the contact with a half smile, but doesn't make a comment, which I'm grateful for.

"Trix do you think you bought enough food?" Dalton—I assume, anyway—says as he steps into the house.

He's tall and broad. He has dark tan skin and shaggy blonde hair. He looks like a surfer.

"For a few days at least," she says with a wink.

Lanya claps her hands together excitedly. "Okay. We have a lot to do and not a lot of time to do it. We have one of the relics here, one coming tomorrow, and the other two are scattered about elsewhere. We'll have to go to them."

"Relics?" I ask.

Being here with this group is like being with a bunch of people who have known each other since high school, but I just met them last week. Their language is all inside jokes and memories and you have no way of connecting with that.

"Did you two tell her *anything*?" Trixie asks as she places her hands on her hips and stares Campbell and Sully down.

"They were too busy to talk, it would seem," Lanya says, wagging her eyebrows.

"*Both* of you?" Trixie gasps, looking at Campbell with a mixture of emotions swimming in her pale blue eyes. Her gaze settles on me with a rage simmering beneath the surface.

"Can we *please* discuss the end of the fucking world or *anything* else?" Campbell groans.

She doesn't like you, Linnie says to me, telepathically.

Ya think? I reply. She's pissed that Campbell hooked up with me, and is not bothering to hide it. I sigh and tell Linnie, *You can go play if you want. Just stay close. I'll come get you when we're done.*

Oh thank god. This is impossibly boring. It looks like you're in good hands, anyway, she says and cackles as she darts away.

"Fine," Trixie says, answering Campbell, and turns back to me. "The relics are four items that you will need to pull your power from when the time for your ascension comes. If you don't have them, you can't use them."

"Okay. You said they're people?"

"They're inside of people."

"Like...they ate them?"

"They were implanted to keep them safe. No one would have thought to look for them there." She's speaking as if all of this makes perfect sense. but I understand none of it.

"You said one is already here?"

Campbell raises his hand.

"Weird coincidence how I was arrested by one of the Relics," I muse, though I don't suspect it was much of a coincidence at all.

"Trix has the sight," Sully says. "That's how Camp and I knew where to find you."

"So, you knew who I was when you saw me?" A small ember of anger flares inside of me. Why would they send me with Murphy if they were supposed to be protecting me?

Trixie answers, "No. We just knew we needed to infiltrate that police department and wait for you. That's the thing about the sight. I only get small pieces. In this instance, we knew you would have something to do with that police department at some point, but not what you looked like. I didn't even know if you were going to be an officer or a prisoner.

"We sent Campbell and Sullivan in to infiltrate the station over a year ago. They knew to keep an eye out, and to watch for your mark. Speaking of which, can I see it? Where is it?" She's bouncing on her toes in excitement.

"Uh..."

"You have the mark, right?" she asks, brow furrowed.

"Yeah, it's just...somewhere kind of private."

"How did these two see it then?"

Images of Murphy attacking me and Campbell killing him flash through my head. Rather than relive it with this girl who clearly hates me, I change the subject which earns me a side eye from Trixie.

"So the relics. How do we get them out of their hosts—or whatever?"

"From what I understand we can't get them out. You'll just have to pull magic from them. Colt will be here tomorrow. He's the second one. He's also amazing. He'd give you the shirt off of his back if you asked, so don't let his thuggish appearance scare you. The third one is a mafia boss who has a manor on the outskirts of the city. We'll have to speak with him next."

"Do you think he'll come all the way out here?"

"No. We'll have to go to him."

"Lanya, Dalton and I will go tomorrow after Colt gets here," Campbell says.

"You'll want to take the Zodiac with you," Trixie says in a sing-song voice.

"No!" Sully and Campbell say, together.

"You won't get his cooperation without her," she says and shrugs. "It makes the most sense, too. I get the impression we won't be using the safehouse much longer."

"What aren't you saying?" Sully asks, suspiciously.

"I can't say definitively, but I don't think we'll be coming back here."

"Taking her with us will put her in unnecessary danger," Campbell argues.

"She's already in danger," Lanya says with a dry laugh. "She has been since she was born, and she's only going to be in more danger the closer we get to the solstice."

Trixie adds, "Archer won't hurt her. He knows what's at stake. But he also won't help her without meeting her."

"Guys, can we please stop talking about me like I'm not here?" I ask in exasperation. "This concerns me and my safety. I want to go. I want to meet him."

"Then it's settled," Trixie says. "We'll go see Archer the day after tomorrow. Colt will want to be there for it. Now you and I need to talk."

She grabs Campbell by the hand, pulls him away from the counter, and drags him out the door. I try to push down the jealousy I feel. Sully gently squeezes my thigh. The pressure grounds me and stops me from following them outside.

Lanya steps away to make a phone call, and Dalton has some things to accomplish with the security of the cabin. I slide off of Sully's lap and spin around to face him.

Keeping my voice low, I say, "You're being a little possessive."

He stands and backs me into the counter, putting his hands on either side of me, boxing me in. "Do you want me to stop?"

"What if I do?" I challenge, lifting my chin.

"You'll have to make me."

I let out some of my ice magic, freezing his feet and hands in place. I duck out from between his arms and run into the bedroom, and shut the door. The sound of shattering ice, and slow footsteps approaching the door let me know he freed himself.

There's no place for me to hide in here. I pry the bedroom window open and jump out. Linnie, sensing my adrenaline, appears at my side.

I'm not in any real danger.

So the hunk of angel meat is just chasing you for fun?

I give her a devious smile.

Well let me know if you need me. She flits away, probably to play with some birds.

I was able to outrun Sully in the city, but barefoot in the woods may be a different story. I take off across the small field behind the house toward the trees. I glance back to find Sully dropping to the ground below the window.

He takes off after me, and I push myself into a sprint. I'm almost to the woods when Sully calls after me.

"You better run as fast as you can, because when I catch you, you're *mine*."

He's a lot closer than I expected. With a breathless giggle, I push forward. I dart between trees, and around brush. My feet sting from the rocks and twigs, but I press on.

I can feel him gaining on me. *How is he so fast?* His footsteps are right behind me, and I feel his fingers graze the back of my shirt. I squeal and sprint just a little faster, but it's futile. He tackles me to the ground, and holds me down with his body weight.

"That tight cunt is mine, Little Witch. Tell me, does the chase turn you on as much as it does me?" He grinds his erection into my ass.

He rips my pants down, and groans before bringing his hand down across my ass cheek. The sting of the sound of his zipper has me practically panting with need.

"You're not even going to fight me? I'm disappointed in you. I shouldn't be surprised. You're such a good little slut."

If he wants a fight, I'll give him a fight. I elbow him in the temple, knocking him for a loop just long enough for me to claw my way out from underneath him. I don't make it more than a couple feet before he grabs my ankle and pulls me back to him. He flips me over onto my back and wraps a hand around my throat, pinning me to the ground.

"Good try, but you're mine, baby girl."

He thrusts inside of me without warning, making me gasp. I don't even pretend to fight him anymore. He slams into me with a punishing force, his grip on my throat tightening.

"Do you want to come?" he asks.

I nod, and he squeezes harder.

"How many times am I going to have to tell you to use your fucking words? Do you want to come?"

"Yes," I gasp when he lets up on my throat.

"Then tell me you're mine."

My eyes go wide, and anxiousness fills my gut. I never settle down with anyone. This is too fast. Sully senses the change in me, and softens his request.

"I'll share you, but I need to know at least a piece of you belongs to me. Tell me you're *mine*." he growls out between grunts.

My heart wages a battle with my brain. I search his eyes for what his intentions are, but all I find there is unbridled need.

He continues pounding into me. "I need an answer, Jinx."

"I'm yours," I concede.

"Say it again," he demands. "Louder."

"I'm yours!" I cry out, desperate for release.

He reaches between us and presses his thumb to my clit and begins working magical circles. "Come for me, baby girl."

I fall apart around him, raking my nails down his chest, leaving bloody marks in their wake.

"Fuuuuuck," he roars as he shoots his load inside of me.

He leans down and kisses me, staying inside of me as he grows soft. He pulls back, and looks in my eyes, searching them for something. His brows are furrowed, like he can't find what he's looking for.

"What?" I ask with a soft laugh.

"Did you mean it? Are you mine?" Gone is the dominant beast who was just fucking me into the dirt. In his place is a vulnerable and soft man.

"I wouldn't lie to you for the sake of an orgasm. But I need to be very clear with you, I will never belong to one person wholly."

"And I would never ask that of you."

He slides out of me, and helps me to my feet. I immediately miss him being inside of me. I pull on my pants and take stock of all the minor injuries I sustained. My arms are scraped up, and I have a bruise on my ass from a rock that was underneath me.

He pulls me into his arms and kisses me slowly, and purposefully. "You're something special. And not just because you're the Libra. I'm disappointed it took me this long to find you."

My cheeks heat at his words. No one has ever spoken so lovingly to me.

"We should head back," I whisper.

He laces his fingers with mine and we walk back to the cabin. Linnie plops down on my shoulder just before we round the corner to the front of the cabin.

The other cop is still arguing with that fairy on the porch, she warns just before I hear their voices.

"We're just talking in circles, Trix. You can't change my mind."

"You're making a mistake and you're going to get your heart broken."

"Why aren't you lecturing Sully about this?"

"Because Sully doesn't catch feelings like you. You're not capable of sharing her. You'll lose your mind. And there's a good chance she won't even make it out of this alive. Besides, I give her about thirty minutes before she's become a cum dumpster for Colt, too."

"That's enough! Stop talking about her like that. I know you're upset, and I'm sorry, but we tried, you had your chance, and you decided not to take it. Stop blaming that on her when you're the one that fucked up."

My heart swells at Campbell sticking up for me. And Trixie obviously doesn't know Sully as well as she thinks she does, because he all but told me he's already caught feelings. I clear my throat as we step into view, and Trixie startles at the sound.

"Where were you two?" Campbell asks, suspiciously.

Sully pulls a twig out of my hair. "We got tired of waiting for you, so we ran off together."

I smack him in the chest. "I'm blaming the succubus."

Campbell gives Trixie a defiant look, then steps off the porch and stands so close to me that his chest brushes mine.

"I hope you saved some energy for me, Buttercup," he says with a smirk. He tangles his fingers in my hair and kisses me like he has something to prove.

Trixie makes an irritated sound and storms into the house. *Great. So much for that friendship.*

Chapter Eight
Campbell

I continue kissing Jinx until I'm sure Trixie is inside, then pull away slowly.

She gives me a seductive look then says, "So have you caught feelings yet?"

"You heard that?" I ask and scrunch my nose.

"Yeah, and I get the feeling that Trixie doesn't like me very much. Is there a history there I should know about?"

"We slept together once a few years ago. She didn't want anything serious. I did. We went our separate ways."

"Do not use me to make her jealous. Kiss me because you want to kiss me. Not because you want to prove something, okay?"

"I did want to kiss you, though. Proving my point was just an added bonus."

I pull a leaf out of her hair, and take note of the scrapes and bruises she has. There's a bruise around her neck that looks like a hand. My eyes find Sully's. He's just as scraped and filthy as she is.

"So what happened?"

"Jinx thought I was being too possessive so she tried to run," Sully says and steps up behind her. "I caught her though. I might have even tamed her a bit."

"It'll take more than a good fuck in the woods to tame me. Good try though."

I tip her face up to mine, "I get you to myself for a little while, later. Okay?"

"Yeah, okay," she agrees, surprising me. "I need a shower. Again." She steps out from between us and goes inside.

Sully wraps his arm around my shoulder. "For what it's worth, I already caught feelings." He pats me on the back and follows Jinx in the house.

I'm in trouble. If he's already in this deep with her, there's no hope for me. I step into the house after them. Trixie is pouting on the couch with Dalton, and Lanya gives Sully a knowing look as he disappears into the bunk room.

"Did you do that?" I ask her.

"Nope. That was one hundred percent them. You two seem rather smitten with her."

"She's unlike anyone I've ever met," I say with a shrug.

"As the Zodiac should be. Just be careful. You can't let your feelings get in the way of destiny," she says in a mystical voice

"We'll make sure she succeeds."

"Even if it kills her?"

"Even if it kills her," I agree. But I don't believe my own words. I already feel so protective of her.

I let myself into the master bathroom as quietly as possible and strip off my clothes. I pull back the curtain to the shower, making Jinx jump in surprise.

"Hey, you," she purrs as I step in behind her.

"Hey back."

She has a massive bruise blooming on her ass cheek, and scrapes all over her body. I grab the soap and begin gingerly washing her body, letting my hands dance across her skin. She spins to face me, and I continue lathering up the front of her body. Her nipples peak under my fingertips.

"I'm never going to actually get clean if you and Sully keep it up," she says with a smile.

"Being clean is vastly overrated," I tease while I admire her delightful curves. "You're so beautiful, you know that?"

She ducks her head and stares at the floor of the shower. "Thank you."

I grab her chin and make her look at me. "Are you okay with Sully and I sharing you?"

"I'm more than okay with that. The question is if you're okay with it. If you're the type to get super jealous, then this isn't going to work and we should just pretend it didn't happen."

"There's no going back for me. There was no going back from the second I tackled you in that alley way. I immediately knew that I couldn't be around you any longer than absolutely necessary or I would become addicted." I kiss down the side of her neck and gently nip at her flesh.

"You put me in jail," she says with feigned annoyance.

"They allow visitation." I lift my head and smile at her, wrapping my arms around her and holding her to me as the water cascades around us. "I will say that seeing the way you and Sully were looking at each other outside the diner nearly made me put him through the window."

"So you are the jealous type."

"A little. But Sully is my best friend, and I share everything else with him."

"*Everything?*"

"Well, never women before, but it was clearly only a matter of time."

She stares up at me through those long dark lashes. This girl will be the absolute end of me—assuming the world doesn't end first.

I kiss her and say, "I said I wanted you to myself for a bit tonight. If it's okay, I would rather just spend time with you. We'll have plenty of time to have sex, but I want some time to get to know you."

"Okay," she says. Her face falls a bit, and I almost regret my request.

"Is that really okay?"

"I'm just not used to people caring about my life. The guys I go on dates with usually just want to trauma dump on me, fuck me, then go home."

"Not to sound like a cliche, but I'm not like other guys."

She laughs. "I suspected that you weren't. Sully's a bit like other guys. But there's something softer about you."

She turns off the water and grabs a towel off of the sink. I retrieve my own and we dry off before entering the bedroom. Sully is laying on the bed. He gives Jinx's naked form an appreciative look.

"Took you two long enough. If there's any hot water left, I'm going to go get clean."

"Don't come back in here when you're done," I say.

"Oh come on. Why can't I join?" Sully whines.

I tip Jinx's chin up so I can look at her. "Because we're having a date."

Her cheeks go rosy, and I wonder how long it's been since she's had a real date—if she's even had one at all. I vow to myself that the second her ritual is over, we'll be going to the nicest place I can afford and having a real honest to goodness date.

I kiss Jinx on the nose, and say, "Wait here," before darting out into the living area.

Dalton, Trixie, and Lanya are playing a card game at the coffee table. I open the coat closet by the front door, and grab a couple of board games. Trixie scowls when she realizes I'm headed back to the bedroom, and not sticking around with her and the others.

Her concerns are probably valid, but I have an inexplicable attraction to Jinx that I can't ignore; even if it means sharing her with Sully. Truth be told, Sully is the only person in the world I would *want* to share her with.

I grab a couple sodas and a bag of chips and precariously place them on top of the stack of board games and fumble my way through the door with full hands.

"Okay, I've got snacks an—"

Jinx is laying on her stomach on the bed, still wrapped in her towel. It's hiked up so I can see her ass cheeks, and she's got a book in her hands—my book from my duffle bag.

"Sorry, I wasn't sure whose clothes, or what I should wear. Not having anything of my own—except what I was arrested in, which is filthy—is kind of putting a damper on things."

"I brought enough clothes that I wouldn't have to do laundry for over a week. Here."

I rifle through my bag and toss her a tank top and a pair of gym shorts. She drops the towel and begins pulling them on. Her cleavage is distracting, and I can see her nipples through the thin fabric of the tank top. I did not think this through.

The bathroom door opens, and Sully steps in. His eyes immediately land on Jinx's chest.

"I told you not to come back in here." I scowl at him.

"I'm going! I just wanted to tell Jinx to have fun on her date," he says and kisses her softly on the lips. "I'm still sleeping in here tonight, so don't get any ideas about keeping her to yourself."

"I wouldn't let him ban you from the room," Jinx says. "Now go."

"Fine," he says with a pout, and heads out the bedroom door.

I set the sodas and the chips on the bed, and hold out the board games. "Ticket to Ride, Clue, Payday, or Monopoly?'

"Oh. I've only ever heard of Clue and Monopoly. I've never played any of them. I guess whichever is easiest to learn."

"Have you ever played *any* board games? like Candyland or Chutes and Ladders?"

"No," she says, glancing at the floor. "Most of my foster families didn't do stuff like that. They just...I was alone a lot."

"Well you won't be anymore. Let's spend some time with that inner child," I say.

She nods, but has a guarded look about her. This conversation must have hit a nerve, and I don't know how to remedy it so things aren't weird.

I sigh, and glance at the games in my hands. "Look, I'm sorry. I just want you to have fun. Let's start over. Let's play monopoly. I think it'll be a good introductory board game for you."

I set up all the pieces and the bank. "Here, choose a player piece."

Jinx's hand hovers over mine as she decides which one she wants. She picks up the ship and holds it in her hand. I select the horse and put the others back in the box, and explain the rules. After a few turns, Jinx is the one to initiate conversation.

"So how did you end up with the cop position? There's so many people involved in this. Did you and Sully draw the short straws?"

"Well, Colt has throat tattoos. Trixie is too conspicuous. Lanya looks more like a forty something trophy wife, and Archer is a mafia boss. Sully and I are unattached and looked the part. What about you? How did you end up at the Naughty Nebula?"

"I didn't start with stripping. I started out turning tricks. That was easier when I was fifteen."

"You've been on the streets since you were *fifteen?*" I ask in horror.

"Yeah. It was out of necessity. The foster system wasn't working out. Once I ditched my last foster family, I met a couple of girls that were older than me. Because I was chubby, they didn't see me as a threat for potential clients. They took me under their wings, and showed me the ropes.

"They taught me how to spy the bad ones, how to not get pulled under the control of a pimp—that sort of thing. Then when I turned seventeen, I got a fake ID and I got a job at a lower scale place. My boss didn't do any real background checks, and I got hired on the spot. It was a real dive off of Jefferson."

"I know the place. Burned down a year or two ago."

"That's the one. I was gone before that happened though. Manny, my boss at The Neb, came in scouting for new talent. He took a liking to me right away. That was about a year after I started stripping. I've been there ever since. I feel bad for bailing on him. I've always been a very dependable employee. He gave me the good shifts because I never no-showed, and never gave him any trouble.

"I don't do drugs. I don't even drink. I was the ideal employee for that club. Most of the girls there were great. A couple fell through the cracks, though."

"And the escort service?"

"I got recruited for that, too. My madame came in one night with a client. He liked to watch me dance while she jerked him off under the table. He made a comment about how he wanted me, and that was that. He was a really good client. She gave me her business card. It took me two weeks to work up the courage to call her. It seemed so...formal after everything I'd been doing for the last five years." She shrugs and ends her turn in the game.

We sit in silence for a while, only talking when it relates to game play. Eventually she says, "I don't want you to pity me. At first things were hard, but they were better than being with my foster families—especially the last one. It taught me a lot of independence and despite all of it, I did really well for myself."

"I still wish you hadn't had to go through all of that."

"Me too. But what's done is done, and I can only use what I learned to move forward."

"You're really something, you know that?"

"So I've been told." She lets out a small laugh. "Usually on my 'dates' with clients, I do all the listening. But I don't know really anything about you aside from how good you are in bed."

My cheeks heat, and my stomach flutters. I pray that she doesn't notice. If she does, she doesn't say anything.

"What would you like to know?"

"Whatever you want to tell me."

"I'm a blood hunter. Did Sully tell you that?" I ask.

"No. He did tell me what he was, though."

"You should see his wings. They're beautiful."

"So what does a blood hunter do exactly?"

"If I take someone's blood and ingest it, I can use a magical connection to them to cause them physical ailments or kill them. I can also use it to track them until it's fully digested which takes several hours because of how my body metabolizes blood, specifically."

Her eyebrows raise in interest. "That's amazing. Anything else?"

"Well...one other thing..." I trail off, unsure of whether I should tell her.

"Spill," she says, moving to her knees, and leaning in.

"I can make them feel immense pleasure as well as pain, by moving the blood to their genitals."

Her mouth pops open. "Do it to me."

"I don't think that's a good idea…"

"Please? You can do a little pain and a little pleasure." She sticks out her bottom lip and gives me puppy dog eyes.

I sigh and put the game back in the box.

"I wasn't feeling it anyway," she says with a laugh. "No offense but if that's what board games are, I'll pass."

"They're not all like that. We'll try something better next time we have the chance to play with Sully." I close the lid and place the boxes on the floor. "Lay down. And it's very important that you follow my instructions. Don't try to talk to me, or ask me for specific things. If I get too distracted, I could really hurt you. Do you understand?"

She nods and strips off her clothes and sits in the middle of the bed. I furrow my brow in confusion. "You could have stayed clothed."

"I figure you should get something out of this too," she says with a flirty smile. She pulls her hair to one shoulder and lays back on the bed.

"What part of 'no distractions' did you not understand?" I scold.

"You'll be fine. I trust you."

"I need a safe word."

"No you don't." She laughs.

"Yes I do. Safe word or no play."

"Pickles," she says, rolling her eyes.

I pull my pocket knife from my jeans and reach for her hand. She places it in mine, palm up. Keeping my eyes on hers, I press the blade to her pointer finger until the sweet and metallic scent of her blood hits my nose.

I place her finger to my tongue and groan. "You taste amazing."

Her eyes go wide as she stares at my face. My eyes go black as the blood magic surfaces. I sit back on my heels and concentrate on the line of magic that now links us together. I reach toward her with my energy, and I can feel the blood flowing through her veins, pumping to and from her heart.

Directing a little extra blood flow to her groin, I watch as her face flushes and her breathing picks up. I send some extra blood to her nipples and make it build in pressure, and stimulating them from the inside. They peak as a result and she moans.

I should have thought this through. Her sounds are going to be enough of a distraction on their own. Pressing on, I continue shifting small amounts of blood against her clit, and adding pressure. She reaches down to touch herself and relieve the intense feeling, but I smack her hand away.

"No," is all I say, and it earns me a glare.

She'll come almost immediately if she touches herself and I want to prolong this. Her nipples are bright pink and swollen from the extra blood, and she reaches up to touch her breasts. I'll allow that.

Right as her hand hits her breast I change my pace and pressure on her clit, and she cries out, and squirms on the bed. She pinches her nipple between her fingers and I have to do a double take. Liquid shoots out of one of them.

"What the fuck?! Pickles!"

I immediately drop the connection between us. It's still faintly there but if I'm not pressing my magic into it, it doesn't do anything.

"Did you just..."

"Lactate? Yeah. I think I did." There's a look of shock and horror on her face that she shakes off. "I mean, the good news is that was one of the best orgasms I've ever had that didn't involve penetration."

She reaches up and squeezes her nipple again, releasing more white liquid. My cock grows impossibly hard at the thought of putting a baby inside of her. I've never wanted to actually reproduce before, and now I've seriously thought about it twice in less than twenty four hours.

"Has this ever happened before?" she asks, staring at her boobs.

"No. I mean, the only person that I ever did this to was a guy," I say.

Her face snaps up so she can look at me more closely. "I didn't know that you were into men."

"Oh...it wasn't a sexual thing. It was more of a prank I guess? I got into a fist fight with a guy in high school, and he called me some gross names, so I surreptitiously took some of his blood, and made him come in his pants in front of the entire tenth grade class."

Jinx stares at me for long seconds then erupts into laughter until tears stream down her face. "That is the best thing I've ever heard," she says once she finally settles down again. "Please do that to Sully tomorrow."

"I will not!" I say, blushing at the thought of making him come the way I just did with Jinx.

"Oh come on! It'll be funny!" she insists.

"I would rather just watch him come on you again, I say and push her back on the bed. Watching her come undone like that has me aching to be inside of her. "I know I said no sex..."

"Shut up and fuck me," she says and kisses me.

And I do fuck her, multiple times for the next several hours.

Chapter Nine
Colt

I've been sitting inside my car so long that the engine is now cold. The Zodiac is inside of the cabin. I just need to work up the nerve to get out of this car, and go inside. Taking a deep breath and steeling my nerves, I open the car door.

I grab my bags from the trunk and walk up to the front door. My stomach coils with nervous energy with every step I take. I twist the knob, and push the door open, and scan the room. Everyone is in the living room area. Trixie is in an armchair, and Lanya is sitting on the chaise with a book. Dalton is in the kitchen getting a snack.

On the couch, Campbell and Sully are sitting a couple feet apart with a green haired girl laying across both of their laps. Campbell is rubbing her feet, and Sully is stroking her hair. Something in here smells familiar. Something smells like...

She twists her head in Sully's lap, and makes eye contact with me. *What the fuck?*

"Hi!" she says, cheerfully. "You must be Colt!"

She doesn't remember me. I grind my teeth together.

"You okay, dude?" Campbell asks.

"Yeah. Fine. You three look comfortable."

Jinx sits up to get a better look at me. She shrugs and says, "Physical touch is comforting to me."

She crosses the room and holds out a hand for me to shake. "I'm Jinx."

I don't take it. Her brow furrows as I stare down my nose at her. I walk into the bunk room and toss my stuff on to an empty bunk. There should have only been two available, but there are four. I poke my head back out of the room.

"Why are there so many open beds?"

"Jinx is sharing with Campbell and Sully," Trixie says, giving me a look that says she's not thrilled with this development. "Actually, she has something she needs from you."

"What could you possibly need from me?" I ask in irritation.

Jinx's face reddens. "We didn't have time to grab my birth control. They said you could get me a script."

"No."

She scowls at me. "No?"

"You need to be focusing on your ascension. Not fucking around."

"Wow," Jinx says, anger flaring in her eyes.

"Dude," Campbell says.

"Don't dude me. Fucking the Zodiac? What were you thinking? Sully I get, but *you*? It's irresponsible."

"We're all adults here, we can do what we want," Jinx says, crossing her arms over her full chest.

She's developed since the last time I saw her. Her curves are outstanding, and the soft features of her face have matured. But I can't get caught up in that. She's already made a choice to be with the other two.

"Whoring around isn't your job anymore. I won't encourage it."

Jinx storms off into the master bedroom, and Sully follows after her. "Good going, dude."

"What is wrong with you? That was super uncalled for," Campbell says and joins them.

"I agree with you," Trixie says with a shrug once the door is closed. "I'm just surprised you feel that strongly about it. I thought you'd be falling into bed with the three of them."

"Not a chance," I mutter and disappear into the bunk room. I pull my phone out and text Niall.

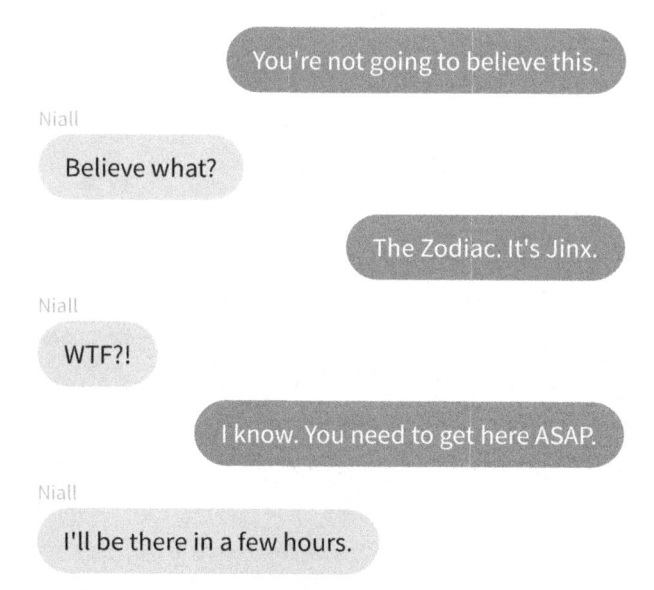

> You're not going to believe this.

Niall
> Believe what?

> The Zodiac. It's Jinx.

Niall
> WTF?!

> I know. You need to get here ASAP.

Niall
> I'll be there in a few hours.

I lay back on my bunk bed and cover my face with my hands. In all my years I never would have expected my former foster sister would be the Zodiac we'd been searching for.

I'm eleven years old. My brother is nine. We share a small cold room in a house owned by our foster parents, Steven and Shelly. We're laying on our bunk beds, reading and doing homework. My stomach growls because for the third night this week, all Steve allowed us to eat was toast.

The door to the bedroom slams open, and Steve storms in with Shelly hot on his heels. "Where the fuck is she?" he roars.

"Who?" I ask? My prepubescent voice cracking.

"That little fucking whore!"

"I don't know what you're talking about!" I shriek as he grabs me by my shaggy hair and hauls me out of the bed.

"Don't play stupid with me, boy! Where is Jinx!"

"I don't know! She went to her room after dinner like always!"

His fist connects with my face, and I see stars. Steve has been emotionally abusing us, and starving us since we moved in here six months ago, but this is the first time he's ever laid a hand on me.

Niall leaps from the top bunk onto Steve's back and starts wailing on his head. He lands a couple of good blows before Shelly rips him off of Steve.

"Get on your fucking knees!" Steve roars at both of us.

We both resist at first, but eventually he wrangles us into submission. He's a lot bigger than both of us. And much stronger. He rips his belt out of his pants and tears our shirts down the back leaving scraps of fabric hanging off of us.

He brings the belt down on our backs repeatedly until he draws blood. Each time we cry out, he hits us harder.

"If I find out you had anything to do with her leaving, I'll do this every night for a month," he spits, sweat dripping down his face.

He continued to abuse us for another year until one of our teachers caught on. I spent every day hoping that wherever Jinx ended up, it was better than where we were.

The fact that she was out whoring herself out, and that she doesn't remember me when her choice irreparably changed my life, makes me furious. He treated her just fine. He even allowed her to sit with them at meals. And instead of being grateful for it, she ran off. She was around fifteen at the time, and she never did anything to help us even though she knew he was neglecting us.

How am I supposed to help this girl when I hate her?

I take the time I need to collect my thoughts and unpack my stuff, then I go out to the kitchen and put on a pot of coffee. After a couple of minutes of it brewing, Jinx steps out of her room and makes eye contact with me. Her gaze shifts to the coffee pot, and she presses her mouth into a thin line.

"You going to forbid me from having caffeine, too?" she snarks.

"That depends, does it turn you into a slut?"

She steps closer to me and lowers her voice so only I can hear her. "All I've heard for the last twenty-four hours is how great you are, and I'm struggling to find the appeal," she says. "Is this shining personality and all the time thing, or is that reserved for girls you've just met?"

I invade her space, staring down at her, my chest nearly touching hers. "This side of me is reserved for entitled little whores who think they can sleep their way out of any problem."

"If that were the case, I could just seduce you into giving me my birth control which I need for more than just pregnancy prevention, asshole. What's the problem? Jealous that your friends are 'fucking the Zodiac'? You know I have a name, right? I'm more than just this fucking curse that's been bestowed upon me."

"That 'curse' is going to save the planet. So get it together, and keep your legs closed."

She reaches up to slap me, but I catch her by the wrist. I'm not expecting her to try anything else, so I'm caught off guard when she knees me in the balls, making me drop to my knees in front of her.

"You don't want to fuck with me," she growls, staring down at me. "I have lived through too much to let pretty boys like you speak to me that way."

She turns on her heel and struts away from me. She thinks that she's won, but this is just the first round. There will be more to come.

Chapter Ten

Jinx

Colt's brother Niall shows up a few hours later, and he gives me the cold shoulder just as bad as Colt does. He's younger than Colt by a couple of years. He's probably just recently out of high school.

I'm not sure what I did to offend them so severely, but they both seem to hate me. Between Trixie being pissed at me, and Niall and Colt hating me, it's going to be a long few months in this cabin.

We're all sitting around the bar in the kitchen eating dinner when Lanya says, "We should come up with some sort of plan for tomorrow."

"You don't think just asking him for the relic or whatever will work?" I ask.

"Archer is a demon. He only trades in deals. We'll have to work something out with him that benefits him. Especially since his body is imbued with the power of the relic."

"What are you thinking?" I ask.

"I don't really have anything to offer him. He might want to siphon off a bit of your magic, or have you do some magic for him. He may send us on some sort of hunt for an object. He's a collector. He likes antiques and oddities."

"Maybe Jinx can just offer her golden pussy to him," Colt says, sarcastically.

"Dude, lay the fuck off," Sully growls at him.

"It's fine. I'm used to being disrespected by men. Comes with the territory."

"It's not fine. He's being a prick for no good reason, and you don't deserve that."

"If she weren't sucking your cock, you would have a clearer head about this," Niall chimes in.

Campbell moves for him, but I grab his arm. "Don't bother. Seriously. I'm not bothered by it." I am bothered by it, but I refuse to let them know that.

"Cause you know it's true," Trixie mutters under her breath.

"Trixie!" Campbell says.

"Enough!" Dalton yells, and slams his fists on the counter. "Everyone just leave her the fuck alone."

"You're not sleeping with her, too, are you?" Niall accuses.

"NO! But it's none of my business who she sleeps with and it's none of yours either. We have more important things to worry about and if this conversation comes up again I'm going to lose it. Let's just deal with these fucking relics and get through the Winter Solstice so that we can save the damn planet and go back to our lives."

Colt and I stare each other down as I wait for him to concede. He breaks eye contact first and I assume that means I've won. The corner of my mouth turns up for a split second before I school my reaction.

"We'll figure out what Archer wants, and we'll deal with it. I'm going to go lay down," I say. I step away from the kitchen island and head toward the bedroom.

"I'll join you in a bit," Sully says and kisses me on the cheek.

I give him a soft smile and leave. The second the door is shut, loud voices erupt in the kitchen and I roll my eyes, trying to tune them out. I'm going to have to see if I can get a phone or something to play music, because I'm tired of being able to hear all of the conversations going on in the house.

The door opens and Campbell slides inside, trying to block out the noise. He crawls onto the bed with me.

"Ignore them. I don't know what climbed inside Colt's ass and died, but he'll come around."

"I don't care if he does or doesn't. His opinion doesn't matter." That's a lie, but I tell it well.

Campbell seems to believe me.

He climbs on top of me, and settles between my legs. "He's probably just jealous," he whispers and kisses me hard, swallowing any protestation I had.

A lot of people look down on me because of my jobs. It's really not something that usually bothers me, but for some reason it bothers me that Colt is judging me for it. But I let Campbell take charge, and distract me.

He slides a large hand under my shirt and toys with my left nipple. He leans back and pulls his shirt off, then helps me out of mine, revealing bare breasts to him.

"You're so fucking beautiful," he says, taking a nipple between his teeth.

He moves down my body and pulls my pants down as he goes. When I'm laid completely bare to him he lays down with his head between my legs, and gently pushes one finger inside of me. He nips at my thigh with his teeth, and I moan softly.

"I want to make you make that sound over and over again," he mutters then spreads my pussy so he has better access.

He presses the tip of his tongue to my clit, and I gasp in pleasure. He inserts another finger, then laps at my clit. He's so good with his tongue.

"Fuck, that feels good," I moan.

He hums in delight with his lips pressed against my aching flesh. The vibration makes my eyes roll back in my head. I press my hand to the back of his head and begin grinding against his face, moaning out as he adds a third finger, stretching me around him.

He pulls away and I whine at the loss. "I was close," I pout.

He lays back on the bed. "Sit on my face."

My eyes go wide at the command. I have had a couple of guys ask me to do this in the past, but it always made me nervous.

"Don't make me ask again. Fuck my face, Jinx."

I move slowly, straddling his face.

He grabs my thighs and says, "I said *sit*." He pulls me down on his face and spears me with his tongue.

He grabs my ass cheeks forcing me to move against his mouth. He dips a finger between my folds, moistening it, then reaches back and inserts it into my ass, making me moan out.

"Fuck," whisper. I grind my pussy against his face, riding his tongue while he works his finger in and out of me. "I'm coming," I gasp. My pussy flutters around his tongue as I ride out wave after wave of pleasure. I climb off of him, his face glistening with my arousal.

"You taste amazing," he says. "Fuck that was hot."

"Your turn," I say, reaching for his pants.

I slide them down and take his thick cock in my hand. I lick the underside of the shaft from base to tip making him groan. I slide my mouth down over the tip and all the way down until he's balls deep in my mouth.

"I'm gonna fuck your mouth, Buttercup. You ready?"

I nod the best I can with his cock still stuffed in my mouth. He slides his hands into my hair and thrusts up into my mouth, hitting the back of my throat over and over again. He grunts and groans as his hips piston up and down. He presses down on my head forcing my nose against his flesh, cutting off my air supply.

I pull back and gasp for air, but he doesn't allow me a very long reprieve before he's forcing himself into my mouth again.

"I need to be inside of your tight little cunt."

He pulls me off of him and throws me down onto my stomach, lifting my ass in the air. He presses at my entrance and shoves himself inside. His pants are still at the edge of the bed. He pulls the belt off of them and brings it down across my back making me gasp out.

"Harder," I gasp–the need for a distraction taking over.

He pounds into me, bottoming out, and brings the belt down across my back again. The sound of him spitting, and wetness at my hole, is the only warning I get before his thumb is inside of my ass. One more blow from the belt is all it takes, and I'm coming again. His thrusts slow and I feel him jerking inside of me as he comes.

He collapses on top of me, peppering kisses down my spine as he goes limp, still inside of me. He slowly pulls out and I flip onto my back. He spreads me open to watch his cum leak out onto the bed.

"God you look good with my cum inside of you," he says, admiring his handiwork.

"Yeah well that's going to have to stop if Captain Stick-up-his-ass doesn't agree to get me my prescription."

His heated gaze meets mine. "The thought of your belly, swollen with my seed..." He climbs back on top of me, and pins my hands above my head. "Please don't freak out again. I won't knock you up, unless that's what you want. I'll talk to Colt about your birth control, but fuck if I don't like the idea of breeding you."

His cock is hard again, and I wonder how the hell he has such a voracious sexual appetite. He scoops his cum up with his cock and slides inside of me and groans. I whine like a needy bitch.

"I'm just going to put that all back where it belongs."

The next morning, we're up before the sun, prepping to drive back to the city to meet with Archer. I step out of the bedroom to find that the only other person in the kitchen is a shirtless Colt.

The tattoos on his throat stretch the whole way down, disappearing beneath his waistband, and I assume they go even lower. The small number thirteen tattoo on his cheek paired with his pierced septum and tongue ring make him irresistible to me. I'm a sucker for a bad boy and he oozes danger from every fiber of his being.

His eyes meet mine and he scowls. "Do you three ever stop fucking?"

"Not if we can help it," I say, pouring myself a cup of coffee.

I am deliciously sore from the night before. After what Trixie said, Sully and Campbell are concerned that something is going to go wrong with Archer, so they wanted to make sure that they made the most of their time with me.

"You're going to have to stop that soon if you don't want to get knocked up," Colt says, sipping his own coffee, and smiling triumphantly.

"We'll just get some condoms," I say with a shrug. Then I set my cup down and step toward Colt. I trail a finger down his bare chest, and add, "Although I do love the feeling of skin against skin. Don't you?"

He grabs my hand and spins me around, pinning my now twisted arm between me and him as he bends me over the counter. He leans down so his mouth is against my ear and says, "Your little tricks won't work on me. I'm not interested in someone who's been used up and discarded at the age of twenty-five."

"You may want to tell that to your cock," I say, grinding my ass against his erection.

He lets out a strangled sound and I laugh. The hate sex between us would be incredible. If only he would give in. He pushes away from the counter and storms into the bunk room. Niall is getting dressed, and he makes eye contact with me right before the door closes. I give him a little wave and he flips me off.

Everyone slowly makes their way into the kitchen while I'm cooking breakfast. I make pancakes from scratch, bacon, and eggs. My very first foster mother taught me how to cook. It came in handy over the years as I cooked and cleaned for me and my foster siblings.

Sully comes up behind me while I'm flipping a pancake, and slides his arms around me. He kisses my neck and cups my breast in his hand.

"You look so good standing here cooking for us. Like a domestic little housewife."

"Is that your thing? Would you like me to be barefoot and pregnant in the kitchen, wearing nothing but an apron as I make you dinner?"

He groans and nibbles my ear, which tells me he would like that very much. I've never lived with a man before, but I could get used to playing house with him and Campbell while we're here. I plate the last of the food, and bring it to the counter. I set the plates down in front of everyone, serving myself and Colt last.

His brow furrows and he makes eye contact. "You made me a plate?"

"You may think I'm an awful person, but I'm not. I'm not going to feed everyone but you."

"Thank you," he mutters, and cuts into his pancake.

He hums softly as he chews, and it brings a smile to my face. I've always enjoyed cooking for people. Especially when they're clearly enjoying it. The fact that my cooking transcends his hatred of me brings me joy.

"Well if you fuck half as good as you cook, I can see why those two are so smitten with you," Lanya says.

Sully leans in and kisses my cheek. "I would say she cooks half as good as she fucks."

I laugh, and glance up to find Colt staring at me with a heated gaze, his eyes trailing down my cleavage. My cheeks heat at his attention, but I look away.

I slowly eat my own food, as anxiety settles in. The way everyone has been talking about Archer, I'm anxious to meet him. They sang Colt's praises and he's a raging asshole. They've done nothing but talk about how terrible Archer is, so if their golden boy is this bad...

We finish eating and get on the road. I'm riding in the passenger seat of Campbell's car. Sully and Colt are in the back. Lanya, Niall, Trixie, and Dalton are in the other car. I had wanted Dalton to ride with us instead of Colt, but he and Trixie are joined at the hip.

We drive in silence for the majority of the trip. About forty-five minutes outside of the city Campbell finally speaks.

"Be very careful about any deals that Archer wants to make. He's a slippery bastard. He'll trick you in any way possible to get more from you than what you bargained for."

"Have you met him before?" I ask.

"A couple of times through The Believers. Plus being in charge of a major crime syndicate will get you all kinds of attention from the cops. He's a scary man. I guess that probably comes with the territory of being a demon, though."

"Lanya isn't scary, and she's a demon."

"That's because Lanya feeds off of lust. She *can't* be scary or she would never eat."

"Fair," I say with a laugh.

"I bet she's good and sated in the cabin," Colt grumbles.

"I expect there's always room for dessert," I say, smirking over my shoulder at him.

Campbell glances at me, but doesn't say anything. What Trixie said about me falling for Colt seems to be getting under his skin. But I warned him that this was not an exclusive situation. We resume our silence for the remainder of the drive.

We pull up to a large set of wrought iron gates. There's a call box off to the side. Campbell reaches out the window and pushes the button on the intercom.

"Can I help you?" a snobby british accent calls through the speakers.

"It's Leon Campbell. Archer is expecting us," he says.

The gates swing open to allow us through.

Somehow this is the first time I'm hearing Campbell's first name. "Leon?" I ask with a giggle. "Wait. Sully, what's your first name?"

"You've been fucking them both without knowing their names?" Colt grinds out.

Sully ignores him and says, "It's Chip."

"Chip?!" I ask with a snort.

"Well, Charlamagne, but Chip for short."

"I can see why you go by Sully," I tease.

"And what kind of a name is Jinx?" Colt snaps.

"We're just joking around," I say. Clearly I've struck a chord with him.

We pull up to a huge estate made of red brick with a black shingle roof and black shutters adorning all of the windows. There are two huge black gargoyles sitting on either side of the front stoop, and the door to the home is massive. I've never seen a private home so large in my entire life. The cabin we've been staying in would fit in this house five times over—maybe more.

When we come to a stop, a man in a tuxedo and a bow tie opens my door for me.

"Miss," he says with a dip of his head. His eyes trace from head to toe then back up. There's a look of distaste in his eyes.

I'm wearing a pair of jean shorts and a T-shirt that Trixie went out and bought me. I imagine that whatever the dress code is for this manor, it is not casual.

"Thank you," I say with a bright smile, stepping out of the car.

He leaves the men to open their own doors. The other car pulls up and the others step out. A man in a valet outfit collects the keys and sets to parking our cars.

"If you'll follow me," the man in the tux says to our group.

"What's your name?" I ask, trying to be polite.

"You may call me Marshall, miss."

"Well, Marshall, I'm Jinx."

"Yes. I've already been informed of that by Master Archer."

I exchange a look with Sully who shrugs. Marshall leads us through the immense front hall of the home and back a long hallway on the first floor. He opens the door to a large room. Linnie flits around behind me, oohing and awing in my head about the decor.

There are three men in arm chairs sitting around the room. Each of them are wearing black button up shirts and slacks, and they each have a handgun visible on their hips. I assume they probably have others hidden on their persons somewhere; maybe some knives, too.

Behind a solid cherry desk is a large man with long black hair and pale skin. He's got a scar over his left eye, and though he shouldn't have vision in that eye, it feels as though it can see right through me. He's wearing a tailored black suit with a red tie. His hands are clasped on his desk as he gives me an appraising look.

"Well come closer little Zodiac. I don't bite. At least not while in this form."

Lanya steps up behind me and places her hand at the small of my back. She escorts me closer as Archer stands. She moves into his space and kisses him on the cheek.

"Lanya, it's been too long."

"Hmm some would say not long enough," Lanya retorts while tracing a flirty hand down his broad chest.

His scrutinizing gaze returns to me. "Your photos didn't do you any justice. Come here. Let me see you."

I swallow thickly and step closer. I can feel the dark energy radiating off of him. He may only look to be around thirty, but he's *old*, and powerful.

His long slender fingers reach for me as I round the desk. In my peripheral vision I see Sully move toward us. I make eye contact and shake my head, stopping him in his tracks. He clenches his teeth together.

"Don't worry, icarast. I won't harm her. So you've come for the relic," he says, brushing his knuckles down my cheek, sending a thrill through my body. "Tell me, what would you offer me in exchange?"

"Is the promise of a future not enough?" I ask with a raised brow.

"I think you can do better than that, little one."

"Seeing as how I was whisked away from my home with none of my possessions, I don't really have much to offer. How about a favor?"

"Jinx!" Campbell says.

"Your boyfriend is right to be concerned. An open ended favor with a demon is a dangerous game to play."

"I'm not her boyfriend," Campbell says.

Archer gives him a skeptical look. "Don't lie to me, mage. I can smell the evidence of your sins inside of her. The angel's too."

My cheeks flush, but not out of embarrassment. "That doesn't make them my boyfriends," I say.

"Everybody out except the Zodiac," Archer commands. "Your familiar, too."

Of course he can see me, Linnie says sarcastically with a sigh. *I'll be right outside if you need me to alert the others of anything heinous.*

"No!" Sully says. "We're not leaving her alone in here with you."

"It's fine. He won't hurt me," I say. For some reason I believe that.

The three armed men usher the others out of the room. Sully gives Archer a glare before the door shuts in his face.

Archer moves closer to me and looks down into my eyes. "I can smell the celestial power radiating off of you. I'm sure the other's told you that I'm a collector?"

"Yes." It comes out as a whisper.

"I don't just collect items. I collect...experiences."

My brow furrows. "Like skydiving?" I say with a laugh.

"Yes. That kind of thing. I would very much like to experience you."

My breath hitches as his fingers graze my breast. "Rig—right now?" I ask in a nervous pant.

He nods. My gaze flicks to the door then back to his eyes.

"And you'll give me the power from the relic?" I ask.

"That depends."

"On what?"

"If I enjoy you as much as I expect I will, I want you at my disposal. We may not have much time left in this realm. If the other Zodiacs can't complete their trials, then this world will end. I'll have a place to go, but you'll be long gone.

"You'll obviously still be free to go about your business. But if you prove to be as delicious as I believe you to be, then I want you here—in my manor—sucking my cocks whenever I tell you."

"C-*cocks*?"

Men never make me nervous, but the last couple of days has had my stomach doing gymnastics like it's going for gold. *It's just because of what's at stake.*

His mouth turns up in the corner, revealing a dazzling lopsided smile. "Cocks."

"Um...the others..." My gaze shifts to the door again.

"You're still free to fuck them. Far be it for me to stop you from having fun."

"Okay," I say.

"One last thing..."

"Isn't that enough?" I ask in exasperation.

"Not quite. You're powerful. Even without the blessing of the Zodiac behind you, I can sense your power. If we all survive this thing, I want you to provide me with an heir."

"What?" I gasp.

"A baby. I want you to give me a child. Do you agree to those terms?"

"Can I talk to the others first?"

"No. This is your choice to make. They can't make it for you."

My heart is in my throat.

He removes his suit jacket and hangs it on a hook on the wall. "What's it gonna be, Little Star? My relic in exchange for renting your womb?"

"Wait, you just want me to hand the baby over to you after it's born?"

He stares at me for long seconds then says, "You would want to be involved? You don't seem like the maternal type."

"I'm not gestating a child for you and giving it up. I was in foster care, and I'm not leaving a baby without it's mother. Plus you don't exactly radiate paternal energy."

"Touche. Yes, well, I suppose custody arrangements could be made. Of course I would have to vet any future friends or partners of yours, but we could negotiate all of that after your ascension. The angel and the blood hunter are acceptable mates, though. That's assuming I'm willing to give you up." His gaze darkens. "Do we have a deal?"

My heart is thundering. This is a huge commitment for something I'm not even sure I believe in. He's hot, and powerful. The others have had me thinking about babies, and as much as it scares me, it also has me panting like a bitch in heat.

"Offer is going once, going twice–"

"Deal!"

"Good girl. Now strip."

I glance to the door then tug at the hem of my shirt nervously before lifting it over my head. I unbutton my shorts and slide them down, and stand in my bra and underwear in front of him. He sits patiently and waits for me to take the rest off.

I slide my panties to the floor then toss them to him. He catches them with a smile, and holds them to his nose and inhales. He watches with rapt attention as I unclasp my bra and drop it to the floor.

"Perfection," he growls. "Now, get on your hands and knees and crawl to me."

I'm a submissive by nature, but I'm a brat. I stand tall and stare him down. He loosens his tie, strips out of his vest, and unbuttons his shirt at a teasing pace.

"I don't like asking for things more than once. If I have to say it again, you'll be punished."

He peels off his shirt revealing corded muscle and a broad chest. His nipples each have a silver barbell through them. There's a delicious trail of dark hair leading from his belly button and disappearing beneath his pants.

I'm so busy admiring him that I don't notice him toying with the tie in his hands. He stalks toward me and loops the tie around my neck and cinches it tight against my throat.

"I said on your hands and knees." His voice is pitched lower, and his eyes flash red. The lights flicker around us.

I stare at him in defiance and a deep rumbling comes from within his chest and I shiver at the sound. His already large form begins to shift and expand. Horns sprout from his head and his skin turns a deep grayish-blue. He pulls the tie tighter around my throat and I begin to feel lightheaded.

"I can do this all day," he purrs.

Finally I drop to my hands and knees and sputter out a cough when he slightly loosens the tie. He leads me back behind his desk like a dog on a leash. He sits in his office chair and stares down at me.

"Take out my cocks and please me," he says.

The button to his pants had popped off when his shape changed. I reach into his underwear and gasp softly as I relieve his cocks of their constraints.

One of them is heavy and thick, and has a bulge at the base. The other is more like a tentacle or a tongue than a cock. The latter wraps around my wrist and squeezes gently as I take the hard, thick, bulbous one into my mouth.

It barely fits in my mouth, and I have to use both of my hands to cover the shaft. He groans as I work myself up and down. He tips his head back in his chair, and grabs a fist full of my hair.

"That's a good fucking girl," he growls. "Put a finger in that tight little cunt for me."

I do as he says, using the hand that doesn't have the tentacle wrapped around it. I moan around the head of his cock and he grunts and fucks my face. All at once he releases me. He drags me to my feet, presses me against his desk and clears it with the sweep of his arm, resulting in a loud crash. Loud voices erupt in the hallway.

His mouth lands on mine, and a forked tongue snakes its way into my mouth. Something trails between my legs, and toward my ass. I open my eyes expecting it to be the tentacle, but I find a tail between my legs. Two large wings are extended behind him. His hands, cocks, and tail are everywhere all at once.

He pulls back and stares down at me. "You taste delicious, Little Star."

He lifts me with ease and sets me on the edge of the desk and gently pushes me back so I'm laying with my head hanging off the other side. He drops to his knees and runs his nose up my slit, making me whimper with need.

"You're so wet for me already." He slides his long tongue inside of me, and moans against my flesh.

One of the others is pounding on the door.

"Jinx!" I think it's Sully, but I can't tell.

Archer removes his tongue and lines his hard cock up at my entrance. "Are you ready for me?"

"Yes," I breathe.

"Beg for it. And I'm going to have you screaming my name loud enough for everyone out in the hall to hear you."

"Please. Please fuck me, Archer."

He rams into me, not giving me time to adjust to him and I scream in ecstasy. His tentacled dick slides into my ass and works in and out of me as he slams into me again and again. His tail slides around and massages my clit and I'm seeing stars as I come for him, screaming his name, just like he said.

He pauses his movements. "I wonder."

"Wonder what?"

I lift my head to watch him with curiosity as he presses into me, somehow stretching me further. The bulbous base of his shaft shoving into me, making me cry out. My reaction has him pausing his movements.

"Are you okay?" he asks.

"More than okay," I gasp and rock my hips upward toward him.

"Good," he growls and starts pumping in and out of me again, shoving the swollen base of his cock into me over and over.

He shoves it in one last time and I'm coming undone for the second time. He roars and an immense delectable pressure builds inside of me as he fills me in both holes.

I let out a breathless laugh and look at him. "Fuck. That was good." I wait for him to pull out, but he doesn't move.

He scoops me up into his arms and sits down in his chair with me on his lap, his cock still inside of me. I look into his eyes and smile.

"Not going to let me go?" I kiss him, running my hands along the horns on his head, making him groan.

"I...can't let you go."

I stare down at him in confusion. The door bursts open, and Sully and Campbell storm inside with guns raised. When they take in the sight before them, they drop their weapons, and their faces go cold.

Colt steps in behind them. "I wasn't serious when I said to offer him sex." He's even more pissed at me than before.

I try to climb off of Archer's lap, but where we're connected, I'm locked in place.

"What is going on?" I ask in a panic.

Chapter Eleven

Archer

She's mine. She took my knot. Her other boys are watching, and they're mad, but that doesn't matter to me. I found a human who could accept what I have to offer. She squiggles on my lap, and I groan. I'm going to come again.

"What's going on? What did you do?"

She tries to move off of me again, and I grunt as I start filling her again with my seed. Thankfully, she's not fertile. This shouldn't result in a child. I want her pregnant, but not until this ridiculous trial is over with.

Lanya steps into the room. "Oh my god, Archer. What the fuck were you thinking? The Zodiac?"

"It was an accident," I say with a shrug.

"Fucking me wasn't an accident," Jinx says with a scowl.

"No, that *was* intentional. Mating you, however, was not." I gasp as I unload into her for a third time. "You feel so good. Can you wiggle again?"

A blush is creeping into Jinx's face. "Can everyone leave, please?"

"No," Sully, Colt, and Campbell all say in unison.

Jinx leans forward and places her forehead on my chest and groans. My hands slide up and cup her tits, my second appendage wriggles in her ass and she gasps.

"Can you come again?" I whisper in her ear.

She sits back up and looks at me, staring daggers at me. "Does this seem like a good time for that?"

"Seems like the perfect time," I say and rub her clit with my thumb.

"Stop that," she hisses and swats my hand away.

"No!" I growl and put my hand back where it was. "Give me one more."

I grab her hips and grind her against me, making eye contact with her boys as I do. She moans when I put my thumb back against her clit. She turns her head to look at the others.

"Eyes on me," I command and grip her face in my free hand. "I want to see you while you're coming all over my cock."

She continues grinding against me, pleasure building inside of her. Her breath comes in quick pants. She grabs my horns and tips my head back.

"I'm going to get you back for this," she gasps.

"I look forward to it. Now come for me, Little Star."

"Fuck, Archer," she moans as she clamps down around my knot, making me fill her even more. She comes down from her orgasm. "How long are we going to be stuck like this?"

"I'm not sure. No one's ever taken my knot before."

"Can someone explain what the fuck is happening?" Niall asks. He's staring at my girl like she's dirt on his shoe, and I want to relieve him of his head.

"Can everyone get the fuck out?" Jinx screams.

"I'm not leaving you alone with him, again." Sully insists.

"Fine. Campbell and Sully can stay. Everyone else out."

I nod in approval. My men escort the others out, and shut the door behind them. Sully and Campbell approach. I snarl at them. Jinx and I are in a vulnerable position, and I don't entirely trust them.

"Just keep your distance, please."

"What the fuck happened, Jinx?" Sully asks.

"We made a deal, and we were sealing it," she says.

"You mated her without her permission?" Campbell asks me.

"I'm not thrilled about it either, but he already said it was an accident," she answers for me as I kiss down her neck and chest.

"What all was a part of the deal?" Campbell asks. He's anxious. He should be.

She tries to turn and face them and the friction has me coming again. I grunt and ride out my fifth orgasm. That seems to be the final one, because the swelling goes down, and I'm able to pull out of her. A waterfall of my cum pours out on my lap, my chair, and the floor.

Jinx breathes a sigh of relief and stands. She turns to face the others and tries to step away, but I pull her back into my lap. She's mine, and if they want her, they can fight me for her.

"The deal was that he would give me the relic in exchange for..." she hesitates like she's embarrassed to say it out loud.

"In exchange for the relic, Jinx had to seal the deal with sex, stay here until her ascension if I decided that I liked her, and give me an heir after her ascension was complete."

Sully's face falls. "I see how it is," he says.

"What do you mean?" she tries to move toward him, but I hold her in place. "Archer, let me go, please," she whispers.

"No."

"You said that I could still have them, if we did this."

"Yes, but that was before that delicious little cunt of yours accepted my knot. Does that greedy pussy need more than me?"

I pull Jinx back against my chest and lay her head on my shoulder. The blush has returned to her cheeks. She wants to go to them, but she wants me to keep touching her. I dip my fingers between her thighs and scoop up some of the mess I've made.

"Open for me," I whisper in her ear.

She opens her mouth and I shove my fingers inside.

"Good girl," I purr, and shift back to my human form. "So you still want the other two?" I ask.

She nods.

"Can you handle three of us at once?"

She bites down on her lip and nods again.

"Well what the little lady wants the little lady gets. You both are moving in here with her."

"It's not safe here. That's why we have the cabin."

"I can assure you that whatever redneck set up you have out in the middle of fucking nowhere is nothing compared to my security here. My home is the safest in the state."

My hand roams up and cups her breast. She arches her back against me.

"Would you stop fucking touching her?" Campbell shouts, getting more pissed by the second.

"I can't," I say, biting her shoulder gently. "I don't think I'll ever be able to stop."

"You're going to have to since the others need to come back in here so we can figure out what the plan is now," Jinx says.

"No. You need a bath. And food. And then we can talk. What do you want to eat? I'll have my cook make it." My need to protect and provide for her is kicking in. This is shit timing. I want to lock her away for a week and not let anyone else see her.

"I'm okay for now," she says.

"No. You need to eat. If you don't choose, I'll choose for you."

She doesn't respond so I text my cook to bring dinner to my room.

"If you'll excuse us, I need to take care of my mate," I say and scoop Jinx up into my arms and carry her, naked, through the manor.

Chapter Twelve

Jinx

"I can walk," I protest.

"Nonsense," Archer growls.

We step out the door and the others are all whispering among themselves. They all glare as we walk past, but none as much as Colt. This whole situation is super embarrassing.

"The shifter is obsessed with you," Archer whispers when we round the corner.

"Shifter?"

"The big one with the tattoos. Are you sleeping with him too?"

"No. He hates me," I say with a laugh. "Not sure what I did to piss him off, but something upset him."

"He doesn't hate you. He wants to fuck you. He was practically screaming his lustful thoughts at us as we walked by. The younger one, though. *He* hates you."

"Oh," I whisper. My mind starts going a million miles a second thinking about Colt and the other three. *No. That's selfish.*

Be selfish for once in your life. Linnie encourages, following behind.

Fuck off, Lin.

"She's right. You're allowed to be selfish. Whatever you want, it's yours," Archer insists.

"I'm mad that you all can see and hear her," I grumble.

"The others can, too?"

"Just Sully and Camp."

"Interesting." He doesn't elaborate on what he means.

He carries me up an entire flight of stairs and into a massive master bedroom with a California king sized bed and an intense mural of heaven and hell on his ceiling. It provides a stark contrast to the otherwise off-white room. He walks past the bed and into the bathroom and begins running water into an enormous bath tub.

"We made such a mess of your office," I say.

"I have people to clean it up. Don't worry about any of that. Just let me take care of you."

My cheeks heat at the thought of someone else cleaning up the mess we made. *What a terrible job to have.*

He waits until the water is a good depth then lifts me into the bath. He climbs in with me and begins scrubbing me down with soap and water. His hand roams between my legs and I gasp.

"I'm just trying to get you clean, Little Star. But if you want to go again, I'm happy to oblige. I won't knot you this time."

"I think I need a little break," I say with a laugh.

"You did have the seed of the other two inside of you. You have quite the appetite. Do you think you can keep all three of us sated?"

My pulse quickens, and my pussy clenches thinking about all three of them on me at once. "I think so," I say.

There's a knock at the bedroom door while we're toweling off, and Archer opens the door to allow the cook to bring food in. There's a steak and potatoes and steamed broccoli along with some iced tea and a piece of cheesecake for dessert. Archer cuts into my steak and tries to feed me a piece.

"I can feed myself," I say with a blush.

"Please let me. It's important to me that I take care of you."

I sigh and open my mouth. He watches intently as I chew and swallow.

"Well?"

"It's so good," I say. "Easily the best steak I've ever had."

Archer beams at me, and it's adorable. The menacing demon is still below the surface, but it's being suppressed by a man obsessed with his mate.

"A stripper from the city is our Libra," he muses.

"You knew I was a stripper?" I ask.

"I know everything there is to know about you," he says. "Well, as much as one can learn from a piece of paper. I know you grew up in foster care. Your parents died when you were young. You took up stripping and then escorting to make ends meet. You were just accepted into university for psychology, and you're currently wanted by the police in connection with the death of an officer."

"That was Campbell. He walked in on another officer..." I look at the ceiling.

I felt so helpless in that moment. I vowed as a teen that I would never let someone violate me like that again, and I almost let it happen.

"What was the other officer trying to do?"

"Trying to rape me."

Archer snarls. I move the plate out from between us, and pull my towel off, and straddle his lap.

"He didn't manage to do anything. Campbell saved me."

"Is that why you slept with him? Out of obligation?"

"No, silly. I slept with him because I like him."

"And me? Did you just fuck me because you felt like you had to?" He cocks an eyebrow at me. His cock grows hard beneath me.

"Well, partially. But, I mean, look at you," I say with a smirk.

"This form is flattering."

"I like your other form better."

He growls and kisses me, sliding his cock inside of me, and shedding his human visage. His cock grows with him and I groan into his mouth.

He pulls away and says, "Most people are scared of this form."

"I'm not most people," I say and kiss him again as I bounce up and down on his cock.

"This mating will be the end of both of us if we can't leave this bedroom," he says, nipping at my throat with his pointed teeth.

"I'm okay with that," I pant, starting to reach the edge of oblivion. His tail wraps around my right tit and his tentacle rubs at my clit. I gasp in pleasure and moan out his name as he rides out his own orgasm.

We lay in bed for a few minutes, his tail tracing circles on my back as he strokes my hair.

"We really need to get back to the others," I say. "Do you have any clothes I can wear? We left mine in the office."

"Give me a minute," he says, shrinking back down to his human state, and pulling on a pair of pants. He leaves the room for about five minutes and returns with a dress.

"Where did that come from?" I ask, sliding it on over my head. It fits okay, surprisingly.

"One of my men lives here with his girlfriend. She's about your size. She won't mind. I'll buy her two to replace that one."

He leads me back down to the office where the others are sitting around talking. A couple of them have glasses of whiskey in front of them. Sully, Campbell, and Colt jump to their feet when we enter the room.

"Are you okay?" Campbell asks, tucking my hair behind my ear.

"I'm actually really good," I say, taking his hand in mine. And it's the truth. At some point I might start panicking about my newly mated status, but I like Archer. A lot.

"He mated you without your permission. That's a serious violation of your autonomy."

I shrug and smile at Archer who is gazing at me lovingly from his office chair. "I was annoyed at first, but I'm coming around. Are you okay?"

"I'm...dealing."

"We can talk about it later?"

He nods, and I step up to Sully. "Are you mad?"

"You're still mine?"

"I'm still yours."

"I'm a little mad, but I'll get over it with a little help." He cups my cheek with his hand and kisses me and groans. "You taste like hellfire. It's like a sinful little treat."

"That's enough. Come here, Little Star," Archer says.

I want to defy him, but I obey. We have too much to do. I step past Colt who is standing with his arms crossed, glaring at me. I still can't sense the shifter on him which is weird for me. I can typically peg a supernatural being from a mile away.

He grabs me by the arm. Archer stands and snarls at him. Colt doesn't even acknowledge him as he sneers at me.

"Don't get yourself knocked up before you start your ascension. You won't be getting my relic, if you do." He releases me aggressively.

I shove past him and move over to Archer.

He pulls me into him and says, "Touch my mate like that again and we're going to have problems. If you won't give her your power, I'll kill you so she can get it out."

"Enough," I say and place my hand on his arm.

He relaxes at my touch, and sits back down in his chair. He pulls me into his lap and nuzzles my neck. The others return to their seats.

"I'm taking you to my room and not letting you leave after this. I already need to be back inside of you," Archer whispers and nibbles at my ear.

"Can we please get this meeting over with? We have three of the relics," I say giving an annoyed look at Colt. "Where is the last one?"

"The fourth is in Blackridge Asylum," Archer says.

His hand starts migrating up my thigh and under my dress. I try to move it away but he squeezes my leg hard enough to bruise, and I have to stifle a moan. When he's sure I'm not going to try to stop him again, he releases me and dips his fingers into my pussy. The desk is high enough that the others can't see what is happening, but by the look on their faces, they know.

"So wet for me, again?" He whispers in my ear.

I try to play it off like he's not finger fucking me in front of a room full of people. "How do we get it from him?" I ask breathlessly?

"Whoring yourself out seems to be going well," Colt says.

I make eye contact with him. There's a hunger in his eyes as he watches me. Having his eyes on me, I'm close. I'm so close. I tip my head back against Archer's shoulder as I fall apart, all eyes in the room on me. Colt stands and storms from the room, with Niall in tow. My cheeks go red, and for the first time in my life I feel shy. I try to bury my face in Archer's shirt, but he won't allow it.

"Don't be ashamed Little Star. That was beautiful," he says and kisses me.

"Can we please get this over with? How do we get the relic?"

Archer chuckles in my ear. "I have a connection at the asylum. I can get him out. The problem is that he's dangerous."

"How?" I ask.

"You've probably heard of him. They call him The Cobra. His real name is—"

"Ranger Stevens," Campbell finishes.

"Yes."

"Who is that?" I ask.

"He's a fucking nut job is what he is," Sully says. "He has mind control and telekinesis abilities, and he doesn't use them for good. We're not letting Jinx anywhere near him."

"I agree," Archer says. "But he only trusts me. I'll have to come with you."

"I want to come!" Trixie says.

"Who will stay here with Jinx then?" Sully asks.

"Colt and Niall can," Lanya says. "I'll be coming with you, too."

"Great. I'll just stay here with the two big grumpy shifters who hate me," I grumble.

"It'll only be for a half a day at most," Archer says, toying with my hair.

"Fine," I say with a pout. "But don't I need to be the one to retrieve the relic? How do I get them out anyway?"

"I'm not one hundred percent sure on that. It's possible you have to cut them out," Archer says as if that's not a horrifying proposition.

Trixie says, "I'm almost positive she just has to pull on the energy from them. They can stay firmly attached to your bodies."

"How did they get inside of you?" I ask.

"Painfully," Campbell grumbles. "We each woke up one night with searing pain after a believer meeting with one of the higher ups. They had said that we would be chosen, but didn't explain what would be entailed."

"So Cobra is also a believer?"

"He is," Sully says. "He got locked up shortly after we were imbued with the power of the relics."

Archer squeezes my knee. "I'll call my contact at the asylum first thing in the morning, and arrange a visit. Let's be done with this stupid meeting and get some rest."

"Can I talk to Jinx for a minute?" Lanya asks.

"Fine, but don't keep her long."

"I wouldn't dream of it."

The others leave, or start speaking among themselves in the room. Lanya takes me by the hand and pulls me into the hallway. She glances around nervously.

"What's going on?" I ask with a laugh.

"You need to be careful," she warns. "Archer is dangerous."

"I think he's sweet," I say defensively. He is my mate, and I want to protect him as much as he wants to protect me.

She lets out a cackle. "Honey, he's not sweet. He's an Archdemon, and he has some of the most evil men in this country under his thumb. Including some of the deniers. He answers directly to the dark lord himself."

"I'm not worried about him, but thank you, Lanya," I say and try to return to the office, but she grabs a hold of my arm.

"I don't think you're capable of properly *satisfying* him. And if you're not, he will find someone else who is."

I pull my hand out of her grasp. "Thanks for the advice, but I don't need it." *Great. Making enemies as I go.*

Archer steps out of the room and gives Lanya a dark look, then turns to me, "Ready to go back to my room?"

"So ready. Can Campbell and Sully come too?"

"I already invited them," he says, and offers me his arm. I take it and we head back to his room together.

Chapter Thirteen
Cobra

The Zodiac is with him; naked and writhing between him and two others. They offer her pain with her pleasure, whipping her relentlessly with a riding crop, taking turns impaling her on their cocks.

I stand in the shadows on the balcony–watching, waiting. I'm stroking my hard length with one hand and smoking a cigarette with the other.

It's been years since I've fucked a woman. Sure, I made due with the male residents, and the occasional health technician. But given my preferences, they wouldn't allow me within a hundred feet of a female.

Archer roars out his release, sliding his knot inside of the girl, and I watch wide-eyed as she actually takes it. Archer spoons her on the bed as the other two come all over her face and tits. Her gaze shifts to where I lurk in the shadows as if, now that they're all spent, she can sense me. I shoot my load on the balcony, staring into her eyes; at her cum covered face.

That's it, Little Mouse. You're ready for me. You just don't know it.

Archer's cell phone rings, pulling her attention from her fate. I know exactly who's on the other line. He answers, still locked inside of her, and shouts. He thought he could keep her from me, but he was so wrong.

The blonde one retrieves a towel from the bathroom and cleans The Zodiac up. Archer thrusts absently into her, and I watch as he spills inside of her again. He mated her. Which means she's different from most humans. But then of course she is. Libra chose *her* as its champion.

Archer is finally able to pull himself free; his enormous cock sliding out of her as her cunt gushes his cum onto the bed. Archer and the other men get dressed. They each give The Zodiac a kiss, and then they take their leave.

The girl goes to the bathroom, and is in there for a while. When she returns, her hair is wet and she has a towel wrapped around her body. She removes the comforter from the bed since it has the evidence of their romp all over it. She flicks off the light, covers herself with the sheet, and falls asleep.

I wait until her breathing slows, and open the door to the balcony without a sound. I leave it open behind me, a cool breeze blowing the curtains inward. She's curled up on her side, sound asleep—likely exhausted from her mating with an archdemon.

Gently, carefully, I climb into the bed and kneel over her, watching her breathe. My cock hardens once more in my pants as I peel back the sheet and reveal her soft curves to me.

I unzip my pants and pull out my hard length and press it to her warm, wet cunt. The wetness gathered there is probably from Archer, but I don't care. I ease myself in and out of her, careful not to wake her. I bite down on my knuckles to stop myself from moaning.

It doesn't matter. She starts to stir, and with a sleepy smile she mutters "I thought you guys had to go to the asylum."

I pound into her, harder and faster. I need to come inside of her before she realizes that I'm not one of the others. She reaches between her legs and rubs her clit, moaning softly. Her breaths come in pants and she clenches down around me. My balls draw tight, and I thrust one last time, spilling myself inside of her.

The sensation wakes her up, completely. Her eyes nearly bulge out of her head when she realizes that it's a stranger taking her, and not one of her boy toys. She tries to scream, but I lay my full weight on her and cover her mouth with my hand.

"Now now, Little Mouse. We wouldn't want to wake the others."

The fear in her eyes shifts to curiosity, then annoyance.

"Do you promise not to scream if I let you speak?"

She nods her head in affirmation. The little liar. I remove my hand and she shrieks at the top of her lungs. The door almost immediately slams open, and two massive tattooed thugs storm into the room.

The smaller one hauls me off of her, and slams me against a wall, pinning me with his forearm against my throat. The bigger of the two climbs into the bed with her. Colt and Niall–they're the most recent recruits to The Believers. I haven't met all of them, but these two I've seen in passing.

"Are you okay?" Colt asks, placing his hand on her cheek and looking her over.

She reaches down and scoops up some of my seed and makes a disgusted face. "Who the *fuck* are you?" she growls, tears streaming down her face.

"I suppose that was quite rude of me," I say; the words strangled from the pressure on my windpipe. "I believe that most people know me as The Cobra."

"How did you get in here?" Colt growls.

"A magician never reveals his secrets," I say with a smirk.

The Zodiac crawls out of the bed and storms into the bathroom, slamming the door behind her. Colt follows and tries to get into the bathroom, but she's locked the door. His panther form is pushing to the surface. He and his little cub of a brother want to rip my throat out, but they can't. Not yet, anyway.

"Jinx, let me in!" Colt yells through the door.

Jinx. That's the name of the pretty little thing that I just fucked. *God I wanna go again.*

"Have you tasted that pussy yet?" I ask Niall with a smile. He thinks he's won with his forearm against my throat, but he couldn't be more wrong.

"No. I have no interest in the bitch."

Nope. That's not going to fly. I knee him in the balls, and his arm loosens on my neck. I bring my palm up into his nose, and he releases me entirely.

"Don't talk about The Zodiac that way."

He tries to pin me again, but I duck out of the way. He's strong as hell, but he's big and slow. Using my telekinesis abilities, I work the tumblers in the bathroom door, and throw it open, revealing Jinx to us.

"Come out, come out Little Mouse. I just want to play."

She put a dress on which is a shame since she's so stunning without it. She tries to slam the door, but I hold it open with my mind, making her growl in frustration. She changes tactics, and marches up into my space and slaps me leaving a glorious sting where her hand connected with my face.

As the pain blooms, so does my smile. "Harder."

Her eyes widen slightly, but she does as I say, and slaps me harder, making me groan.

"Not bad, but I think you can do better."

She pulls back a closed fist and attempts to punch me, but I catch her wrist and pull her flush against my body. She lets out a little gasp of surprise.

"Let her go!" Colt yells and reaches for her.

One look in my eyes has him stopping short. Shifters are so easy to control. They do everything with brute force and never work on their mental shields.

"What are you doing here?" she demands.

"I heard you were ready for me. Well, as ready as anyone can be for me."

"So you decided to come in here and assault me in my sleep?"

"Well, I waited so long to meet you that I didn't want to be a disappointment to you. I don't see what the issue is. You got an orgasm out of it."

She tries to shove me off of her, and Colt growls.

"The big kitty has feeeelings for you," I tease. "I can see why, though. You're scrumptious."

I pull her in for a kiss and she resists at first, but eventually gives in. She tastes like candy and hellfire. Niall tries to sneak up behind me, but I pull his feet out from under him, making him land flat on his back.

Several sets of footsteps make their way up the stairs, and I'm face to face with the people that put me in that horrific place to begin with. Jinx attempts to go to Archer, but I pull her back into me. I reach in my pocket and retrieve the box cutter I stole from the storage shed at the asylum.

"Ah ah, Little Mouse. You're staying with me, for now. I need some reassurance before I let you go back to him. And believe me when I say that I want to see you back with him more than you could ever know."

"Give me my mate," Archer growls.

"You can have her back as soon as you swear to me that you won't send me back to the asylum. Putting me in there was shady fucking business, and I will not go back. They kept me sedated. Did you know that? Drugs upon drugs for days so that I could barely move. It was vaguely reminiscent of my childhood. Happy memories."

Archer's face betrays no feelings of remorse. And that hurts more than anything.

"You're too dangerous to be out in the world," Lanya says, stepping toward me and releasing a little of her succubus magic on me in an attempt to seduce me.

"Keep that up and I'll fuck The Zodiac again in front of you all."

Jinx blushes as every eye in the room settles on her.

"Again?" Archer growls.

"I was asleep. I thought he was one of you, coming back for more."

"Make a deal with me, Archer, or I'll kill every person here not strong enough to fight my abilities. Well...technically I'll make them kill themselves, but same thing really."

"I don't care about anyone here but her. Do what you want."

"Archer!" Jinx says in horror.

He shrugs. "You're the only one that matters to me."

"Thanks a lot," Lanya mutters.

"The others matter to *me*. Make the fucking deal," Jinx says.

"Fine. In exchange for not killing anyone here, I will not send you back to Blackridge Asylum."

"Or any asylum or any prison."

"Or any asylum or any prison," he adds.

"And you won't lock me in the dungeon."

He rolls his eyes. "And I won't lock you in the dungeon. I will not do anything to you that could be considered imprisonment."

I know better than to allow for loopholes in deals with devils–especially him. Archer advances. He takes my face in his large hands and kisses me. A small peck would do, but Archer and I have a history. He swipes at the seam of my mouth with his tongue and I grant him access. He growls into my mouth, then smiles and pulls back, looking down at Jinx, who's still pressed against my body.

"You like that, Little Star?"

Chapter Fourteen

Jinx

My face heats. I've been caught. I did like that—very much. I'm still horrified at the fact that Cobra assaulted me, but watching him and Archer makes me feel needy. I won't admit that though.

"No. I'm getting a shower." I pull away from Cobra and shoot him a dirty look. He gives me one of his unhinged smiles.

"Get some rest, Little Mouse. You're going to need it."

He is insane. When Archer said he had escaped, I saw the concern in his eyes. He and the others left fully believing that the security at the estate was enough to keep him out and I trusted their judgment.

"I'm taking Cobra down to the office to have a conversation with him. I'll post one of my men outside the door. Just tell them if you need me." Archer kisses me on the forehead.

He grabs Cobra by the scruff of the neck and leads him out of the room. Everyone else follows except for Colt, Sully, and Campbell.

"You okay sweet girl?" Sully asks.

"No. I feel violated." I wrap my arms around myself.

"Do you want some company?" Campbell asks.

"I don't think so. I think I just need some time alone."

I've never had anyone to look out for me except for Linnie. After my foster dad assaulted me when I was a teenager, she had stood watch every night for several years. I feel like I'm going to need her to do that again for a while.

"We'll go join the others then. Let us know if you need anything."

Colt looks like he wants to say something, but he leaves with the others and I go and get a shower to wash away my feelings. I get dressed and step back into the bedroom. About an hour later, Archer, Sully, and Campbell return. We all get into the large bed, and eventually, with their comforting touches, I fall asleep.

I roll over in the bed and reach for the guys, but there's no one there. My heart skips into a panic when I realize that I'm alone. My dreams were plagued with my foster dad's face, and it's made me a little jumpy. The door to the bedroom opens and Archer enters with a purpose—he's in his human form.

He crosses the room and climbs into bed with me, wrapping me in his arms. "What's wrong, Little Star."

"Cobra sneaking in here last night brought back some bad memories. That's all."

"Memories of what?" he growls.

"It's all in the past. I don't really want to talk about it."

"We're going to talk about it. Anyone who has hurt you is going to pay. The only reason Cobra is still alive is because you need him for your ascension."

"You two seemed to have a special bond," I say, bitterly.

"Are you jealous?" he asks with a smirk.

"I just didn't like seeing you kiss the man who just assaulted me like he was your lover, too." I pout.

"It seemed like you liked it," he says and trails his hand over my curves. "It *seemed* like you liked it very *very* much."

I chew my lip. "It was a little hot, but that doesn't change what he did."

"Cobra is not sane. His brilliant mind is fractured from things that happened to him as a child. He's not all together there. I'm not going to excuse what he did, but he saw you with me and assumed that you were to be...shared."

"That's a really weird thing to assume. Unless...You've shared women before, haven't you?"

"And men. And we were together without anyone else. He was my—what's the word that humans are using for it these days—partner."

I feel my face flush. "It doesn't change the fact that he sneaked in here and fucked me without my permission."

"He said you came," he teases.

"That doesn't make it better."

"Well, don't expect an apology from him. He will never concede to having done anything wrong."

"He said that you were the reason he was locked in the asylum?"

Archer lets out a heavy sigh. "When we were chosen to guard the relics, it was because of our strength; not because we're good people. When Cobra found out that we would be meeting you soon, he got weird. He started talking about how you belonged to him, and how he was going to break you in and possess you. He was obsessed. So we decided it was safest to put him in the asylum until we could find you and make sure that you were prepared for him."

My brow furrows. "But you claimed me and made me promise to have a baby with you. Isn't that the same? That feels a little unfair."

"You asked her to give you a baby?" Cobra asks, stepping into the room.

Archer didn't shut the door behind him. Cobra has a pained look on his face. He waves his hand and the door slams shut and the tumblers click it locked. Archer stands and puts himself between me and Cobra. I move to a sitting position, pulling my knees and the blanket up to my chest.

"I did," Archer says.

"You never wanted a baby before. You've known her for two days and decided that you wanted to have a baby with her?"

"I never said I didn't want a baby, Ranger. I told you that I didn't think you were stable enough to raise a baby with me. And initially Jinx and I weren't going to raise a baby together, but then she took my knot, and that all changed.

"And anyway, she still has to complete her ascension. I'm not getting her pregnant before then. I won't put our child or her at risk."

"Should I go?" I ask, feeling like I'm intruding on a very private conversation.

"No. You can stay. I'm clearly the one who isn't wanted here," Cobra says. He turns to leave.

"Ranger, wait!" Archer moves toward him.

Cobra rounds on Archer, "Don't 'Ranger' me. I thought that you locked me up in there because you didn't trust me with The Zodiac. But you just wanted me gone. You dumped me in there like a pile of trash. I might be crazy but I still have feelings." He pauses and takes a deep breath. "I never imagined that you didn't actually want me anymore."

"Wait," I say, interrupting their conversation. "Is that how you broke up with him? By throwing him into an insane asylum?"

"He didn't even visit once I was in there," Cobra adds indignantly.

"Archer!" I snap.

"Oh no! You two don't get to gang up on me."

"We could gang up on her instead," Cobra jokes.

But I know he's just trying to hide how hurt he is. I do the same thing.

"I'll apologize to him as soon as he apologizes for assaulting you last night," Archer says and crosses his arms over his chest like a petulant child.

"I'm not going to apologize for that. It might just be that I've been locked up for the last three years, or the fact that she was full of your cum, but that's the best pussy I've ever had. Taking it while she was asleep was the cherry on top. The only thing it was missing was you, fucking me from behind."

My breath hitches at his words, and Archer's head snaps toward me. "You're turned on."

"I am not!" I protest.

"Don't lie to me. I can feel it through the bond. You were turned on when we kissed last night, too. Do you like that? Do you want to watch me fuck him? Would that make up for what he did to you last night?"

I suck in a breath through my teeth, making a hissing sound. Heat pools in my belly, thinking about watching them together.

"I'll do it if she lets me eat her out while you do," Cobra says.

"No. You can watch her touch herself, but you can't touch her. That'll be your punishment for breaking her trust; and mine." Archer grabs a fistful of Cobra's hair and leads him to the bed. He throws him face down and rips down his pants. "Bedside table, princess. There's a bottle of lube in there. And some zip ties."

I drop the blanket from my body and reach for the bedside table. I toss Archer the lube and he catches it one handed. He does the same with the zip ties. With expert fingers he zips up Cobra's hands as I watch, enraptured.

"Spread your legs Little Star; right in front of his face, but just out of reach. I want him to smell your dripping cunt, but not be able to touch it."

He releases his massive cocks and pours a generous amount of lube onto the thick one and some onto Cobra's ass. He lines himself up with Cobra's hole. This is exactly what I need. To feel some piece of control while Cobra doesn't have any. To take back the power that felt lost after last night.

"Touch yourself, beautiful. I want to see you get off while watching us."

I follow his command and dip a finger into my wet pussy. "Fuck him," I say, but it comes out as a pant.

"Dirty girl," Cobra mumbles into the blankets.

His eyes meet mine and he groans as Archer begins pushing into him, stretching him out. Archer works in and out of Cobra's ass going a little deeper each time. Cobra gasps and I can't tell if it's in pain or pleasure or both.

"You have always been able to take me so well, Ranger."

"Not as well as Jinx does," Cobra says. "I saw her take your knot last night." He moans as Archer sinks all the way up to his knot. "Let me taste that pretty cunt, Jinx. Please," he begs.

I consider giving in to him, imagining what his long split tongue would feel like on my clit.

Archer growls and says, "Look at me. Don't listen to him. Don't reward him for his bad behavior. He needs to be punished. If you wait, I'll fuck you good and hard when I'm done with him. Or we can call the others in."

He's grunting between words, his eyes glued to where my fingers stroke my clit. Cobra tries inching forward toward me, but Archer yanks him back by the hips and slaps his ass.

"Just a little taste Archer, please."

"No, not a single touch until we both tell you you're allowed. And don't you dare come until I tell you to."

Disobedience flashes in Cobra's eyes, but he ultimately follows through. With his eyes and Archer's glued to me, I'm almost there.

"Don't come yet, Little Star. Wait for me." He slams into Cobra's ass three more times. "*Now!*"

"Fuck, Archer!" I scream.

We both come at the same time. Cobra is struggling to hold back his own orgasm. I can see his cock weeping beneath him, desperate for the sweet release that it would give him. Archer pulls out of him, and his cum spills onto the bed.

"Please. Please let me come," Cobra begs.

"What do you think, Jinx? Does he get to?"

"Hmmm not yet. Go get cleaned up then give me your knot. I want him to watch me take it."

"She's just as sadistic as you are," Cobra says with an appreciative smile.

"Is it any surprise I was able to mate her?"

"No. It's no surprise why you chose her, either."

Archer goes into the bathroom and turns on the sink to wash himself off. Cobra sits cross legged on the bed and leans back on his palms. His cock is jutting straight up into the air dripping with precum. I can't help but glance at it. He notices my attention and smirks, making a blush rise in my cheeks.

Archer returns and his gaze darts between the two of us. Cobra smiling like a maniac, and me trying desperately to look anywhere but at his throbbing member.

"You want to suck his cock, don't you, Little Star?"

"No," I lie.

"Yes you do. If that's what you want, I'm not going to hold you back, but I'm going to fuck that tight little cunt while you do it. Go on. Put it in your mouth."

I crawl toward Cobra and he spreads his legs for me, a neediness in his eyes. I press my tongue at the base of his shaft and clean up the mess he's made of himself, savoring the salty flavor. Cobra's hips buck toward my mouth, desperate for more.

Archer settles in behind me and presses at my entrance. I whine and push my hips back impatiently while I wait for him to sink into me.

"Such a greedy little thing, aren't you. Suck his cock like you mean it, pretty girl."

Eager to please I suck Cobra's cock into my mouth until it hits the back of my throat. I hold him there and hollow out my cheeks before I begin moving up and down. Archer plunges into me hard and fast.

"Your mouth is the most amazing place my dick has ever been. and I once fucked Archer while that tentacle penis thing he has fucked my asshole, and his tail tickled my balls."

"Stop fucking talking," Archer growls.

Cobra groans as I gently squeeze his balls and moan around his thick shaft.

"Don't be jealous, big guy. It's not your fault that you can't compare to the heaven that is her mouth."

"I said shut up!" Archer yells, and he grabs Cobra by the throat.

"Harder," Cobra moans, and I can't tell if he's talking to me or Archer.

Archer slams into me, his knot stretching me as I suck Cobra's cock hard and fast. His face turns purple in Archer's grip and I think for a second he might pass out. Instead his hips jerk, and his cock twitches as he spills his load into my mouth. I swallow him down and he groans as he watches.

Archer thrusts into me one last time, his knot locking into place as I come for him. We collapse on the bed, and he kisses the back of my neck.

"Fuck that was good," Cobra says. "You're perfect, Little Mouse. I could just eat you up."

He laps at my pussy where Archer is connected to me and I tremble at the sensation causing Archer to come again inside of me. I really need to get back on my birth control before a baby happens by accident and for real.

I hear voices in the hall and realize that Cobra never shut the door after he tried to leave. The faces of the rest of The Believers appear in the doorway.

"I'm getting really tired of everyone seeing me naked, I grumble."

"You'd think you'd be used to it, being a hooker and all," Niall snaps and storms off.

Lanya and Trixie glare at me like I'm ruining their entire lives. Dalton's eyes are glued to where I'm joined with Archer, his mouth hanging open. Eventually he snaps it shut.

"We'll wait out here until you're decent," Dalton says and ushers the others away.

"So you're having consensual sex with him after he violated you?" Colt asks.

Which is a fair question. But something about him feels right. It's the same feeling I have with Campbell and Sully. And he let me be in control for a little while, which helped me trust him.

"He was properly punished," I say with a shrug. "Besides, if he had just asked in the first place, I probably would have fucked him willingly," I add giving Cobra a leveling stare.

It doesn't phase him one bit. "I like taking things that don't belong to me. And you are more valuable than anything else I've ever taken."

He climbs up my body and kisses me, slipping his split tongue into my mouth. His declaration is romantic in a demented sort of way. I nip at his bottom lip and he grinds his hard cock against me. How these men are able to just keep going and going is beyond me.

I push back on Archer and he comes a final time and softens inside of me. He pulls out and I pull away from Cobra just as a loud crack sounds from the doorway, making me jump. Colt punched a hole in the hallway wall.

I stand and grab a towel from the floor and clean myself up before tossing it in the hamper, and pulling one of Archer's shirts over my head.

"Would you stop fucking every male you come in contact with?" Colt shouts.

"It's not *every* male seeing as how I haven't fucked you," I snap back. "Why are you so concerned about who I sleep with?"

"Because you're supposed to be *better* than this Minxy!"

"What do you—" My brain catches up to the nickname he just used, and my stomach drops. How did I miss it? The tattoos and the chiseled jaw are a far cry from the chubby prepubescent boy that I used to live with.

"Max?" I step toward him with an outstretched hand.

"Don't touch me," he says and steps away from me.

"I don't...What did I do?"

"You left us!" he growls. "In that place, with Steve. Do you know what he did to us after you—it doesn't matter. What matters is that you abandoned us. And I had hoped that it was for a good reason, and that you got out and made something of yourself. But you're just a fucking whore." He storms out of the room as silent tears fall down my face.

"You two know each other?" Sully asks softly, placing his hand on my shoulder.

"Not any more, apparently," I say, wiping the tears from my eyes. I clear my throat and shake off the pain. "So what do we do now? We have the relics all in one place, but what's the next step?"

"Are you sure you don't want to talk about what just happened?" Campbell asks.

"No. I want to figure out a plan so that Ma—Colt can leave."

"That's not going to happen until you complete your ascension."

"Can't he just stay somewhere else until this is done? Can't we figure out how to get the relic out? Maybe we could put it in someone else."

"The runes that contain the magic are carved into their bones. You have to pull what you need from them directly. I'm afraid that separating them isn't an option," Trixie says.

"How do you know?" I snap. This information seems to be coming at a convenient time.

"I had a vision last night. Get decent and we'll make as much of a plan as we can. I still don't have a location."

Chapter Fifteen

Jinx

We aren't able to solidify anything, yet. Without a location for the ritual, making plans for the ascension is useless. Trixie says it's likely somewhere nearby since we were all chosen from the city, but she can't be sure.

At breakfast the next morning, Colt takes one look at me and storms off upstairs with his plate. I don't see him again until after lunch when Archer calls a meeting.

Campbell, Sully, and I enter Archer's office less than ten minutes after he texted to say that we all needed to come down, but we're still the last ones there. Colt glances at me, then angles his whole body away from mine. Every fiber of my being is begging me to go to him, but I hold my ground. I won't beg and plead for him to give me a chance to forgive me for whatever he thinks I did. If he won't talk to me, there's nothing I can do.

"Nice of you to join us," Niall snarks.

"Can it," I snap, earning me a snarl from Niall.

We had never been close when I lived in the house with them, and Steve and Shelley. His name had been Pete back then. I had treated him and Colt with the same amount of respect, but Colt and I were always closer; likely because we were closer in age.

"Stop being rude to my mate," Archer warns. "I won't say it again."

"It's fine, Archer. I live in peace knowing that with a tiny little spell I could have the little kitty whimpering in a puddle on the floor."

"One stab and I could, too," Cobra says, pulling his pocket knife from his pants.

"Put that thing away. I'm not actually going to do it. Unless he gives me a reason. Which I would *love* for him to give me a reason," I say, staring Niall down.

Colt stares at his phone in blatant disinterest. He's gone from hating me to pretending I don't exist, and I don't know which is worse.

"Can we just get this over with?" Dalton whines. "There's a game on in thirty minutes that I would like to watch and all the drama is making me itch."

Archer nods. "Right, well Trixie has had another vision. She said that somewhere..." he pulls out a map and sets it on the table. There's a large circle drawn around a portion of the map. "...In this vicinity, is our likely ritual site."

"The vision wasn't any more specific?" I ask.

"They never are," Trixie says with a shrug.

"So how do we find it? That's what? Five hundred square miles? How are we supposed to find something that small in an area that's half the size of Rhode Island?" Sully says.

"Well, some of this area is developments. Some of it is state game lands. I assume that the spot won't be in a housing development, but you never know. It might be in someone's basement," Campbell observes.

"We'll start making outings and covering the area to see if we can sense the power of the ritual site," Archer says.

"*That's* your plan? That will take forever!" Niall says, throwing his hands in the air.

"I figured we could start with the more obvious areas like cave systems and the like," Archer says as if it's perfectly reasonable.

"There's got to be a better way. Maybe we can just wait for another vision. How often do you have them?" I ask Trixie.

"The closer we get to the solstice the more frequent they are. I expect the next couple will reveal the location. Or at least pretty close to it."

"Then let's give it a week or so and regroup, then," I suggest.

"But what if the vision never comes?" Sully asks. "There's a lot riding on this."

"A week won't put us that far behind," I say.

Archer places a hand on his chin and gazes at the map. "Okay. We'll give it a week, and if we don't have further clarity by then, we begin searching. You're all dismissed."

He sits back at his desk and begins searching the map, I'm sure looking for the ritual site. I want to help him, but I *need* to talk to Colt. I walk up behind where he's talking to Niall and tap him on the shoulder.

He doesn't even turn to look at me. "Go away Jinx." He sounds tired.

Frankly, so am I.

"I need to talk to both of you."

"You *need* to fuck off," Niall snaps, and grabs Colt by the arm and escorts him out the door.

Feeling deflated, I approach Archer. "When will you be done for the day?"

He leans back in his chair and laces his fingers behind his head. "I can be done whenever I want. That's the beauty of being in charge."

I feel like a child asking their father to come and play with them. I hate admitting that I need anyone's attention. But right now I want to cuddle up with all of the guys and watch a movie or something.

"What's wrong, Little Star?"

Tell him! Linnie urges.

I swat at her, very aware that Archer can see and hear her.

"Yes. Tell me."

"I hate that. We need to figure out a way for her to go back to being *my* familiar."

"I could already see her when you first entered my office. Now I can hear her too. Your familiar is my familiar," he says with a smile.

"I'm still upset about Colt and Niall," I pout.

"Colt will come around, Little Star. Niall I'm less convinced about, but Colt will. He's connected to you by the Zodiac blessing. He can't stay away."

I nod. He kisses me, and pulls me into his lap. His hand slips under my shirt and he runs his nails gently up and down my back making me melt into him.

"Let me finish up a little bit of work so I can focus solely on you, and then I'll be up to give you whatever you need."

Cobra, Sully, Archer, and Campbell spend the next three days pampering me, fucking me, and hanging out, getting to know me and one another. I've never had anyone who really cared about my well-being, let alone asked me what my favorite color was.

One afternoon, we're lounging in bed together when Archer says, "Your birthday is coming up in about a week and a half. What would you like to do?"

"Wait, when's your birthday?" Cobra asks.

"October thirteenth, but I think the better question is 'how does Archer know that'?"

"I told you that I looked you up when I found out your name. And besides, we're all Libras. I'm assuming it has something to do with strengthening your Zodiac power."

"Even you, Sully?" I ask turning to face him.

"Actually, yes. My birthday is two days after yours, and I share one with Camp."

"Archer and I share a birthday too. We're on the cusp," Cobra says."

"Colt and I share a birthday," I say softly. "Whatever we do, can we try to involve him?"

"Whatever you want," Archer agrees, kissing me on the forehead.

"Thank you. Thank all of you for being so cool about all of this."

"You were made for all of us, so of course we're going to try to make this work," Sully says.

Archer's phone dings, and he picks it up to look at it. "Trixie had another vision," he says and morphs back to his human form and begins getting dressed.

"I wish you would stay a demon," I grumble.

"I'm always a demon, sweet thing. Besides, if I stayed in that form, we'd never get anything done because you cannot keep your hands off of me."

I roll my eyes and stick my tongue out at him. Cobra catches my tongue between his fingers.

"Hey!" I protest to the best of my ability around his fingers.

"I have better things for you to do with that tongue," he says and kisses me, biting my lip and sucking on my tongue.

"Meeting! Now!" Archer scolds.

"You're a party pooper," Cobra says and boops Archer on the nose, as he climbs out of bed.

Sully and Campbell get dressed on the other side of the bed, and I sit under the sheet with my knees pulled to my chest, watching them all. If they don't all stick around after my ascension, I'm not sure how I'll handle it. But I know that I'm going to do my best to enjoy this time with them while I have it.

"Come on, Buttercup. We've got stuff to do." Campbell reaches for my hand, and I happily take it.

Four sets of eyes roam over my naked body as I get dressed.

"Take a picture, it'll last longer," I mock.

Archer holds up his phone seconds later and the shutter noise goes off.

"Delete that!" I yell.

"But you just said..."

"I'll take a better naked photo for you later. That was probably terrible!"

"It wasn't. I'm keeping it. But I'll still take you up on your offer of more pictures."

I groan and chuck a sock at him. "Let's get this meeting over with."

We meet the others back in the office. I enter first and overhear Trixie saying, "All she does is roll around in bed with them. What was Libra thinking, making a whore the chosen one?"

"Probably that it was better than someone who has a stick shoved up their ass, but what do I know?" I ask.

Cobra snickers behind me. "Do you want me to squish the pixie? Cause I'll do it," he says, wrapping his heavily tattooed arms around my waist and kissing my neck.

"No. We need her. Maybe after the ritual."

"Speaking of which, what was your vision about?" Archer asks, ignoring the conversation.

He's started letting me handle my arguments myself, which I appreciate immensely. But it means that he pretends that people aren't speaking at all sometimes so that he can keep his temper in check. I love that he wants to stick up for me—that they all do—but sometimes a girl needs to fight her own battles. He just needs constant reassurance that I'll tell him if there's something I can't handle.

Trixie drags her glaring gaze off of me and folds her arms over her chest. "I've narrowed the site down to mountains. That's all the more specific I've got."

"We're in New York. There are three mountain ranges," Campbell says with a groan.

"My suspicion is the Adirondacks," Trixie says, pointing to a piece of the map. "The Appalachian Mountains are outside of the circle. And I don't know...it just feels like the Adirondacks to me."

"I trust your intuition. We'll wait another four days and see if there's any more information to be gleaned," Archer says. "Good work," he says to Trixie.

I know he's just trying to remain diplomatic, but I scowl at him for praising her. "If she doesn't get another vision, then what?" I ask.

"Then plan B. I hope you like hiking, Little Star."

The next couple of days are more of the same. I miss going to work, and being cooped up in the mansion is starting to get to me. Having this much downtime means having time to reflect on everything. My memories invade my brain like parasites wanting to take control of me and make me *feel* things that I haven't felt in years.

The guys are all busy writing up hiking plans, so I sneak out of the office, grab a blanket from the bedroom, and go outside to sit in the cool air to clear my head.

What's wrong? Linnie asks.

Everything. I want to go home.

I think this is your home now, babe. And these guys can do a better job of protecting you than I ever could.

I don't need saving Linnie.

But you do need love. No, you deserve love, Jinx. More than anyone I know.

Why didn't you warn me about Cobra? I finally ask the question that's been bouncing around in my brain for days.

She plops down on the railing of the porch and sighs. *I was actually gone when he first arrived. I had gone off to play in the woods while you were playing with your boys. There are a couple of birds out here who are a lot of fun, and they've been keeping me company while you've been spending time with the guys.*

I came back the second I felt your distress, but it was too late. I haven't strayed far since then. I'm sorry.

"It's okay. You shouldn't have to babysit me every second. One of these days you'll be able to go do your own thing, and I won't have to rely so heavily on you," I tell her, aching at the thought of her not being around.

*"Nonsense. You'll never be rid of me. At least not if I have anything to do with it. But I really want you to think about things, Jinx. Really *think* about them. These men can keep you so happy, and you'll never have to go back to stripping. I know you tell yourself and them that you like it—"*

"I do like it, Linnie. Most nights, anyway."

"But it takes a toll on you. With these guys, you can focus on school and get a job somewhere that really makes a difference. Imagine being able to work with kids who grew up like you, Colt, and Niall."

I rest my arms across one of the beams of the railing, and rest my chin on my hands. Growing up in foster care was impossibly hard. I had good families and bad ones. I pushed the buttons of the good ones until they sent me away. The bad ones I reported to my teachers the second they acted up.

There were so many times that I wanted to run away but I never had the courage until my last foster home—the one with Colt and Niall. All this time, and all these years later and we've finally been reunited. Colt was the best thing about that foster home. He was the best thing about any of my foster homes. My heart shreds itself into pieces, and without realizing it, I'm crying; feeling my fucking feelings again.

Chapter Sixteen
Colt

After dinner one night, I stalk out the back door and strip off my clothes on the patio. I need to run. Archer has a couple other unregistered shifters working for him and he has a space for them to run behind his massive mansion where they won't be seen by any locals. When I'm completely naked I let the beast in me take over. Large paws hit the dirt, and I'm running through the trees.

Tonight I'm on the hunt because I'm feeling vengeful.

Everything about that nut job telepath makes me want to rip him to shreds. Every time I see his hands on Jinx I want to remove them from his body and force them down his throat. Actually, that's what I want to do to all the guys she's sleeping with.

Archer mated her without her permission. The cops jumped on her the second they rescued her from the station. She's always been meant for me, and instead she's been out stripping, and hooking, and now sleeping with the other relics? It's too much.

The sadness in her eyes when she realized who I was—it nearly broke me. She does seem to care about me, at least a little. Every sad look, and quiet attempt to speak with me breaks my resolve to hate her just a little more.

Something moves ahead of me—a deer. I crouch low to the ground and slink up behind it. I close in on it, one silent step at a time before I pounce. Claws and teeth gnash into this flesh. Blood pours from the wounds I created, and fur goes flying.

Once it takes its last breath, I feed. Nothing tastes better than raw game while I'm in this form. I chew it for a while and savor the kill. There isn't much hunting to be done in the city, so I cherish these times where I can get out and get a good session in.

Nearby running water catches my attention. I move through the woods silently until I find a stream, then I step into the flowing water and wash myself clean. Feeling refreshed and tired, I head back to the house to get dressed, and go to bed.

The perimeter patrols are moving around the grounds. I want to eviscerate every single one of them for letting Cobra in to attack Jinx. Not that it matters since she let him into her bed, anyway.

I catch her scent when I'm close to the edge of the woods. When I get to the tree line, I find her sitting on the edge of the patio with a blanket wrapped around her, kicking her feet. She looks beautiful in the moonlight. I watch her for about a minute before I realize she's crying. A blanket-covered hand moves to wipe the tears away.

The beast inside of me is still in charge, and the urge to protect her takes over. I step out of the woods. still in my shifted form. She doesn't notice me right away, my coat letting me blend in the darkness. When I get closer I realize that she's not just crying, she's sobbing.

I break into a run. When I'm twenty feet away she gasps when she sees me coming, and I shift back into my human form. I pull her off of the patio and wrap her in my arms.

"What happened? Why are you crying?"

She pushes me away, and puts distance between us. "Nothing that you can fix." She pulls the blanket off of her shoulders and hands it to me. "Cover yourself."

She's trying hard not to look at me. I don't take the blanket from her. Instead I grab my clothes and pull them on. Once I'm dressed I face her again to find her staring at the sky, tears steadily streaming down her cheeks.

"Please tell me what's wrong," I say, softly.

"Why? So you can tell me how shitty I am and how I probably deserve it? No thank you. If you don't mind, I came out here to cry alone, in peace. You're kind of the last person I want to be around right now."

"No."

She spins to face me, the fire returning to her eyes, and extinguishing the sadness. She marches up to me and pushes me in the chest. She's not strong enough to move me. But to make her feel better, I take about a half a step back.

"Why are you so fucking difficult?!" she yells at me. "Just leave me alone!"

"No," I say again, this time with a chuckle.

This time she balls up her fists and hits me in the chest. "Go away!" she shrieks and starts hitting me over and over again.

I let it happen a few times before I grab her wrists and pull her into me. Gentle but firm I say, "That's enough. I'm not leaving you alone out here. Not when I found you sobbing by yourself."

Where my hands meet her skin begins to feel exceptionally hot to the point that I have to let her go. Small flames are licking up her forearms. Then without warning she holds her hands in front of her and releases a blast of air that sends me flying backward through the air and into the pool. Thankfully it's heated. I pop my head up above the water. She's standing over me with her hands on her hips.

"You don't get to treat me like shit, and then act like you care, fuckface. Let's just get these trials or whatever done so that we never have to see each other again."

I place my palms on the edge of the pool and push myself up. "There's just one problem with that."

"What's that?" she asks defiantly crossing her arms over her chest.

"I don't want that."

I grab a hold of the front of her shirt and pull her into the pool with me. She lets out a shriek as she tries to avoid the water and fails.

She lets out a frustrated growl and splashes me. "What the fuck, Max!"

"You started it," I say with a smirk. "And it's Colt now. Max died a long time ago."

She's wearing a white T-shirt and I can see her pretty pink nipples right through it now that it's soaking wet. I glance at her face and realize I must have been staring, because she's watching me with a raised eyebrow. I've been caught. A look of sadness falls over her face again.

"Why were you crying?" I ask.

She sighs. "You're not going to drop it are you?"

"Nope. So you might as well tell me."

"Because everything changed so fast. One second I was meeting with a client, and everything was fine; the next I was arrested, assaulted, kidnapped, and told that I was the key to saving the planet. Now I have a mate, and I don't know what's happening to my apartment, and I have to do this ritual. I just want to go home."

"You would rather go back to the city than stay here with your mate in this ridiculously huge mansion?"

"No, but I don't want to be some sort of kept woman either. I want to work, and to earn my way. I was doing okay for myself."

"You were sleeping with men for money," I growl.

"Please don't start. Please."

"I just don't understand."

"You haven't *tried* to understand. You've been on the offensive and treating me like shit since you arrived at the cabin." She faces the side of the pool and rests her arms on it. Her feet don't quite reach the bottom here.

I grind my teeth together to stop myself from saying anything else insensitive. I want to believe that she has a good explanation for it. "Then help me understand. Because I've spent the last ten years hoping that you got out and ended up somewhere good. I was hoping that all of the shit that Steve put us through because you left was worth it because you managed to become something."

She whispers, "What did Steve do to you?"

"We don't need to talk about that right now. I want to know about you."

She mindlessly trails her fingers through the water. "Do you know why I left there?"

"No. It didn't make any sense to me."

"Do you remember how Steve started giving me special treatment? Letting me eat dinner with them, giving me chocolate, buying me new clothes?"

"Yeah. You would sneak some of the chocolate to us when he would give it to you." I smile remembering the few really good times that we had in that house.

She nods, but doesn't return my smile. "He was grooming me."

My stomach drops. I should have known. Steve was a total creep when it came to young girls. I take too long to respond so she continues.

"Three days before I left, Shelly went to a friend's house for the evening. Once you and Pete...Niall...whatever, were in bed, Steve invited me to come watch TV with him on the couch. He gave me a drink and told me not to tell Shelly. It had alcohol in it. It apparently also had a sedative in it.

"My powers had just started to surface, and the coward that he was, he didn't want me using them against him. When I told him I didn't feel good, he told me he would help me to my room."

"Jinx, I—"

"When we got to my room, he told me that I couldn't sleep in my clothes or they would get wrinkled. So he started stripping me. Once I was naked, he started groping me. Then he got undressed. I tried to protest, but I was so tired and out of it.

"He pinned me to the bed, and forced himself inside of me. When he finished he pulled out, told me to clean myself up, and that he would see me again the next night. The next morning, Shelly found the blood on my sheets and thought that I had started my period. She made me do chores to pay off the sheets that I had 'ruined'." Her face is placid as she stares straight ahead. It's like she's told this story a thousand times.

"I vowed that night that I would never let another man control me that way without my permission again. I never drank. Never did drugs. And I used sex as a tool; not as a means of intimacy. I lived on the streets for a while, running from truancy officers. With the help of some people I met on the streets, I got a fake ID and enrolled myself in high school. I graduated, and spent the last several years building a small life for myself.

"Now. What did Steve do to you?" She's not giving me the choice to back out of this conversation, and if I don't tell her I risk hurting her even more.

"When he realized you were missing, he assumed that Niall and I had helped you escape. He came in, and beat us relentlessly. He did that every night for months. Eventually Mrs. Simpson—the science teacher—figured it out and told someone, but it was hell."

She's crying again. She was able to tell me the story of her own pain just fine, but hearing mine has her in tears. She moves through the water and places her hand on my cheek.

"I'm so sorry. If I had known, I would have taken you two with me. We could have figured it out together."

"I'm sorry for assuming you just abandoned us. Not a single day has gone by where I haven't thought of you. When I walked into the cabin and saw you there; saw them touching you—"

Her mouth is on mine, as she wraps her legs around my waist. I pin her against the side of the pool and kiss her with purpose. She tastes so sweet and I want to devour her.

She pulls back and looks at me through wet lashes. "If I ever see that son of a bitch again, he's a dead man."

I slide my hand into her hair and kiss her again, grinding my erection against her warm center. She gasps into my mouth and I smile at the effect I'm having on her.

I pull back, "You won't get a chance to kill him if I see him first."

"Let's make a deal. Whoever kills him wins and the loser has to take the winner on a date."

"Deal," I say.

"Should we seal it like Archer and I did?" she asks flirtatiously and kisses me again.

"That depends, do you want me to mate you?" I ask jokingly, kissing down her neck.

She doesn't respond, so I pull back to look at her. Her smile has dropped, and her mouth forms a silent 'O'. Her breathing has picked up, and her pupils are blown so wide, I can hardly tell that her eyes are blue. *Does she want me to mate her?*

"I was mostly joking," I say, worried that I've upset her somehow.

"I know but for some reason the thought of you mating me..."

"You don't want it?"

"No, it really turned me on. I think I do want that."

"I'm not going to do it until you're sure," I say, kissing her forehead. "And I'm not going to have sex with you in this pool. I don't want my first time to be in the water."

"Y-your first time?" she asks.

Shit.

"I meant *our* first time," I say, trying to play it cool.

"Don't lie to me, Colt." She drops her voice to a whisper, "Are you a virgin?"

I chew the inside of my cheek and stare at the sky, not wanting to admit the truth. I can't make myself speak so I just nod my head.

"And you were about to have your first time in the pool with *me?*" she asks indignantly.

"The pool was not ideal, but there's no one in the world I would rather slip myself inside for the first time than you. It's always been you, Jinx. Even when we were kids." I cup her cheek and kiss her again. I pull her bottom lip between my teeth and suck lightly before releasing it. "I'm in love with you. I always have been."

"Colt..." she starts and sighs deeply, her brow furrowing. She unwraps her legs from around my waist, and hoists herself up onto the side of the pool. "We were just kids. And that was a long time ago. I'm a different person now, and so are you. And up until twenty minutes ago, you hated me. You don't love me."

"I never hated you!"

I step between her legs, and looking up into her eyes. She's starting to shiver from the cool night air. I need to get her inside.

"Can we go inside and talk about this, please?"

"I don't think there's much else to talk about, Colt. I'll never be able to tell you that I love you, and I think you've got feelings for a person that doesn't exist anymore."

"No. I have feelings for you. I love *you*. Because you're my mate. The one fated to me by the gods."

Chapter Seventeen

Jinx

A nervous laugh bubbles out of my chest. "I'm sorry, I could have sworn you said...fated? Since when?"

"Please let me take you inside and get you dried off, and then I promise I'll tell you everything."

"Fine," I grumble and stand up.

Colt pushes himself up out of the pool and follows me into the house. We have to walk past Archer's office in order to get to the upstairs, and unfortunately the door is open.

"I smell my mate!" he calls lovingly from his desk. "Come in here Little Star."

I push the door the rest of the way open, and Archer gives me a warm smile until his brain registers that I'm soaking wet.

"What happened? Why were you crying? Why are you aroused?"

"I went for a swim."

"By yourself? In your clothes?"

"With me," Colt says as he steps into the room behind me.

"You finally gave in, pussy cat? Good for you. I hope it was good. Was it good for you, Little Star?"

"We didn't have sex, Archer," I say, my face flushing at the attention his men are giving me.

"You left her frustrated?" Archer asks Colt. "Well that just won't do." He looks at his men. "Out!"

The three of them get up and leave the room shutting it behind them. Archer sits down in his office chair and looks at the two of us expectantly.

I walk behind the desk and place my hand on Archer's cheek. "Colt and I have to have a private conversation. We're going to go upstairs and dry off and talk."

"Fine," he says with a pout. "But if you have sex I'm going to be really disappointed that I didn't get to watch. The tension between you two is delicious."

"We'll let you watch next time," I promise. And I realize that I'm not only expecting that we'll have sex, but that there will *be* a next time.

"Go. Have your fun while I finish my paperwork. I'll see you in a few hours. Send the goons back in when you leave."

I kiss him, dripping water all over his suit, but he doesn't seem to mind. I return to where Colt is standing. He looks irritated, but he doesn't say anything.

We grab some of my clothes from Archer's room then he leads me to his room and opens the door for me. Niall is inside.

"What the fuck are you doing here?" he snaps.

"Enough, Niall," Colt growls. "Can you give us some privacy?"

"Not you, too. Why is everyone so obsessed with her? Is her pussy made of cookies?"

"I said enough!" Colt roars.

Niall ducks his head in submission.

"I'll explain everything to you later, but we were wrong about her. *I* was wrong about her," he says and he looks at me with apologetic eyes. "Jinx and I have a lot we need to talk about and we need someplace where the others won't interrupt us, so please, just go down to the kitchen for a bit, or the game room. I'll text you when we're done."

Niall grabs his coat aggressively and storms out of the room without another word, slamming the door behind him.

I step into the attached bathroom and pull off my wet clothes and hang them over the shower curtain rod to dry. Colt steps into the room while I'm still naked, and leans against the door frame, and watches me with hungry eyes.

"You're so fucking beautiful," he says, eyes roaming up and down my body.

I pull my tank top on and a pair of Archer's boxers and step back into the bedroom. "How long have you known?" I ask, crossing my arms over my chest.

"Since forever. I mean I didn't know for sure as kids, but I was pretty certain. After you, no one else felt right. I kissed a few girls. Even went to first base with a couple of em. But none of them *felt*...right.

"Then I walked into the cabin and I smelled you, and I knew. And seeing you—*my* mate—cuddled up with two other guys just set me off. Especially after feeling like you had abandoned us all those years ago. And then you mated the fucking demon."

"I wouldn't have done that if you had just *told* me."

"And what about the others? Would you have stopped fucking them, too?" he asks, skeptically.

"I...don't know," I answer, truthfully. "Before you showed up I had told Sully that I was his. I was Campbell's, too. A piece of me belongs to them, and I think I knew that from the second I met them. They just fit."

I lay back on the bed and cover my face with my hands. *Why didn't I think any of this through?* I'm not a monogamous person. And I'm a stripper. And a call girl. And now I'm mated to a demon, and in relationships with three other men. Is that what they are? Relationships? Colt climbs onto the bed with me. I pull my hands away and watch him as he holds himself over me

"I can accept you for you, Jinx," Colt says, his voice barely above a whisper. "Every piece of you. If you'll have me after the way I've been treating you."

There's a question in his eyes. He wants my permission to touch me. He wants my permission to love me. He wants my permission to *mate* me. My skin erupts into goosebumps, and my breath hitches as he runs his thumb along my bottom lip.

I take his thumb into my mouth and suck on it softly, and his eyes roll back into his head. That's all the permission he needs. He reaches over his head and pulls his shirt off in one swift movement and tosses it to the floor. Then he grabs the top of my tank top and rips it down the center.

"So dramatic," I say with a chuckle.

"You have no idea how torturous it has been watching you with the others. Seeing you with Archer's cocks buried in you. Hearing you fuck those two fucking cops back at the cabin. Every single time you touched me, or looked at me, I nearly came in my pants. It's been the worst week and a half of my life."

He grabs my hands and yanks his belt out of his pants. He moves so quickly that my brain doesn't register what's happening until my hands are tied to the headboard. Once they're secure he yanks the boxers off of me and discards them. He grabs rope—fucking *rope*—out of his bag, and gives me a devious smile.

"What are you doing?" I ask, and try to scoot away from him.

"Torturing you the way you tortured me," he says, and grabs one of my ankles in a punishing grip. "This will be a lot easier on you if you don't fight me, baby girl."

He ties my foot with one end of the rope, then ties it to one of the bedposts. Then he pulls out a knife and slices through the rope, effectively cutting it in half. Then he ties my other foot to the other bedpost.

He crawls up between my legs and kneels before me. He's holding something behind his back. "I know you like pain. I've heard and seen how the others fuck you. Do you want that from me?"

"Yes," I say, and it comes out desperate and needy.

"Good. I'm going to fuck you raw. But first..."

He pulls a pair of my underwear out from behind his back, and I look at him in confusion before he stuffs them in my mouth. The underwear wasn't the only secret he was holding behind him. In his other hand is a riding crop. That's all it takes. I'm instantly wet for him.

His nostrils flare and his eyes turn cat-like. "You're fertile already. All that mating with the demon must have triggered it. Should I put a kitten in you, baby girl?"

My eyes go wide and I try to spit the underwear out of my mouth, to no avail. He smiles, his teeth turning to fangs, and he kisses up the inside of my thigh. I try to talk around the makeshift gag, but it just comes out as muffled nonsense.

"I want to breed you so bad," he growls. "I want to pour my seed into you over and over until you give me a baby."

He slaps the inside of my thigh lightly with the riding crop and I moan and squirm beneath him. He does the same to the other thigh and I try to move toward him, desperate for him to touch me.

"You're such a good little whore for me, baby girl. But you've had a lot of practice, haven't you?"

He brings the crop down harder on the inside of my thigh and I cry out in pleasure.

"I like when you can't talk back," he says with a devious smile. "What do you say? Should I breed you, and mark you as mine?"

I take too long to answer and he holds the crop above my aching pussy.

"You just need to move your head. Yes or no?"

I want him to mark me. I don't want a baby right now.

Whack! The crop makes contact with my clit and I cry out, tears forming in my eyes. He rubs it gently with his free hand, easing the sting.

"You have thirty seconds to answer me or I'm taking what I want. Holding back for the last few days while you paraded around here naked, and fucked every man in sight was torture. You get no more courtesies from me." To emphasize his point, he lands one more blow with the crop on the inside of my thigh.

He pulls his hard cock out of his boxers. I hadn't noticed it before, but he's got jacob's ladder. I groan, staring at his large cock. Fuck, I want him inside of me. I'm so mad at him for not helping me with the birth control situation. I'm mad at myself for not asking Archer to help me.

He doesn't give me the full thirty seconds. He presses the tip of his cock at my entrance and stares down into my eyes. "How does it feel to know that yours is the first and only cunt that my cock will ever see?"

And then he thrusts himself inside of me, the piercings dragging up the inside of me, until he is fully seated inside. He groans and presses his forehead to mine, then he gently moves his hips, testing the waters, sliding in and out of me with ease.

"This is even better than I ever imagined it would be," he says and pulls the underwear out of my mouth.

Before I can say anything, his mouth is on mine, and his tongue is seeking entrance. I grant him access and suck on the tip of it. Our kissing is frenzied, and feral. He slams his hips against mine, pleasure building within me. He pulls back from our kiss and wraps his hand around my throat, squeezing like he still hates me—like he wants me dead.

It's like he can sense what I need; like he can read all the darkest pieces of me, and I forget myself in the moment with him. For right now, it's just me and Max...me and the boy I used to know.

I start to see stars, and the lack of oxygen paired with his abusive thrusts sends me over the edge. He pulls his hand away from my throat and without ever slowing his movements, he grabs his knife off the bed and cuts his belt, freeing my hands.

He sits back on his knees, pulling me up onto his lap, giving me some of the control he had taken from me. I ride him hard, bracing my hands on his shoulders. He presses his nose to the space where my neck meets my shoulder and inhales. He gives me no warning before he sinks his teeth into my flesh, marking me as his own.

The mate bond sends a thrill through my body, and I clamp down around him, coming again, as he spills himself inside of me. We stay like that as our breathing settles. I take his beautiful face in my hands and kiss him softly, pulling his bottom lip between my teeth. His massive hands are resting on my thighs. I pull away from him, and smile.

"I love you, Minxy," he says, gripping my thighs as though I may run.

And I want to.

I bite the inside of my cheek and look at the ceiling, willing myself not to cry. Why did he have to ruin a perfect moment?

"You don't have to say it back, but I needed you to know. It's always been you. And now you're mine."

"Max...Colt...I've never told anyone I loved them before in my life. Not even my parents. Not even Linnie. I feel like saying it to you now would be a lie."

"Then don't. Just know that when you're ready to admit to yourself how you feel, I'll be here waiting."

I nod, and slide off of his lap, his cum making a mess of him as I do.

"I can't believe you came inside of me," I complain.

My mind starts racing with all the possibilities of me getting pregnant. I had sex with Archer this morning, and Cobra last night. I groan and cover my face with my hands. Colt starts laughing, and I uncover my face to find him doubled over, nearly in tears.

"What's so funny?"

"You're not fertile," he says. "I can't believe that worked. I told you I was going to get you back for the shit you've put me through the last few days. The look on your face was way better than you getting annoyed over a delayed orgasm."

I grab a pillow and hit him in the head with it. "You asshole," I say with a laugh. But inside I'm surprised at the amount of disappointment I feel. Maybe starting our own weird little family wouldn't be so bad.

Chapter Eighteen

Jinx

I fall asleep in Colt's room, cuddled up with him, enjoying our new bond. A few hours later the door to the bedroom opens and the light comes on, rousing us both from our sleep.

"Well, glad to see you got your whore hooks into my brother, too," Niall snaps. "I'll be staying in one of the other guest rooms," he says to Colt and starts aggressively throwing his clothes into a bag.

"Don't be like that," Colt says. "Jinx and I talked things out, and she had a good reason for leaving us."

Clutching the blanket to myself I sit up and watch as Niall grabs his charger and his laptop. I don't have anything to say to him if he doesn't want to at least hear out my side of the story. I'm sorry for what happened to them, and I regret leaving them behind, but there's nothing I can do about it now.

"Yeah, what could have possibly made it okay that she caused us to get beat by that fucker every—what the fuck is that?"

His eyes are on me, and for a split second my brows furrow in confusion. Then realization hits me. I reach up and touch the mate mark on my neck.

"She's mine," Colt says firmly before kissing the sensitive spot, making me shiver.

"You fucking mated her? *Her?* She belongs to you *and* half the city. What were you thinking? I can't believe you. Either of you."

He doesn't allow Colt any time to explain before he storms out of the room. Colt sighs and kisses my head.

"I need to go talk to him. I won't tell him your side of things, but hopefully I can talk him into hearing you out. Will you be okay without me?"

"I should go find Archer. He's probably wondering why I didn't come to bed. Come find me when you're done?"

"I'll always find you, Minxy," he says and my belly flutters. I'm not sure how I got so lucky, but I'll have to count my lucky stars later.

We get dressed, and Colt goes on a mission to find Niall while I head off to the bedroom to look for Archer. I step inside, and find a note on the pillow.

Little Star,

I had some business to take care of in the city, but I should be back in a couple of hours. I was going to wake you, but you and the kitty cat looked so cozy together. I didn't want to disturb you. I took Cobra and the piggies with me. I'll see you in a bit.

Archer.

I set the note down on the bedside table and head down to the kitchen to grab something to eat. I snag a piece of fruit and the cook shoos me out of the kitchen and into the dining room to wait for breakfast. Lanya and two of Archer's men are sitting around the large dining room table speaking in hushed voices. They stop talking as soon as I enter the room.

"What's going on?" I ask, not liking the vibe of the room.

"You know how Mars was sucked into the void a while back?" Lanya asks.

"Yeah. Something about a wormhole or something," I say then take a bite of my apple. I don't tend to keep up with current events.

Lanya clicks her tongue as if I've displeased her. "Well, it looks like the moon might be next if we don't get this rift stitched up."

"Campbell said that I couldn't do my ritual until the Winter Solstice. Is there anything that we can do in the meantime to try to prevent it from getting worse?"

"We basically need everyone to stop using magic, but that's not going to happen unless the council members pull their enormous heads out of their asses."

"That tends to be the case with people in power. They don't care how their actions are affecting other people."

"Yes, well I was thinking that maybe you could try to appeal to them."

"You mean try to talk them into not using their magic? I don't foresee that going well," I say with a laugh.

"You never know. That pussy of yours seems rather persuasive," she spits at me.

"I'm not up for sale. I'm not offering myself to the supernatural council, because quite frankly, fuck those guys—figuratively speaking. I know you're upset about Archer still, and I'm sorry if you had some sort of claim to him. I didn't exactly ask to be mated to him. But you can't just ship me off to someone else to get rid of me."

"This isn't about me and Archer. This is about the fact that you seem to be able to convince the men around you to cater to your whims. I know a couple of the council members and they might be willing to change their tune if you offered them what you offered Archer."

"Absolutely not. From what Campbell and Sully said they want me dead. I'm not going anywhere near them."

Lanya sighs heavily. "Shame. I didn't want to have to do this the hard way."

"What do you mean?" I ask, and then the world goes dark.

Chapter Nineteen

Sully

Campbell and I meander down to Archer's office after dinner to talk to him about Jinx and about our plans to make sure she succeeds in her ascension. I knock gently on the door, and Archer calls for us to come in.

His men are sitting in their usual spots. They're all demons, and they give me the creeps. They hardly speak unless they're by themselves and then when anyone else walks in they immediately stop talking.

"How can I help you boys?" Archer asks, not looking up from his paperwork.

"We wanted to talk about Jinx," Campbell says.

"What about her?" Archer asks, giving us his full attention and folding his hands on his desk.

Campbell and I share a look then return our attention to Archer who lets out a small chuckle.

"You're worried about her and your positions in her life. I get it," he says clasping his hands behind his head and leaning back in his chair.

"She's something else. I want to reassure you, just as I did with her, that your relationships with her are safe. She likes both of you very much. And if you're willing to abide by my rules—which there aren't many—I think that the six of us can co-exist peacefully."

"Six?" I ask.

"Yes. She's taken a liking to Cobra, and it seems that the panther has finally decided to stop sulking and get his dick wet. They're upstairs romping around as we speak."

Campbell clenches his fists at his sides. He didn't want to share her even with me, and now he has to contend with three others as well.

"It's what she wants. And if you want her, you'll let her have it," Archer says matter of factly. "Give us the room please," Archer says to his men, and they get up and leave.

I assume they're going to wait just outside the door, just in case Archer needs them. Why he needs these guys hanging around is beyond me. He's a powerful ancient demon. He's way stronger than anyone else in this house except for maybe Jinx. I wonder if she even knows how powerful she is.

"I can handle sharing her with all of you. If she wants it, I plan to mate with her as soon as her ascension is done," I tell them, plopping down in one of the chairs.

"We're going to need a bigger bed," Campbell grumbles, coming to terms with the fact that she belongs to all of us.

"I've been meaning to do some redecorating anyway. Why don't we all go tomorrow and pick out stuff for the bedroom; including a new bed? It can be our way of telling her that we accept this relationship for what it is. We'll leave Colt behind. I expect he'll want to celebrate their mate bond a little longer."

"Mate bond? He mated her? How do you know?"

"I can feel him at the periphery of my subconscious. It's almost like she's a bit of a conductor connecting us together," Archer explains.

"Will I feel you if I mate with her?" I ask.

"Probably, though I don't know how your bonds work."

"Did you know that Colt was her foster brother?" Campbell asks.

"I did. But it wasn't any of my business."

The door slams open and Cobra struts into the room with a cigarette hanging out of his mouth. "Having a meeting without me? Where's our Little Mouse? Do you think she's ready to play?" he asks, rubbing his hands together.

"She's playing with Colt right now. Will I do?" Archer asks, standing and grabbing his suit jacket from the hook on the wall.

"Can't we go play with them? Please. You wouldn't let me taste her," Cobra pouts.

"Because you didn't deserve it. Let her and the kitty have fun." Archer looks to me and Campbell and gestures for us to stand and leave. "We'll see you boys in the morning. Cobra and I have some lost time to make up for."

Campbell and I head back to our room. I immediately start stripping out of my clothes for bed. I'm standing in my boxers checking my phone to distract me from being separated from jinx and I can feel Campbell's eyes on me.

I slowly shift my gaze to him. "What's up?"

"I fucking miss her, man."

"Get a grip. It's been like four hours since we saw her at dinner," I say with a laugh.

"I know. It's pathetic," he mumbles and sits down on the bed. "You know, out of everyone I could be in this with, I'm glad it's you."

"I'm glad it's you, too," I say. "Now enough sappy shit. Next thing you know, we'll be spooning each other in her absence."

"Would that be so bad?" he asks, uncertainty lacing his voice.

I stare at him, mouth slightly ajar. "Are you that hard up for our girl?" I say with a laugh, trying to play it off like it's not a big deal.

I'm into men, but I never thought Camp was. I've always found him attractive, but never thought he would be interested.

He stands and tentatively takes a step toward me. "The last few days...I've realized a few things about myself. I think I've always known, but until we shared her, I wasn't able to really confront those feelings.

"The way you took control of us, the way you didn't hesitate before cleaning my cum off of her...that was so fucking hot, Sully."

"You liked that?" I ask, and close the gap between us.

I brush my thumb over his bottom lip. He swallows thickly, and nods. He runs his hands down my bare chest, and I shiver as my skin breaks out in goosebumps.

I drop to my knees in front of him. Staring up at him, I grab a hold of his belt, a question in my eyes. He nods, and brushes his fingers through my hair. I unbuckle his belt, and unbutton his pants before pulling them down, along with his boxers. He's already half erect. I wrap my hand around him and work it up and down.

He groans, and I smirk up at him. All those long nights patrolling. This fantasy has crossed my mind more than once. I take the tip into my mouth, and swirl my tongue around.

"Fuck," he moans, closing his eyes and tipping his head back.

He puts his hand on the back of my head and gently rocks his hips forward. When I don't protest, he does it again, a little harder. He gains some confidence and begins properly fucking my mouth.

His eyes find mine. "Your mouth feels so fucking good."

I reach down and slide my hand in my underwear and begin stroking myself. I don't want to push him to do any more than he's comfortable with tonight, but I need to get off.

His thrusting becomes more frantic, and with one last jerky motion, he's spilling down my throat. His legs are trembling as he pulls out of my mouth. He smiles down at me, and lets out a breathy laugh. His eyes land on my hand running up and down my cock.

"Tell me what you need," he says, stroking my cheek. "Whatever part of me you want, please take it."

"That's a dangerous offer, Camp."

Even from my position on the floor, I hold the power. I never would have guessed that he was a bottom. His gruff demeanor, and quiet resilience always pointed to a pleasure dom or a soft top. But the way he follows directions, the way he offers every piece of himself, shows he's neither of those things.

He treats jinx like she's delicate; fragile. She's anything but fragile. But she needs someone who will treat her with softness and remind her that she doesn't have to do this alone anymore.

And maybe he needs that softness too.

I hold my hand out, and he pulls me to my feet. I slide my hand under his shirt and kiss him with the same soft passion that he gives Jinx. I slide my boxers off and he steps out of his pants. I pull him to the bed and lay down. He eyes me with hungry curiosity while I touch myself.

"Come here," I whisper, and pat the bed next to me.

He strips off his shirt exposing all his hard muscle to me. This isn't the first time I'm seeing him naked, but it's the first time I'm allowing myself to appreciate it. He climbs into bed with all the gracefulness and confidence of a newborn giraffe, and I chuckle.

"We're going to start slow." I roll into my side, and scoot closer to him so that I can kiss him again.

I press my front to his, giving myself just the tiniest bit of friction, and his breath hitches at the contact.

Without my asking, he reaches between us and takes me in his hand, stroking me lightly. I groan into his mouth, spurring his confidence and he tightens his grip. He watches his hand work my cock, and I allow it for a minute before I grab him by the chin and make him look me in the eye.

"You have no idea how long I've wanted you to touch me like this," I growl, and his eyes go wide at my confession.

His mouth crashes onto mine, and he kisses me hard. Our tongues tangle together before he sucks on my bottom lip, and that pushes me so close to the edge. He pulls back and tries to look back down at his hand but I catch his chin one more time. I want him to watch my face as I come for him.

"Camp," I groan before I shoot my load all over my stomach.

The last little bit gets on his hand and he brings his hand to his mouth and licks it off.

He lays on his back and tucks his hand under his head. He stares at the ceiling with a furrowed brow, and I start to worry that I pushed too hard.

I prop myself up on my elbow and look at him. "You know, if that wasn't everything you were expecting, we don't have to do it again. It doesn't change anything for me. I'm just happy you trusted me with that."

"No. It was great," he says with a genuine smile. "Just...I was trying to figure out when things changed. I mean, I think I've always been a little in love with you. I'm just not sure if it became romantic before

Jinx and I didn't notice, or if it was strictly platonic until she came along."

"Does it matter?" I'm worried he's overthinking it.

"No. Not at all," he laughs. "And having you is going to make it easier to share her with the others."

"Oh, a handjob and a blowie and you think you 'have me'?" I tease.

He smiles and says, "I do. Cause I think you're just as in love with me as I am with you."

A loud knock sounds on our door at five in the morning. I grumble under my breath and shuffle to the door holding a decorative pillow over my junk.

"What?" I snap as I open the door to find Archer on the other side.

Instead of his usual tailored suit, he's sporting jeans and a henley. His long black hair is pulled into a bun on his head, and he's got Cobra with him.

"You boys ready to go shopping?" Archer asks with an amused and knowing look.

"Does it look like we're ready?" Campbell groans from the bed. "Why so early?"

"Because I want to be able to get back and spend the day with Jinx. I cleared my schedule for the whole day so I could shop and play."

I decide to drop the feigned modesty and toss the pillow aside as I go to pull on some clothes. Campbell's eyes roam hungrily down my body as I stroll across the room.

"No time for that I'm afraid," Archer says to Campbell, leaning against the door frame. "Later though. And I daresay that Jinx will be just thrilled with this development. She got quite turned on watching me with Ranger." He lovingly ruffles Cobra's mop of curly blonde hair, and Cobra swats his hand away.

Campbell climbs out of bed begrudgingly, and gets dressed along with me. We're about half dressed when Trixie and Dalton show up in the doorway.

"Why is there so much noise at this hour?" Trixie pouts.

"We're going shopping," Cobra provides.

"Ooooh for what?" She asks, her face lighting up.

Campbell and I exchange a look. Trixie hasn't been very welcoming of Jinx.

"Jinx is moving in permanently so I'm surprising her with a room redecoration. She also needs a new wardrobe."

"And all four of you need to go?"

"All four of us are involved with her and will be sharing the space with her, so yes," I answer, crossing my arms over my chest defensively.

"Don't forget Colt," Archer adds. "Do you think he'll want a cat bed? Is that insensitive? We'll get one to be safe. He can return it if he doesn't like it." He has the whole conversation with himself.

Trixie just gapes at Archer for a minute then asks, "Can I come? I want to get her something as an apology for how I've been acting. I was just feeling protective of you two, but I realize now that it was unnecessary. She seems to care about you. All of you. And it's not unheard of for supes to practice polyamory."

"I knew you couldn't hate her forever," Campbell says with a beaming smile. "I'm okay if you come."

"Fine by me," Archer agrees. "We'll have to take the SUV if we're all going. I'm gonna go pull it around front. We leave in five."

Archer makes the executive decision to drive us two hours away to shop. I understand why, but it doesn't make it any less irritating. Shopping in the actual city might draw unwanted attention.

Campbell and I initially protested since the last time we left her she was assaulted by Cobra, but Archer assures us that his security was increased and that a newly mated panther is the best protection she could ask for.

Archer has decided to make the bedroom 'dramatic'. He hired a guy to come paint one of the stark white walls a dark teal color.

"What do you boys think? Charcoal or elephant grey for the bed frame?" He asks as he's flipping through a catalog of color choices.

"Definitely elephant," Cobra insists.

"I still can't believe they make a bed larger than a California king," Campbell mumbles.

"It should fit us all," Archer says. "I hope so anyway. We can always get a twin bed and shove it on the end if it doesn't. Or I'll just have something custom built." He hands over the credit card to the employee and writes down the address for the delivery.

The employee is staring at us like he can't quite figure out what's going on, but he doesn't say a word.

Trixie helps us pick out clothes and curtains and art for the walls. Archer, the psychopath that he is, has all of Jinx's measurements already so we know exactly what sizes to buy her. The amount of wealth that he has amassed over the years is nauseating.

"Can we go get a soft pretzel at the place next door before we go?" Trixie asks.

"I'll buy you two for all the help you gave us. I know what I like on Jinx, but she certainly has different tastes than me," Archer says, squeezing Trixie's shoulder.

We load up the SUV and go next door to the pretzel place. I'm itching to get back to Jinx, but a snack couldn't hurt. We each grab a pretzel and Camp and I split a tropical smoothie.

"So what happens after the ritual then?" Trixie asks.

"What do you mean?" Campbell replies with a mouth full of pretzel.

"Do you guys go back to working at the station? I'm sure Jinx isn't going to want to stick around."

"She will," Archer says. There's no question in his voice.

"How can you be so sure?" Trixie asks. "I bet she's planning an escape even now. Can't make a whore into a housewife."

Archer snarls at her, attracting the attention of everyone around us. Once they've all returned to what they were doing he says, "I will cut your tongue out of your mouth and force feed it to you if you say anything like that about Jinx again. You are living under my roof, and you are only good to me for as long as we're looking for the ritual site.

"If you think for one second that I can't find another pixie with the sight, you've got another thing coming. And the next one won't be so fucking obsessed with a man who doesn't even want her that she does something as stupid as insulting and arch demon's mate right in front of him."

Trixie trembles under Archer's gaze. He somehow has the restraint to keep his voice quiet.

"Maybe we should talk about something else," Dalton suggests, looking like he's about to shit himself.

Trixie puts back on the mask of indifference she was wearing before Archer verbally eviscerated her. "I just don't understand why you all think she'll change for you," she says and looks directly at Camp.

"We're not asking her to change anything for us. That's what you're not getting," I say. "If she wants to return to the Naughty Nebula after this is over, she can do that. We love her, and we want her to be happy."

"And does she want the same for you all? Or is she just using you to fill some void while she's stuck in the mansion? And why do you all have to change to suit her needs. Campbell would have never even considered sharing a woman before Jinx came along."

"I wouldn't be so sure about that," I say with a laugh.

"Why are you being so snotty about her?" Campbell asks. "I thought we went through all of this at the cabin, Trix. I feel like I can't explain this in any way that you'll understand."

"You're right. I don't understand. Because a year ago, you were ready to move in with me, and now you're panting after a girl who you've barely met who is sleeping with four other men. It's pathetic."

"Yeah and a year ago you wanted nothing to do with a serious relationship and now that I've moved on, and am happy with Jinx and Sully, you're acting like a giant bitch."

He says the last bit a little loud and people start staring again.

"We should go," Dalton mutters.

"Fine," Trixie says and stands and throws the rest of her pretzel in the trash.

We follow her outside and pile into the SUV. The tension in the car feels like it's going to suffocate us. Once we're on the road, and headed back toward Jinx, I'm able to unclench my jaw, and un-ball my fists. From the time we started shopping until the time we're back on the road takes less than two and a half hours, but I'm anxious to get back to her. Shortly after we merge onto the highway, Campbell falls asleep on my shoulder on the way home as I draw lazy circles on his thigh with my finger.

Trixie has been his friend for a long time, and her being so rude toward Jinx is really wearing on him. He just wants them to get along. All of the friendships we'd forged at the station are now gone. He had to sever his relationships with his friends when we joined the believers so we didn't put anyone else in danger. I'm just happy that he at least has me.

We're about forty minutes from the house when Archer's phone rings. He jabs the button on the center console to connect to the Bluetooth.

"Colt! I was wondering when you would wake up. How's–"

"Jinx is fucking gone!"

"What do you mean she's gone? What happened?"

"I was having a conversation with Niall, and she went downstairs to have breakfast, and when I went to join her, your cook was dead, and Jinx, Lanya, and your three goons were gone. I'm freaking the fuck out, Archer."

Archer's knuckles are white as he grips the steering wheel in blind rage. He hits the gas to get us back to his estate faster. In my periphery, Trixie is smirking. I don't say anything because I don't want to spook her. But I'm convinced that she knows something, and she's not telling us.

Chapter Twenty

Archer

If Lanya has touched one single hair on Jinx's head, I will grind her up so small that you won't even be able to smell the sulfur wafting off her bones. I've been skeptical of her since the moment she joined The Believers because she always was a fan of doing whatever she wanted—everyone else be damned. As demons we don't have to worry about the world ending because we can just go back to the hells where we belong.

I make it back to the estate in record time, and find Colt sitting on the steps of the mansion. I basically throw my keys at the valet as I'm stepping out of the car.

"How the fuck did you let this happen *again*?" I demand, storming up to the steps.

"Niall came in all pissy this morning because I mated her, so I went to talk to him. She was just going down for breakfast, and I assumed that you were here. I had no idea that you all had left! So *maybe* the next time you're planning a multiple hour long outing, you can give me a little bit of heads up!"

I clench and unclench my fists. He's right. I should have told him directly. But his brother knew. I told Niall on our way out that we were leaving.

"How long were you and Niall talking?"

"A couple of hours. I explained to him why I mated with her, and we had a long discussion about him being nicer to her since she was family now. Then we played a couple rounds of pool."

"How did they get her out of the house without making a sound? Jinx would have put up a fight," Campbell says.

"If they were able to sneak up on her and subdue her somehow, they wouldn't have," Sully says. "Trixie, you're the closest with Lanya out of all of us, did you have any idea she was going to pull something like this?"

Trixie frowns. "No. I had no idea."

That's a lie.

"She seemed so excited that we finally had the Zodiac. She just wanted to get the ritual done."

Another lie.

Sully gives me a look, and his eyes flit to Trixie. He knows something. There's a reason he asked her that question. Pixies can phase out of this realm at will, so if we're going to catch her, we need to be smart about it.

"Right, well, my office then. Let's discuss what we can do to get her back. Colt, go get Niall. No one but this group and him are permitted in that room."

Trixie pulls out her phone and begins texting someone. I pull it out of her hand and she scowls at me.

"Everyone, hand over your cell phones. I don't trust any of you right now, and we need to be sure that we're keeping any information about this situation within our ranks. I'll throw mine on the pile too so that you know that I can't contact anyone."

Everyone passes me their phones. I grab a large mixing bowl from my now bloodied kitchen and toss them in. The cook is still laying on the floor practically decapitated. Aside from Jinx being taken, that's the biggest show of disrespect. Loren was a good man, and he didn't deserve any of that. It also took almost a decade to break him in after the last one quit.

The shift is threatening to take over again, so I take a deep breath, and head to the office. Everyone is standing around arguing with each other over whose fault it is that Jinx is missing.

"ENOUGH!" I yell when I enter. "We won't get anything accomplished if we're fighting among ourselves. It's no one's fault that she's gone except Lanya and whoever she was working with. And trust me, I will find every single one of them and slaughter them, myself."

I say the last part and make pointed eye contact with Sully so he knows that I'm aware of what he was trying to tell me.

"I just can't believe she would betray us like this," Dalton says.

"She is a demon, and demons are known to be tricksy and evil," I say.

Trixie pales a little at the use of the homonym of her name. Sully positions himself behind her, and I grab my phone out of the pile.

"I thought we weren't allowed to touch our phones," Niall protests.

"You all can see what I'm doing. I'm just pulling up a GPS app on my phone."

"Why?" Cobra asks, crossing his arms over his chest.

"Because I inserted a tracking device into Jinx after you broke in."

"You did *what*?" Colt demands, jumping to his feet.

"Oh calm down. She was asleep while I did it, and it's proving to be useful."

"We're going to have a talk about this later with Jinx present," Sully says through clenched teeth.

"She'll thank me for it once we have her back. Go ahead Sully."

He pistol whips Trixie in the back of head rendering her unconscious. I wanted to make sure that the tracker was still working properly before I had him take her out.

"What the fuck?!" Dalton yells.

"She had something to do with it, I'm just not sure what. Were you in on it too?" Sully asks, pointing his gun at Dalton and pulling back the hammer.

Dalton is a low level mage. He could probably get out of this situation using magic, but he wouldn't make it far before he was completely drained of energy.

He holds his hands up, "No. Of course not. I don't want our planet to get sucked into that damn rift. How do you know Trix was involved?"

"Her behavior. I suspect she went with us to the store to stall us. She took an awfully long time picking out curtains," I say. "Then there was the sudden craving for a fucking soft pretzel."

"The one thing I'm curious about," I say and turn my attention to Niall, "Is you. Did you know? Were you in on it?"

"No. I hate her, but I don't want her dead."

A lie.

"I can smell your sins, shifter. Do you want to try that answer again."

"What is he talking about?" Colt asks his brother. "What are you lying about? The part where you didn't have anything to do with it or the part where you don't want her dead?"

Niall stares at his brother defiantly. I give him plenty of time to fess up.

"Both," I say when he doesn't answer.

Colt tackles Niall to the floor, breaking the chair in the process. His eyes are glowing, and his teeth are elongated. His panther is taking over in defense of his mate. He begins punching his brother in the face until he's bloodied and bruised. Niall tries to fight back but he's no match for his brother. Campbell and Sully let him wail on Niall for about thirty seconds before hauling him off.

"Why the fuck would you do that to her? Why would you hand her over to the council?"

With two swollen eyes and blood pouring down his face, Niall yells, "Because she's a fucking whore! She left us! Left *you* to get beat night after night in that fucking house."

"She left us because she *had* to!"

"That's enough," I say, placing a hand on Colt's shoulder. He looks like he's about to cry, and I understand that the betrayal of his brother must sting like a bitch. "We don't have time for this right now. You can do whatever you need to him when we get back. I'll lock him and Trixie in the basement and we'll handle them later. I promise, you get first dibs."

Colt nods, and shrugs his way out of Campbell and Sully's grasp. I nod to Cobra who takes control of Niall's mind, forcing him to walk to his own cell, while I carry Trixie down behind them.

My cells are warded, salted, and made of Unobtainium. They won't be able to escape.

We hop back into the SUV, Colt taking Trixie's place, and we head toward the flashing beacon in the middle of nowhere.

I have Cobra pull up satellite images while we're on the drive. There's an old farmhouse with several outbuildings in the area where Jinx's tracker is showing active. If the Council has anything to do with this, then there's likely high tech security surrounding the area.

"I've known Lanya for years, and while I was surprised that she was a part of The Believers, I am a little surprised that she went this far."

"Why couldn't you detect her lies like you could with Niall?" Colt asks.

"Demons are able to cover it up better. Succubi in particular can emit a pheromone that sort of covers lies or hatred with lust. And since she was constantly hitting on me, I assumed that it was genuine lust. Bitch. I'm going to rip her wings off and force feed them to her," I grumble.

"If I don't get to her first," Colt says.

"I have some plans for her, too," Cobra adds.

"They've likely got cameras set up all around the property. We'll have to sneak in if we want to get to her without them noticing."

"We can do that. Colt can go first in his panther form. He'll look less conspicuous than the rest of us."

"I can fly, and carry Cobra in," Sully says.

"I can make myself invisible," Campbell mentions offhandedly.

"You can do what?!" Sully asks. It's the first I'm hearing about it too.

"I just need blood from one of you."

"Blood mages, man," Cobra says. "You can have a little bit of mine. I like to bleed."

I bite down on my tongue so I don't moan at the thought of slicing his beautiful pale skin and watching it turn red. I wonder if Jinx would be into that as much as we are.

We pull off at an access road about a mile away from the house and park in the trees just off the access road. We cover the car with branches and foliage to make it less conspicuous, then we set off on our trek to the house to save our girl.

Chapter Twenty One

Jinx

I wake with a start and bolt upright. I'm in a bed with my feet in shackles that are chained to the floor. I shift my gaze around the sterile white room. Linnie is flitting around the room in a panic.

Where are we? I ask

About forty five minutes from Archer's. In the woods. The succubus and that fucking pixie have been working for the council this whole time.

The guys?

Are not here. I imagine they're losing their minds about you being gone.

Any way out that you can see?

No. And the room is made of solid Unobtanium. They know I'm in here.

Fuck!

I pull at the chains as if I'm strong enough to break them, but I'm not. I know I'm not. Archer could probably break them like they were made of floss. I wonder for a second if he can feel my fear through the bond. Colt, too. I'm not a shifter or a demon, so while I'm tied to them, I don't have the same bonded abilities that they do.

I try to use my ice magic on the chains, but it never surfaces. *What use is having magic if I can't fucking use it?*

I glance around the room for a point of weakness, but I don't find any. There are cameras in every corner and there's a PA speaker embedded in the wall.

I look at the camera directly ahead of me and flip it off while sticking my tongue out. I'm going to kill Lanya and Trixie if I ever get out of here.

"Oh good. You're awake," Lanya's sultry voice filters through the PA system.

"I hope you realize how fucking dead you are when I get out. And I *will* get out."

"Oh I don't think so, sweetpea. That room was specially designed for you. You're not going anywhere."

"Archer will find you. And when he does..." An unhinged laugh escapes me as I imagine Archer carving Lanya into pieces.

"We'll see. I know I interrupted your breakfast, so I'll be sending some food down, shortly. I hope you're hungry. Then after breakfast, you'll have a nice visit with an old friend."

My stomach twists into knots. Does she mean an old friend of hers or mine?

Linnie, can you get out of here?

I don't think so, why?

I need you to get to the guys. Tell them what you can.

I'm not leaving you.

I'll be okay. It's our best shot. Please go.

Absolutely not. I'm sure they'll find you. We just have to be patient.

You're probably right. I just am scared about what will happen if I'm stuck here too long.

The door pops open and a man in a suit drops a tray on the floor before backing out of the room as if I'm a rabid raccoon who may attack. Linnie hides behind my back until the door is shut securely once more.

My chains reach just far enough for me to pick up the tray which contains toast and eggs. I never had the opportunity to eat this morning, and who knows how long I was unconscious. My stomach grumbles at the smell. I take it back to the bed and nibble on it while sorting out my options.

My heart aches in the absence of my mates. I hope that they're not too stressed out about where I am. I know that I can survive and get out of this place, but it's questionable about what state I'll be in when I do.

What I *do* know is that Lanya is fucking dead the next time I see her. I take the small carton of milk and drink it. I laugh softly to myself thinking about how it looks like the ones they used to serve with school lunches; as if they think I'm a child. But they're going to find out how wrong they are about that. I finish it and place the tray back on the floor.

Taking a deep breath I lay back on the bed and cover my face with my hands. The guys will find me. They have to. After about ten minutes, an important looking man in a suit steps into the room followed by—

"Steve?" I gasp.

He's much more cleaned up than he was the last time I saw him. When I was living in his home, he routinely had several days worth of stubble, and walked around in jeans and a sweat-stained white tank top or T-shirt.

"Did you miss me?" he asks with a slimy smile. "You're even prettier than when you lived with me. You've got a little more meat on your bones now."

"Yes, well, it's amazing what being fed more than seven meals a week will do. What are you doing here?"

"You caused a lot of headaches for me, Jinx. I had a hell of a time finding you after you abandoned us. During our first night together—"

"You mean the night you *raped* me, you fucking pedophile?" I snap.

Anger flashes in his eyes at my accusation. "Please. You wanted it. Always strutting around in our house wearing those shorts and tank tops. Your nipples were practically begging for me to touch them. Anyway, I saw that mark on your ass. I knew immediately what you were and I contacted the council.

"There was a bounty out on your head. They paid me a handsome sum that day and then kept me on their team as I continued to search for you."

"Why am I here?" I ask the other man.

Steve is clearly *not* the one in charge. Suit Guy gives me a broad smile as if he wants me to trust him, but I would rather shove a hot poker in my vagina than take anything that this guy has to say to heart.

"We have to keep you here until the Solstice. We figured out that is when your ascension is supposed to take place. Once the Solstice is over, and you're no longer a threat, Steve can have you, and the money we promised him."

Steve stalks toward the bed with an evil grin on his face. "We can pick up where we left off, Jinx. Shelley's gone and you're mine. We can start a family. You can give me the child she was never able to bear."

"It was probably your fault she couldn't get pregnant you impotent fuck," I say and spit in his face.

"I'll leave you two to get reacquainted. You have an hour before we meet the others," the man says to Steve, then he approaches me. "Oh, and little witch, if you hurt him or try anything to escape. I'll kill your boyfriends. All of them."

"I'd like to see you try," I laugh.

"I don't have to try. I have bombs rigged in the demon's mansion. Just one little *push...*" He presses his forefinger to my nose. "And they all go up like the fourth of July."

My stomach turns sour, but I refuse to show any weakness. I need to get out of here. I need to help my guys—my mates. The man in the suit leaves me alone with Steve who just stands there, checking his watch.

"Trying to decide what you're going to do with the other fifty eight minutes after you rape me?"

"Just seeing how long I have before the drugs kick in."

"You need viagra now?" I snark then I realize that he's not talking about drugs for him. He's talking about drugs for me. The fucking milk.

"You're a fucking coward," I say, my vision starting to blur.

"You're a powerful witch. I know my limits."

"Yeah, and when I was just a teenager?" My words are slurring.

"I couldn't risk you screaming and waking those boys. But now you're here and you're all mine. And you will be for the rest of our lives."

"Max is going to kill you," I grumble, my head falling back on the pillow as he climbs on top of me and begins taking my clothes off. With any luck I'll be unconscious before he's able to actually put his pencil dick inside of me.

I close my eyes, and try to think of anything else. Vague memories come in flashes. *My parents took me to a park when I was a child. They left me on the swing set and went to talk to their drug dealer on the corner. The only reason they took me was to get their fix.*

It's a year or so later, and I come home from first grade and my parents are both dead on the floor. The official report was a bad batch of drugs. Something was laced in their heroin.

I'm in my first foster home. The family's daughter doesn't like me. She pushes me down a flight of stairs and I break my arm. Social Services puts me in a new home. I move several more times until I finally get to Steve and Shelley's when I'm fourteen.

Colt and Niall are already there. They give me the ins and outs of living with the Cutlers. I have nightmares every single night while I'm there. One night I wake up to a warm body in the bed with me. I roll over to find a chubby ten year old Max laying next to me.

"You were screaming," he whispers. "You scream every night."

"I'm okay," I say, and try to give him a reassuring smile.

"You're lying," he says with a furrowed brow.

"I will be okay. I always am."

"I want to stay with you," he says with a pout.

"You should get back to your brother. I'll be fine by myself."

He slips out of the bed and pads quietly to the door. With one last sad smile he leaves my room.

A month later I wake at six am to Shelley screaming in my doorway. "What the fuck do you two think you're doing?"

I open my eyes and find Max in my bed, fear in his eyes.

"He had a bad dream. I told him he could stay here until he felt better. We must have fallen asleep," I say. I don't know why I didn't tell her the truth.

"I don't care what kind of dreams you're having. It's inappropriate for a boy and a girl your age to share a bed."

"He didn't feel comfortable coming to you and Steve, so he came to me. That's all it was, I swear."

"Yeah and like I'm going to believe a slutty little teenager like you. You were probably taking advantage of him."

"She was not!" Max yells. "She would never!"

Shelley grabs him by the scruff of his neck and drags him to his room. I don't see him for three days. When I do, he won't make eye contact with me for a week.

I'm seventeen and I manage to lie my way into a job at a club. It's lower end, but it's something. My first night on the pole, I make over two hundred dollars. I'm sore for three days after that night. Slowly my muscles and stamina build.

I'm nineteen and I get my first offer for A legitimate call girl service. I don't take it. Instead I go home and set up a webcam in my shitty little apartment and begin taking my clothes off on screen. When the second offer comes for a better call girl service, I accept.

I meet my first client. He's a man at least twice my age. He wants me to call him daddy. It's nothing that makes me too uncomfortable. The next guy, however, wants me to piss in my underwear and then shove it in his mouth while he's tied to the bed. He calls me several more times after that. Each time providing me with a gallon of water.

I wish I could say that was the strangest experience.

I'm twenty two and I get offered a job at an upscale strip club. The owner saw me dancing at the first place I worked and asked me to come audition at the Naughty Nebula. He tells me that they've been looking to 'diversify' for their clients. What he means is he wants a fat girl on the poles.

Between those two jobs I manage to get a nice apartment and a bicycle to get me to and from work. No more public transit means that I don't have to get stared at by creeps on the subway.

I'm twenty six. I'm meeting with a client at a hotel bar. He's wearing a button up shirt and a pair of khakis. Something about him feels off. We step out of the bar after a couple of drinks and he pulls me into an alleyway and asks me to go down on him. He says he has a thing for doing it in public.

I pull his cock out of his pants and seconds before it touches my lips, there's a flashlight on me, and a cop telling me to put my hands up. I run. Campbell catches me.

Images of the guys flash through my head, and all I want is to be surrounded by them and their love. Colt told me he loved me. Something no other person has ever said to me in my life.

His face and the face of the others are the last images swimming through my brain before the world goes black.

Chapter Twenty Two
Cobra

We approach the barn where Jinx is being kept. There are a lot more guards positioned directly outside the building than throughout the woods. Colt has been able to stealthily pick off most of the ones we came across in the woods, his panther form lending better camouflage than what we have in human form.

I can mind control several people at once. The problem is that I need to be within a very specific range to do it. The plan is for Archer to create a distraction since he has self healing abilities while I sneak onto the roof of the building and get close enough to take out our targets.

Campbell, invisible next to me, whispers, "I suspect we'll have about two minutes after we alert them to our presence before they're sending people out of the house, so we need to move quickly. I'll stay outside with eyes on the house to pick off any extras."

I nod. "I can manage all the guys surrounding the building, if we can get them close together."

"I'll get Jinx," a now naked, human Colt says.

"I'll come with you," Sully chimes in from above. He stayed high enough that he was above the cameras, but not so high up that he was above the treeline.

We move slowly through the woods, careful not to make a sound. Once we're as far as we're comfortable going, Archer conjures a fireball and lobs it at a bush that's next to the farmhouse, far enough away from the barn that it won't risk catching the barn on fire in case that's where Jinx is being held.

Yelling erupts from the men guarding the barn. There's got to be a dozen of them. Some begin working to extinguish the fire while others watch their backs, eyes trained on their surroundings for the threat.

"Back to your posts," one of them yells once the fire is out. "Protect the asset at all costs!"

They walk back to the barn in formation. Idiots. I reach out with my mental abilities, and one by one each of them raises their pistols to their heads and pulls the trigger. An amused sound escapes me as I delight in the mess it makes.

I go to climb off of the roof when a *bang!* sounds, and a sharp burning pain tears through my shoulder. My gaze drops to my shirt, and blood is pouring from a bullet wound. I missed one. How did I miss one?

I shift my gaze frantically around the area, but I don't see anyone. I reach out with my abilities, and find someone's consciousness not far from where I stand. I take control of him as well, and he raises his gun and shoots himself in the throat. At first the only way I can tell that I succeeded is by the blood that coats the ground, but slowly a man comes into view. A horrific gurgling emits from his throat, and I jump from the roof of the barn to loom over him while he dies.

I crouch down, and pull the gun out of his hand. "I know that I should feel bad for taking your life, but the truth is that I don't. You took something that belongs to me, and now hell is going to rain down on all of you. You're just a puppet in a game being played by people much more powerful than you."

The light fades from his eyes as his blood coats the ground. I walk around the building to find Archer in his demon form. He's holding a man up by the head and squeezing. A nauseating crack followed by the squelching of his brains can be heard throughout the small clearing surrounding the house.

He sniffs the air, and his head snaps in my direction. A growl rumbles out of him when he catches sight of my injury. He bounds over to me and gently inspects the wound.

"Who did it?" he growls.

"He's dead. Don't worry. Let's go get our girl."

We enter the barn. It's large, and the entire interior has been remodeled to look almost like a hospital or a psychiatric ward. My gut churns thinking about being stuck in Blackridge. I'm still mad at Archer for that. I'll get over it eventually, but he's going to need to do a bit more groveling.

Campbell stays outside while the rest of us search the barn. She's not in any of the rooms here.

"Where the fuck is she?! I can smell her." Colt roars and throws a cot across the room he's in. "JINX! LINNIE!"

There's additional gunfire outside.

"Keep looking," I say to Colt.

Archer and I go running out of the building to find about eight more men with guns coming for Campbell. Between the three of us we should have no issues dispatching them. I just have to hope that Colt and Sully are able to find Jinx.

I take out two of the men, then one of them catches my eye. At first I think that Niall somehow followed us out here, then I notice the crows feet and laugh lines. Paired with the specks of silver in his dark hair—this has to be their father.

I take control of him, and walk him over to me.

"Who the fuck are you?"

"None of your fucking business," he growls. "Let me go and fight me like a real man."

"The thing is that you have your strengths and I have mine. Mine just happen to be better than yours." We're far enough away from the others that they can't hear us. "Your boys think that you're dead."

"They were supposed to have a better life than me, but here we are on opposite sides of the same coin. Now you're going to let me go, or I'll blow up that farmhouse. I don't care if Max is inside or not."

"His name is Colt, now, fuck face," I say and punch him square in the nose.

I'm not sure why I'm feeling so protective over the big dumb shifter, but his skeevy dad is pissing me off. Mr. Panther starts cackling as he's laying on the ground.

"You have no idea what is waiting for you. You may get her back, but we'll take her out eventually."

"You'll have to go through your son to get to her."

"I'll do whatever it takes," he says and spits on my shoes.

I swing my leg back and kick him in the jaw. Quick footsteps *thud thud thud* on the ground behind me. I spin around to find a huge demon coming for me. I duck out of the way as his fist swings toward my face.

It's enough of a distraction that I lose my control over Colt's dad. He stands and grabs the demon by the hand. "To headquarters!" he shouts.

I attempt to gain control again, but they poof out of existence leaving me alone. The others have neutralized the rest of the men.

"Cobra!" Archer yells. "I could use some help!"

I jog over to them. "We have a problem. We need to get back to the house as quick as possible."

"Hopefully Colt and Sully find her soon."

I take over with the guy he has on the ground. Telling Colt and Niall about their dad is going to be uncomfy. I don't want to do it. But they deserve to have some warning. I just hope they don't try to shoot the messenger.

Chapter Twenty Three
Colt

Sully and I tear the barn apart, and I cannot find anything that would indicate her presence aside from the vague scent of her.

"What good is having a shifter mate if he can't fucking find her?" Sully snaps.

It stings, but he's right.

Focusing on the connection, and the scent, I discover a small closet that I didn't bother checking it thoroughly because it was too small for anyone to fit inside comfortably. In the closet, under a rug is a hatch that has a ladder. I practically slide down the ladder, and Sully is right behind me.

Not wanting to waste any time I jump the last few rungs, and land on the white tile floor. I'm still not wearing any clothes. I didn't want to bother with them in case I needed to shift quickly.

I sprint down the hall in the direction of the smell, and skid to a halt in front of a door with a small window. Everything here is so white and sterile. They've been building this for years.

I don't even look through the window before I yank the door open and to my horror I find Jinx on the bed, with a naked Steve on top of her, cock inside of her. She is unconscious. Linnie is crushed in a pile of blue blood and bones on the floor next to the bed. *Fuck!*

"Get the fuck out!" he yells over his shoulder, but his eyes connect with mine and he realizes that he's not safe anymore.

Everything inside of me wants to rip his head from his body, but I won't. If anyone deserves this kill, it's Jinx. If she wants it, that is.

I rip him off of her and throw him to the floor and begin punching him in his stupid mustached face over and over until he's no longer conscious. Sully pulls a pair of handcuffs out of god knows where and Restrains Steve. I run over to where Jinx is chained to the bed and check for a pulse. She's still breathing. I open her eye lids. Her pupils are blown. He drugged her with something.

One at a time, I grab the chains that are attached to her feet and pull as hard as I can, breaking them from where they're attached to the floor.

I scoop Jinx up into my arms and hold her bare skin to mine. "Minxy, I need you to be okay. So wherever you are right now, I need you to just come back."

A tear slides down my cheek and rolls down her chest. I hold her close to me and breathe in her scent, trying to calm myself down. She'll be okay. She has to be.

I allow myself a minute to collect myself, before jumping into action again. I throw her over my shoulder and begin back up the ladder one handed. I walk out of the barn and toward the farmhouse where Archer and Cobra are standing in front of a man in a suit who is kneeling on the ground with his hands on his head.

Archer's eyes find me and Jinx, and he runs over. I've never seen the demon look shaken before this moment. Cobra stays where he is, so

I assume that he's controlling the fuckwit on the ground or else he would be joining us.

"She's alive," is all I can manage to say.

Archer holds out his arms to take her, but I shake my head.

"Please let me take her," he says. "Just for a minute."

I sigh and hand her over knowing exactly how he's feeling right now. "You can have her for a minute, but I need you to go down into the basement of the barn, and collect the asshole who drugged her and was assaulting her when I walked in. I don't think that Sully can carry him up the ladder by himself."

"I'll fucking kill him, then nobody will have to carry him," Archer growls as he rubs his face against Jinx's hair, breathing her in the same way I had.

"No. His fate is for Jinx to decide," I say firmly. "It's our old foster father."

Archer nods in understanding, and I appreciate his willingness to surrender control to Jinx.

"Where's Lanya?" I ask.

"Not here. But trust me, once I get my hands on that traitorous bitch, I'll rip her to shreds. I've known her for decades. I never would have expected her to do something so foolish."

Archer hands Jinx back to me, and I clutch her to my chest. "Linnie is dead," I whisper. "Her body is in the room where I found Jinx."

"No," Camp says, and anguish takes hold of his face. "Jinx won't survive that. Familiars are too important."

"She can and she will. She's strong," Archer assures him with a pat on the shoulder. "I'll collect her body along with the rapist."

"Can I kill this guy, now?" Cobra whines to Archer, as Archer makes his way to the barn.

"Not yet! After we get him back to the estate and question him!" Archer calls over his shoulder.

"You're fucking lucky," Cobra mutters to the man on the ground.

"We're going back to the estate? Is that even safe with Lanya knowing where Archer lives?" I ask

"They can't actually come after him at his house without causing a huge uproar between the humans and the demons," Cobra explains. "The second they set foot on his property, they violate a century-long agreement with the devil himself."

"Why do I not know about this?"

"Eh demon politics aren't really made known unless you run in powerful circles. I only know because Archie spilled during pillow talk one night."

"Good to know. Do you think we can keep her safe there until the ritual?"

"My guess is that we'll regroup then move to a safe house elsewhere. But that's really up to Archer."

I'm not going to argue. Strategy isn't my strong suit. I've always been an enforcer, and that's fine with me. The rest of it comes with too many headaches.

Eventually Archer returns with Sully in tow and Steve thrown over his shoulder. Sully has a sheet in his hands that he wraps around Jinx, giving her some semblance of modesty.

We make our way through the woods back to the car. I carry Jinx the whole way, cradling her to me. I'm scared that if I let her out of my arms for even a second she'll disappear again. It's my fault she was taken in the first place.

Within an hour we're pulling back into the estate. The others take Steve and the suit to the cells, and I carry Jinx up to the master bedroom and get her in the bathtub. I take my time to clean her of any traces of Steve. It won't be enough to erase the psychological damage, but I can't do nothing. I dry her off, and put her in the bed, tucking her in tightly. I'm about to crawl into bed with her when Cobra taps me on the shoulder lightly.

"We need to talk," he whispers. "Just the two of us, then we can involve the others."

He looks serious, which is causing me anxiety. Cobra is never serious about anything unless it has to do with Jinx. I nod and follow him out of the room. Sully and Campbell are in the bathroom if Jinx needs anything, and I imagine that Archer will be up soon once he's done dealing with whatever he's dealing with.

Cobra leads me out into the hall and says, "Your room or mine?"

I narrow my eyes at him. "This isn't a sex thing, is it? Cause my door does not swing that way. I am firmly team vagina."

"No it's not a sex thing," he says with an eye roll. "If it *were* a sex thing, I would want Jinx or Archer involved. It's just a conversation."

"My room then," I say and lead him down the hall. Once the door is shut I turn and face him. "Why are you being so cryptic?"

He runs his hand through his shaggy blonde hair and sighs. "This is really hard to do. I am not good at delivering bad news unless I don't like you. And even though we've had our issues—"

"Just spit it out. You're making me nervous."

"So you told us a while ago that your parents were dead?" he asks.

"Yeah, why?"

"Your dad isn't."

"What the fuck are you on about? If this is some kind of joke, it's not funny," I say.

"It's not a joke. I swear. I know how bad parents can really fuck you up, and I would never joke about this. Your dad was at the farmhouse."

I stare at him, trying to decide how truthful he's being. He has no reason to lie about this. I may not like the guy, but I don't think that he's making it up, either.

"Did you kill him?" *Please tell me you killed him.*

"No. I was going to bring him to you to deal with, or at least make a decision about, and some demon fucker bamf'd him out of the area. I just didn't want you to be blindsided if we come up against him again."

My knees don't feel like they can support me anymore. I plop down on my bed, and put my head in my hands. "Thank you for telling me. If it's okay, I would like a moment alone," I say.

"Okay," Cobra says. His footsteps move toward the door, and pause. "Just...Archer and I are here for you if you need us. I'm sure Sully and Campbell are, too. We may have our differences, but we're all a part of this, now. Jinx is the center of our weird little family. I'm sure that with time, we'll come to love each other just as much as we love her. Take your time. Sort your brain out. Then come to bed."

He doesn't wait for a response before he leaves. I give myself a couple of minutes to mull over what he just told me, then I get changed into some gym shorts and head back to the master bedroom.

Cobra and Archer aren't in the room, and Sully and Campbell are still showering together. I crawl into the bed with Jinx and snuggle up next to her. I need her to wake up so that I can properly hold her. For now I'll take what I can get.

In time, the rest of them join us. It's cramped in the bed, but I would rather have all of us here for her when she wakes up. She needs the comfort of all of her mates after the ordeal she just went through. And the worst isn't even over. I don't expect that she'll handle the news about Linnie well, so I'll have to keep my own baggage to myself until she's done grieving.

Chapter Twenty Four

Jinx

A scream erupts from me as I sit upright in bed. Within seconds there are comforting hands and strong arms surrounding me. My head is pounding, and I feel awful. Slowly the memories filter back in.

The white room. The chains. The drugs. Steve.

My eyes focus on Colt, and tears stream down my face as a sob escapes me.

"Shhhhh. It's okay baby girl. I've got you. We've all got you. You're safe. And you will never be without at least one of us by your side. I promise that we will never let them near you again."

"Steve?"

"In the cells."

"You didn't kill him?"

"I wanted you to have the choice to do it yourself, but say the word and I'll go do it right now. No questions asked."

My eyes wander to the rest of the guys. They're all here. All five of them. I hate the look of pity and worry that they all wear. All of them except Cobra. Cobra looks like he wants to go on a killing spree. And he probably does.

"Please stop looking at me like that," I request.

"Like what, Little Witch?" Sully asks.

"Like I'm going to break if you breathe too hard. I'll be okay."

"You will be. But it's okay to not be okay, beautiful. You can lean on us for a little bit then get back to kicking ass tomorrow," Archer offers.

"You don't have to do any of this alone anymore," Campbell says. "None of us do."

My brain slowly catches up to what's happening. They're all in the bed, mostly naked, or completely naked. My eyes trail down Campbell's body to where his fingers are laced with Sully's. Cobra's resting his head on Archer's shoulder, and Colt has his hand resting on Campbell's outstretch leg.

"What did I miss?" I ask, rubbing my temples.

Archer brushes stray strands of hair out of my face. "The five of us came to an agreement. We decided that we're okay sharing you because we all care about you. We were actually going to surprise you yesterday—"

"Yesterday? How long was I out?"

"About ten hours. We all sort of took turns staying with you, then all climbed into bed about an hour and a half ago. You had enough rohypnol in your system to tranquilize a horse," Sully says.

"I had my personal doctor come and check you out because we were all worried when you didn't wake up within a couple of hours. You even slept through me giving you a bath," Colt says.

"Thank you," I whisper. "All of you."

Archer presses a kiss to my hair, and pulls me into his lap. He's strong, and possessive without being overbearing. Colt rubs my back in soothing circles, and I welcome the caring touches.

"So what now?" I ask.

"You don't need to worry about that right now. Let's get you something to eat, and something for that headache, and get you feeling better first. Then we can work out a plan," Campbell insists.

"Where's Linnie?" I ask.

They all exchange worried glances.

"She was in the cell with me, wasn't she there when you got there?"

"She was," Archer says, softly, placing a large hand on my knee.

Realization falls over me. I reach out for our connection, but it's not there. A whole piece of me is gone.

"No," I whisper. "No! Who did it?"

"We suspect Steve."

A sob bubbles out of me, and I lay back on the bed. She connected with me to protect me, and likely died doing just that.

"How am I supposed to live without her?" I ask in a whisper. "I haven't been without her in over ten years."

"Whatever you need, we'll help," Colt reassures me. "And we'll deal with Steve and get revenge for her."

My body is wracked with pain and guilt. I know she insisted on staying with me, but I should have pushed harder for her to leave. The one thing I know for certain is that I want Steve dead more than I ever have.

My brain and body are tired. My head hurts and my body is starting to feel like I'm covered in fire ants—as if my body's memory of my familiar is being scorched away from my skin a tiny bit at a time.

After a day, I break out in a rash and a fever. Even if I didn't feel like death physically, my soul hurts too bad to leave the bed. My Linnie is gone. I didn't get to say goodbye.

The door cracks open and Campbell tiptoes to the bed and sets a glass of water on the nightstand. He gingerly pushes my sweaty hair off of my forehead.

"You're burning up. We need to do something to break the fever."

"I don't think we can," I say through chattering teeth. Despite my temperature being high, I have full body chills.

"I'll get you some meds and see if that helps. I tried to heal it while I was asleep, but it wouldn't work. I doubt the meds will work, but I have to do something. What about a bath? Just lukewarm?"

"No. Not right now."

"Jinx..."

"I said 'not right now', Campbell." I insist with all the fight I have left in me.

"Okay," he whispers, and stands to leave. Before he's even made it two steps, he turns back to me. "I know you hear us, but you don't really *hear* us. We are here for you. Through thick and thin. So when you're ready, we'll listen."

And then he walks away.

I wake up some time later, and the fever has broken, but the pain is just as bad as it was before I fell asleep. There's a dixie cup with some tylenol in it and a glass of water next to the bed. I sit up and throw the pills back and follow them with the water. Once the glass is empty, I drag myself from the bed and shuffle to the bathroom.

If I feel bad, I look worse. My eyes are sunken with dark circles, my face is pallid, and my hair is stringy and gross. A shower sounds like torture right now. I can't even drum up the energy to brush my teeth. I use the bathroom, and return to the bed, and pull the blanket back up to my chin.

The door opens and shuts and I don't even bother to see who it is. I want to be alone right now.

"Jinx?" Archer's voice hits my ears.

I jump, my body giving away the fact that I'm awake. "I would like to be alone, Archer."

"No."

I half roll over to face him. "What do you mean 'no'? You said you would give me whatever I needed."

"I don't believe it's in your best interest to continue to spend time alone, unbathed, and unfed. I've given you forty-eight hours, and while I don't expect you to stop grieving, I do expect you to stop wallowing. I will not be taking 'no' for an answer, and if you don't peel yourself out of that bed, I will do it for you.

"The sheets need to be changed, you need to be bathed, and you need a proper meal in you. Now, *get up!*"

"I said I wanted to be *alone!*"

"And you don't get a say in it anymore. I don't like to repeat myself, and I've already done it once. You have twenty seconds."

"I'm not getting out of bed."

"Ten seconds, Little Star."

"You can't make me!"

"Five seconds."

"Archer," I warn.

"Time's up," he says and he crosses the room and looms over me.

I hug the blanket to myself, but he rips it off with ease. I'm exhausted and weak from not eating. And he's an ancient being that's practically a demigod.

He pulls my underwear down and rips my shirt off of my body as I smack and claw against him like a feral cat. Unphased, he scoops me up into his arms and carries me into the bathroom and turns the shower on.

"Put me down!" I shriek.

"We can do this the hard way, and I can try to get you clean while I hold you, or you can stop acting like an overgrown toddler and let me run a bath for you. I will not let you—my *mate*—waste away any longer. Let me help you!"

"I don't want help. I don't deserve your kindness. I don't want to feel anything. My best friend is gone, and it's all my fault!"

All of the emotions that have been building in me for the last two days come pouring out of me in violent sobs. My arms go limp as I give up fighting against Archer's hold on me. He holds me against his chest, and shushes me like a crying baby.

"None of this was your fault. You couldn't have known that Lanya would take you. You had no way of stopping any of it. And Steve was the one who killed her, not you."

My sobbing eventually slows to soft hiccups, and Archer sets me on my feet.

"Are you ready to stop being so difficult?"

"Never," I mutter.

"Okay, are you ready to let me take care of you?"

"For now. But if I say I want to go back to bed, you have to let me."

"As soon as the maid changes the sheets, that's fine with me."

He draws a bath for me, dumping in bubbles and bath salts. When I step toward the tub, he picks me up again. This time I let him. With me safely in his arms, he steps into the enormous tub and cradles me in his lap as he begins washing the grime off of my body.

After he washes the front of me, he spins me around and begins washing my back and my hair. His fingers massaging my scalp feel amazing, and I nearly fall asleep as he's working the shampoo through my hair. To keep myself awake, I decide to actually talk about my feelings for once in my life.

"A book I read in fourth grade talked about familiars and their connection to their earthly tether. They find their human in desperate times, summoned by magic the human doesn't usually realize they're casting.

"They can be released back into their realm if both parties agree, but the connection remains in case they ever need one another again," I explain. Then a smile creeps onto my face.

"Linnie never once wanted that. She cared about me deeply, and I cared about her. She was comfortable, and real, and just always there—a fact that I started to take for granted at some point. I never even told her I loved her."

"I'm sure she knew, and I'm doubly sure she wouldn't want you to beat yourself up over that."

"No, but I'm still going to. I should have cherished my time with her more. Did you know that nearly fifty percent of humans don't survive the death of their familiar? They either die from the pain of the lost bond, or they waste away to nothing."

"You're stronger than those people."

"No I'm not, Archer. I would let myself waste away if I could. But between you all being incessant about taking care of me, and the fate of the world resting firmly on my shoulders, I have no choice." My voice is placid, but firm. I know what I'm saying is true. If the guys weren't here, I would probably have killed myself already.

"The physical pain I'm feeling is nothing compared to the mental anguish. Everything hurts. *Everything*. And I honestly don't know how much longer I can handle this. I believe that the worst is over, but it doesn't make the leftover pain any more bearable."

He spins me around to face him. "You'll get through this. I swear to you that I will do anything I can to help. You just need to tell me how."

"We can start by making a plan. I hate that everything is so up in the air."

"Can we get you back to some semblance of normalcy before we dive right back into the end of the world?" he asks with a laugh.

"I would rather deal with it now."

"It doesn't matter how good of a plan we come up with, the Solstice is still over two months away. It's a lot of 'hurry up and wait' right now."

"We could at least search for the site."

"Let's talk about this after you're fed and we're with the others."

"Fine, but only because we really need their input before we make any major decisions."

"I'll take it."

After several hours of making sure that I'm okay, pampering me, and insisting that I eat my weight in every food I can possibly think of, the guys are finally willing to lift the ban on shop talk.

We're all sitting around in Archer's office. He insists that I sit on his lap any time we have a meeting in there.

"It's so distracting," I protest.

"This is my throne, and I insist that I have my queen with me while I sit on it," he says.

"Queens usually get their own thrones."

"You have one. My lap."

I sigh and give up, leaning back into his chest as he trails his fingers in feather light touches down my stomach and up my thighs. He sighs too, but his sigh is because he's content and happy with me touching him.

"So what are we doing with the hostages?" Cobra asks eagerly.

"That's up to Jinx. Lanya is the only one I get to call the shots on and that's only because a human determining her fate would break the accord."

"Let's start with an easy one," Sully says. "What do we do with Steve?"

"Dead," I say, instantly. "I don't care who does it. I just want it done."

"That one is mine," Colt says. His determination in his voice sends a shiver through me.

"Okay, and Trixie?" Campbell asks. His voice is soft.

The betrayal he's feeling is written all over his face. I pat Archer's hand and leave his lap to go to Campbell. I position myself between his knees and place my hand on his cheek.

"You can decide on that one if you want. I know that you saw her as a friend."

"No, I don't think that I'm the best person to make that choice. Someone further removed from the situation should decide."

I nod and pull him into me. He wraps his arms around my waist and nuzzles my stomach before planting a kiss just above my belly button. He stares up at me with his beautiful blue eyes.

"I missed you," he mumbles into my skin.

"I was only gone for a day," I say with a laugh.

"That doesn't change the fact that I missed you."

Archer clears his throat, clearly annoyed that I'm not perched in his lap. "You can be all cutesy later. She's mine while she's in this room. Next order of business: Niall."

"What about him?" I ask, returning to Archer's lap.

"He was the reason Colt was away from you, and you were able to be taken."

"Well yeah, but he didn't know. He was just spending time with his brother."

Uncomfortable stares pass between the guys, and I look to Colt who's cradling his face in his hands.

"He distracted me on purpose," he finally says.

"So they could take me?" I clarify, unable to believe that's what I'm hearing.

He nods.

"I need to talk to him. Now. The others I don't give a fuck about. They can all rot. But I need to have a discussion with Niall.

Archer pulls his phone out of his pocket to text one of his guys. I chuckle to myself as he types out *'bring me the bad kitty'*. He puts his phone away and nuzzles his face into my neck while we wait. After about five minutes the door to the office opens, and two of Archer's men bring a handcuffed Niall into the room and push him to his knees in front of the desk.

I stand from Archer's lap and round the desk to stand before him. He looks up at me with such venom in his eyes. I haul back and slap him across the face. He slowly returns his gaze to me.

"I know that you thought that you were protecting your brother by getting rid of me. But in the future you need to get all of the information before you go around making decisions that could impact the entire fate of the planet, dumbass."

"You were just going to fucking leave us again. Just like you did last time, you worthless bitch."

Snarls erupt around the room, and I hold my hand up to silence the guys. "I know you're all feeling protective of me, but Niall just doesn't have all of the information," I say, having a seat on the desk in front of him. "If you're open to hearing everything, and then deciding how you feel, then I think we'll be in good shape. Your other option is to go back to the cells until the Solstice is over. Your choice," I add with a shrug.

Archer scoots forward in his chair and runs a finger down my spine giving comfort through his touch. I keep my eyes trained on Niall.

"I feel there's very little you could say that would excuse what you did, I'll hear your side of things."

"Good."

"Not that I have much of one," he scoffs.

I ignore his snark. "When I left it was because I had to. My choice was to leave and try to make it on my own on the streets, or stay, and be sexually assaulted by Steve. Or worse."

The hard glare that Niall has been giving me since he first saw me in the cabin cracks for the very first time, but doesn't break. "You're lying."

"I'm not. Steve is a monster, and he's going to be dealt with tonight."

"He's here?" Niall's gaze lands on Colt who is glaring daggers at his brother.

"Yes. Because of you, he managed to get his hands on Jinx, again. And he killed her familiar."

The pain of losing Linnie resurfaces, and I have to take a second to compose myself.

"I know now, that if he had kept a hold of me as a teen, he would have sold me to the council. After he raped me the first time, he made a comment about how I was going to make him a lot of money. I thought he was going to sell me into sex trafficking. But he explained it to me yesterday; before he raped me...again."

Horror takes over Niall's face as he realizes just how deep the damage of his betrayal goes. He goes white as a sheet, then a little green.

"I didn't know."

"I know you didn't. That's why I'm giving you the chance to apologize."

"Why didn't you tell me? Why didn't *either of you* tell me?" He demands, his eyes falling back on Colt.

"She didn't owe you *or me* her trauma. And it wasn't my story to tell, so that's why I didn't tell you."

"And you never gave me the opportunity. Neither you nor Max told me who you were. And then by the time I found out your real identities, you were completely refusing to listen to anything I had to say."

He looks as though he might cry. "I'm sorry, Jinx. I never would have...Trixie and Lanya said that you were going to abandon him again and break his heart, so..." He's having a hard time forming a full thought. He's had a long few days just like the rest of us.

"I know that you were protecting your brother. But the thing is that he doesn't need your protection. He especially doesn't need protection from me. I'm here to stay. Come hell or high water, no matter what happens with the ritual, I'm sticking around. So you better get used to me," I say with a smile.

"Okay," he says, casting his eyes to the floor. "But can you do me a favor?"

"Anything."

"Can you try to stay clothed when I'm around?"

I snort in amusement. "If you barge into a room where I have a reasonable expectation of privacy, I can't make any guarantees."

"I'll figure out how to knock first," he says with a grimace.

Archer comes around the desk and tips my chin up so he can see my face. "Satisfied, my love?"

"Yeah, let him go."

Without taking his eyes off of me, he makes a small gesture to one of his guys who takes the handcuffs off of Niall and helps him to his feet. Niall rubs his wrists where the cuffs were digging in. He steps toward me and Archer growls at him.

"It's fine," I whisper.

Niall approaches, and Archer watches him like a hawk. I hop off the desk, and Niall pulls me into a hug. I hesitantly return it. I understand his reasoning, and I forgive him, but I'm still upset that he set me up.

"I'm sorry, Minxy," he whispers into my hair.

"I'm sorry, too."

"Okay that's enough touching," Archer says, pulling Niall off of me by the scruff of the neck.

"I have four other mates, and they're constantly touching me. Niall is where you draw the line?"

"Yes. You forgave him, but I haven't. And I already have to share you enough. Next order of business is the man in the suit. He wouldn't even give us his name, and didn't have any identification on him. Even still, he's our best bet at finding Lanya."

"I vote you do what you need to to get the information from him, then kill him," I say, casually earning me surprised glances. "Look, my entire life people have been taking advantage of me, and it's gone too far this time. I want all these fuckers dead. I think I became a little bloodthirsty after Camp killed that bastard cop at the precinct."

"Your wish is my command," Archer says, kissing my hand, then up my arm in a very 'Gomez Addams' gesture. "The last thing on the agenda, we need to move to one of my hidden estates. We did a sweep of the premises, and the one piece of information that we got out of Steve was that there were some bombs planted in the mansion by a couple of my ex-employees. We located them, and removed them. We'll be safe here for another week—two tops, but they'll eventually send assassins. The question is, do we want to go to the mountains, or the desert?"

"Which is closer to where the ritual is supposed to take place?" Campbell asks, ever the strategist.

"The mountains. It's in the Adirondacks which is where Trixie said that the ritual was to take place, but who knows if she was to be believed."

"Well I guess we have two people to torture, then. But if it's not too far from the ritual site, I vote mountains."

"I think you'll like it there. It's cozy, and there are fireplaces, and the master bedroom has an amazing view."

"So she'll have something nice to look at while we fuck her senseless," Cobra says with a devious smile.

I want to go back to the bedroom, and fall into bed with all of them, right now. I want my ascension to be done. It was my idea to have this meeting, but I'm so tired of all the planning and politics of being *the chosen one*. It's exhausting and I just want to enjoy my mates.

Archer is staring at me with a raised eyebrow, eventually he says, "I think that's enough business for right now. We'll carry out the executions in about—" He glances at his watch. "Five hours. For now, I vote we go give our mate what she's craving."

Chapter Twenty Five

Jinx

Archer throws me over his shoulder like a fucking caveman and despite me protesting, he carries me all the way up to the bedroom and throws me on to the bed. The others close in around me, and my heart starts thundering in my chest.

"Don't act so surprised, Little Star. I could smell your arousal while we were in the office when Cobra mentioned about fucking you senseless, so I plan to do just that. Hold her down."

He says the last line so casually, and the others move toward me as Archer starts stripping. Cobra has a menacing look in his eyes as he prowls toward me.

"Don't...don't touch me," I say, my voice wavering.

Colt and Cobra each grab one of my arms and pin me to the bed while Sully and Campbell each take a leg. I try to thrash beneath their hold, but they won't let go. My breathing picks up, and I begin to legitimately panic.

"Let go!" I yell.

Archer is completely naked, and standing before me in his beautiful demon form. He crawls onto the bed and straddles my waist and rips my dress down the middle.

He places a large hand on my chest and says, "You are in complete control here, Little Star. You can use your magic, you can tell us to stop, and if you really mean it, we will. But I want you to take a couple of deep breaths, and prepare yourself to be completely taken care of by all five of us. Are you ready for that?"

My mouth suddenly feels very dry. My gaze shifts to each of the guys. They're all wearing an expression that says that they fully agree with what Archer just said. They want me wholly and completely, and only if I want them back. I return my attention to Archer and nod.

"That's a good girl."

He shifts back down my body and settles with his head between my legs. He pushes my panties to the side and runs his long tongue up my slick center, making me gasp in delight. The others take turns stripping, they never leave me with more than one limb free at a time. Once they're all bare they hold me in place as Archer begins feasting on my wet center.

He pulls away from me and I whimper desperately craving more of that devilish tongue and what it can do. He chuckles deeply as he slips a single finger inside of me.

Even in my line of work, I've never been with this many men at once. Threesomes were as far as I got. Usually I was acting as a buffer between two men who refused to admit they loved each other.

Archer expertly works his thick finger in and out of me, curling it against my g-spot and making me whimper. Colt takes my hand and places it on his hardening cock, and I begin stroking him. Cobra shifts forward and allows me to take him into my mouth.

Archer growls and removes his finger from me so he has both hands free to tear my undergarments off.

I pull my mouth away from Cobra. "You need to stop doing that. I won't have any clothes left."

"I'll buy you more, now suck his cock."

Archer moves back off the bed, and pulls up a chair. He watches, entranced as the others shift around me, closing ranks. Sully moves between my legs and takes a nipple between his teeth, making me moan around Cobra's hard length. Cobra grabs the back of my head and forces my face against his pelvic bone, cutting off my air supply.

"Your throat feels like satin against my cock, Little Mouse." He grunts and begins thrusting in and out, cutting off my air each time.

While I'm distracted, one of the others throws my legs over their shoulders and slips inside of me. I'm unable to see past Cobra's arm to see who it is, but I would guess Sully by his movements.

"Lick her clit while I fuck her," Sully says, and I'm assuming he's talking to Campbell. He drops one of my legs down so that Campbell has better access.

The flat of his tongue presses to my clit, making me moan again, this time with Cobra's cock fully seated in my mouth. He gives a few more jerky thrusts and spills down my throat.

"My stamina will get better the longer I'm not locked up," he says, but there's no hint of embarrassment in his voice; just resolve. He leans down and kisses me, shoving his tongue inside of my mouth and swirling it around to taste himself.

I pull away and glance past Sully. Archer is casually stroking himself while watching us all play. My eyes land on where Sully is deep inside of me, and Campbell is lapping at not only me, but at Sully's shaft every time it slips out.

"Fuck!" I cry out, coming undone, and squeezing Colt's cock in my hand.

Sully pulls out of me, and I whine. "You didn't come."

"Not yet, Little Witch. On your hands and knees."

I flip over and do as he says, presenting myself to him.

Instead he says, "Fuck her, Camp."

Archer joins Cobra on the bed, and kisses him, laying him back so we're parallel to one another. He turns and gives me a wink and one of his wild smiles. Archer grabs a bottle of lube out of the drawer and pours some on himself before shoving his bulbous cock into Cobra's ass, At the same time, Campbell slams into me, making me cry out.

Glancing over my shoulder I find Sully fucking Campbell as Campbell fucks me, and I tense around Camp at the sight. These guys are all so fucking hot, and watching them with each other takes it to a whole other level. Colt grabs my chin and forces his dick past my lips, careful not to hit my teeth with his piercings.

"Eyes up here, Baby Girl."

The way he commands the room—commands me to follow his orders—there's so much alpha energy in this room, that it's nearly suffocating. I flick my tongue across the barbells in Colt's shaft, making him groan in delight.

"Fuck, that tongue."

He stares down at me with his beautiful hazel eyes and takes control of my mouth, just like he did my body the first night we were together.

Camp's breathing goes ragged, and he pumps me full of his seed. Sully follows right after filling Camp with his own. Colt grabs my hair and pulls me off of him, and flips me onto my back.

"My turn," he purrs and slips himself inside of me, using my spit, and Camps cum as lubricant.

Cobra reaches over and squeezes my breast, and I turn my gaze to to his face. He's staring at where Colt and I are connected as he pinches my nipple between his thumb and forefinger.

"Come for him," Cobra says, his gaze meeting mine. It's almost pleading, like he needs to see me get off again.

"You heard him," Colt growls, and rubs delicious circles on my clit.

My back arches off the bed, but my eyes never leave Cobra's. I hadn't realized that Archer's tentacle had been squeezing Cobra's cock the entire time. He shoots ropes of hot cum all over his stomach and chest. Archer and Colt empty themselves inside of us almost simultaneously, and collapse on top of us.

I laugh breathlessly and Colt pulls out of me. That was quick and rough, and so hot. It was everything I needed to not feel any emotions for a little while.

My mind drifts, momentarily, to the fact that I'm back here with them. They saved me.

Realization dawns on me. "How did you all get to me so fast?"

The guys exchange worried and annoyed glances. I'm starting to get really annoyed by them communicating silently with one another. Archer slips out of Cobra and begins cleaning them both up. Then he lays down between us, facing me, and propping himself up on his elbow.

"I've waited centuries for you, do you know that? I never thought I would find what I have with you. You can't ever know quite what that felt like, but I suspect you know some of the same loneliness that I've experienced. We've all experienced it.

"I've had Cobra, but the screws he has loose make him…difficult to deal with." He gives Cobra a crooked, but loving smile. "So I need you to keep that in mind when I confess what I need to confess."

"I don't like where this is going."

I push myself up to sitting and Archer mirrors my movements before taking my hands in his.

Archer sighs and kisses me, then he says, "I put a tracking device in you."

"You...did...*what*?" I snap and push him back off of me.

He pulls his hands away and holds them up in surrender. "I know you're mad, but I would do it again. It saved your life."

I interrupt his thoughts with a slap across the face.

"Okay, I might have deserved that," he says with a deep chuckle.

I haul back to punch him in the chest but he grabs me by the wrist and pins me back to the bed.

"Let me go!" I yell. I've never been so angry with someone before. This is why I don't trust people. They always disappoint me in some way or another.

"No. I don't think I will, Little Star."

"How could you?" I demand.

"Because if I ever lost you, I would incinerate this planet myself. You're *mine*. I claimed you. The others did, too. And we have a responsibility to protect you and keep you safe. And this week, we failed; even with all of the precautions that we put in place."

"You microchipped me like a fucking dog, Archer! I'm not your pet. I'm not a toy. I'm..." I trail off, unsure how to finish that sentence.

"You're what, Jinx?" he asks with a smirk. "You're my mate. But what else. The angel hasn't mated you yet. What are you to him? What about the blood mage? What do they mean to you?"

"Stop pushing me!"

"Archer," Sully says softly.

"No! She needs to admit to herself and to us that she cares about us." The determination in his voice has been replaced with desperation.

"Of course I care about you! But what happens when this is over? You all go back to your lives? What if I get attached and you... No one ever sticks around. Now take this fucking tracking device out of me!"

"I'm not going anywhere. And I'm not taking the microchip out. I've told you over and over again that you belong to me. You're moving in here. You're not stripping or escorting anymore. Anything you want in the world is yours. Just say the word. You. Are. Mine."

We stare each other down; me in defiance, him in frustration.

"I'm not going anywhere," Sully says, and it breaks some of the tension.

I turn my head to look at him as much as I can while being pinned to the bed.

"You're it for me, Jinx. Well, you and Camp," he says, squeezing Campbell's thigh.

Campbell gives him an adoring look, and I have so many questions about their situation. But I don't want to talk about it here in front of everyone.

"I'm staying, too. Archer offered us a place here, and I will gladly take it if it means being with you. I'm even starting to grow fond of the rest of these fuckers," Campbell says, ruffling Colt's hair.

"And you know that wherever you are, is where I belong. Archer may have mated you first, but so did I. You're mine. You were always destined to be mine. The universe tried to tell us that when we were kids. We were just too young to understand," Colt says, trailing a finger down my cheek.

My eyes land on Cobra who has been suspiciously silent this whole time. It's unlike him to be this reserved.

"I'm not giving up that pussy," he says with a smile that doesn't reach his eyes.

I slip my hand out of Archer's now loosened grip and sit up, pushing Archer back as I do. I scoot over to where Cobra is sitting on the bed.

"There's something you're not saying. What's wrong?" I ask, straddling him.

A combination of Campbell and Colts cum slips out of me and onto Cobra's lap and if he minds, he doesn't say anything. He places his hands on my ass cheeks and gives me another half-hearted smile.

"What's going on with you?"

"Nothing we need to worry about right now. We can figure it out when the world is safe."

"Promise?"

"I promise," he says, and kisses me hard.

He's come twice tonight, and I imagine that he'll be pretty well spent for a while, but I lament at the fact that he's the only one who hasn't been properly inside of me, yet—with the exception of the night that I didn't know it was him.

I pull back and look him in the eyes. "We need some one-on-one time, soon."

"You don't have to convince me. I'll do whatever you say, Little Mouse."

I nod and slide off of his lap and face Archer. "I still want you to take the tracking device out."

"I don't think he should," Sully says.

"What?" Campbell and I say at the same time.

He shrugs. "Look, in any other circumstance, I would feel like it was a gross overreaction. And after your ascension we can reevaluate, but for now? I say leave it in. You're going to be with us at all times, anyway. You'll never be anywhere where at least one of us isn't present, so there's no real invasion of privacy right now."

"Why don't we microchip all of you?" I ask, crossing my arms over my chest.

"I'd be fine with that," Sully says. "We could all use a little extra protection."

"Yeah, I'm in," Colt says.

"You guys would do that?"

"I would do *anything* for you, Minxy." Colt says. "I think you keep underestimating just how much I care about you."

"Alright," Archer says, clapping his hands together. "Five microchips coming right up."

Chapter Twenty Six

Jinx

We take a nap together, all naked sweaty limbs, then get ourselves cleaned up and presentable to interrogate the prisoners. I put on a pair of ripped jeans and a black crop top before pulling my hair up into a bun on the top of my head.

"Are you sure you're ready for this?" Colt asks, slipping his hands around my waist, and making eye contact through the bathroom mirror.

"I've never been so ready for anything in my life. I've played this day out in my head so many times."

"And you still want me to be the one to do it?"

"Niall can join you. I'm sure he would love a piece of him. But yes. I want to see you tear him to shreds."

He nods and kisses the top of my head. "I'll take him down. And then I'll fuck you into oblivion afterward as a celebration."

I smirk at him through the mirror. The idea of him fucking me, bathed in Steve's blood makes me hum in delight. I don't really recognize myself anymore. There was a time in my life where I wouldn't wish death on anyone, but maybe the older I get the more I realize that there are certain people who just don't deserve to live anymore.

"Let's round up the others, and get this over with."

The basement of the house looks like a high-tech prison. In my periphery, Cobra's posture changes. I reach out and lace my fingers with his. He spent so long in Blackridge, that I don't blame him for being on the defensive.

"You're not trapped here. You'll come back upstairs with the rest of us once this is all over," I reassure him. "Even if Archer hadn't made that deal with you, I would never let him lock you up again."

He squeezes my hand and nods. He may be a psychopath, but he's my psychopath, and I'll be damned if he's ever allowed to be locked up anywhere ever again.

Archer comes to a stop outside of a cell and pulls a ring of keys out of his pocket. For a moment I think they're just typical keys, but upon closer inspection, they're skeleton keys and they look like they're made of unobtainium.

He turns the key in the lock, and pulls the door open. Inside is Trixie. She looks ragged, and her normally adorable blue hair is stringy and greasy from not being able to bathe or use her magic.

"Here to bring down my judgment?" she spits.

"We've got some answers to torture out of you first," Archer says with glee.

"You might as well kill me, because I don't know much of anything. I was a late addition to the council."

"How late?" Campbell asks, stepping out from behind me.

"Lanya recruited me after my last vision."

I glance at Archer. "Is she telling the truth?"

"She is."

"Why?" Campbell asks. "You know what's happening with the planets. You know what happened with Mars, and what's continuing to happen with the others. Why would you risk giving Jinx to The Council when you know that it's going to ruin everything?"

"Turns out I'm easily persuaded," she says with a shrug.

"I'm so disappointed in you," Campbell says, and walks away.

Trixie's face falls before she returns to the cool mask of indifference. She's trying to be brave, but she's terrified.

"I'm keeping you alive for now, in case you have another vision. I'll be asking every day, and the second you lie to me, I'll know, and I *will* torture the information out of you. Then as soon as this is over, Jinx gets to decide your fate the way you decided hers."

I give her a snarky smile and step out of the room. Archer locks it up and brings us to the next cell. Dalton. They decided to lock him up just until they were sure that he wasn't involved. I think that Archer was just pissed that Dalton is close to Trixie, and wanted to punish anyone even associated with her.

"You're alive! Thank the Stars," Dalton says when his gaze falls on me.

He's a mess. He looks like he's aged ten years in the last few days.

"She's alive," Archer says. "I'm gonna ask one more time. Did you know anything about what Lanya and Trixie were planning?"

"Nothing. I've been sick over it for days. I've been wracking my brain trying to figure out how I missed it, and I just can't find any possible hints in their behavior that would have..." He turns his attention back to me. "If I had known, I would have stopped them. My girlfriend is pregnant. Our partner is with her, keeping her safe until this is all done, but I want the world to last long enough for me to see my baby grow up.

"You have to believe that I would never ever risk your life for any reason. You're the only hope I have for seeing my son become a man, and to grow old with my partners."

"I believe him," I tell Archer.

"I do, too. Come on out," he says to Dalton. "You go home and spend time with them. I know Jinx will succeed, but I don't know the other Zodiacs and I cannot speak to their abilities. We may not have much time left on this planet."

"Thank you!" Dalton says, and shakes Archer's hand. "You have my number if you need anything. My weaponry is still in the basement and is yours until this is over."

"Take care, Dalton," I say and pat him on the arm.

He walks away through the hall and throws one last glance over his shoulder before he heads up the stairs. I hope for all of our sakes that this goes smoothly, but I cannot imagine the fear of trying to bring a child into a world that you know could possibly not exist in a year.

"Are you ready?" Archer asks after Dalton is out of sight. He means for Steve.

I inhale deeply through my nose and expel it through my mouth before nodding. "Let's just get it over with."

Archer unlocks the next cell. Steve is sitting in the corner on the floor with one knee pulled up to his chest. His gaze immediately lands on me.

"There's the whore," he grumbles.

"Indeed, here I am. I've brought some old friends."

Colt and Niall step up behind me. Steve's nostrils flare, and he clenches his teeth together. He knows what's coming.

"You're not going to fight against me yourself?" he spits. "You're just a scared little girl–just like you've always been."

"That's funny coming from a man who had to drug me twice in order to overpower me. You know you can't win against me at my full strength. But no. I'm not scared of you. I just don't like getting my hands dirty. The boys don't mind, though."

They begin to strip off their clothes, and Steve begins sweating so bad that he soaks through his shirt in a matter of seconds, plastering the wet material to his skin.

"Up!" Archer commands, and hauls Steve to his feet. "We'll do this in the execution chamber. I like to keep my prisoner cells clean. I'm not a complete barbarian."

Archer leads Steve down the long white hallway and through a large iron door with bars over the window. I step inside the enormous room. Rather than a normal square room, it's round and recessed into the floor like a gladiator pit. There are rust color stains painting the stone in a macabre pattern, telling the stories of all who died before.

Naked, Colt and Niall step past me toward the pit. They each grab one of Steve's arms and drag him kicking and flailing into the center of the circle.

"You sure you want to watch, Little Star? No one would think any less of you if you wanted to step away."

"I'm positive."

"Steven Cutler, you have been sentenced to death under the bylaws of the Human-Demon Accord of 1789 and the Supernatural Protection Act of 1939."

"On what grounds?" Steve demands, trying to sound tough even though his voice is trembling and he looks like he's going piss his pants.

Archer smiles. He's enjoying this, thoroughly. "Well since you asked...One, conspiring to kidnap a supernatural. Two, unlawful imprisonment of a supernatural being for your own benefit. Three, unsanctioned intercourse with an Archdemon's mate."

Steve's eyes nearly pop out of his head at that piece of knowledge.

"I guess no one told you," Archer says with a laugh. "The Zodiac is bound to me. Normally it would be me rending your soul from your putrid body, but Colt and Niall here called dibs. Seems you spend a lot of time beating the shit out of them as children, so they owe you."

Steve's beady eyes shift to the brothers.

"You don't even know who we are, do you?" Colt asks. "That's the thing about bullying children. One day they'll be bigger and stronger than you." Colt pushes him down on his knees.

The sickening sound of cracking bones fills the air as the guys begin to shift into their panther forms. Their sleek black coats shimmer under the stage lighting above the pit. their paws hit the stone as they begin walking a circle around Steve who has now *actually* pissed his pants.

"Any last words, shitbag?" I ask, earning a chuckle from Cobra.

Sully and Campbell each place a comforting hand on my shoulders.

"Yeah, fuck you, you no good whor—AARRRGGGHHHH-HH!!!!"

His words are cut off by a shriek of pain as Colt sinks his massive teeth into Steve's forearm. Niall simultaneously rips into Steve's calf. The metallic scent of blood hits the air. I watch, enraptured, as they rip and tear, pulling flesh and sinew off of his bones.

He's still barely alive, horrific gurgling groans coming from deep in his chest, when Colt places a massive paw on Steve's chest and bites down on his neck, nearly decapitating him.

The sounds stop. Eerie silence falls over the pit as the blood continues to spread in a massive puddle on the floor. The only sounds are Niall and Colt's heavy breathing.

Colt pads across the floor to me and I crouch in front of him and scratch his ears. A loud purr rumbles in his chest, and then he shifts back to his human form. His long lean muscles are covered in blood, obscuring the tattoos covering his skin. His face and mouth are decorated in scarlet. He still looks like a feral animal as he stares down into my eyes.

"Colt?" I ask

He pounces, entangling his hands in my hair as he puts his mouth on mine. Then he shoves his tongue into my mouth so I can taste Steve's blood. It's horrific. It's obscene. It is so fucking sexy.

"Okay little kitten, We still have one more person to interrogate and kill."

"I think I'll sit this one out," I say. "I want to go lie down."

Steve is dead, but I'm not sure how much difference that makes when Linnie is also gone. Steve stole my innocence, my trust in men, my ability to connect on an intimate level, and now my familiar. I feel as though he got off too easy with a simple death.

"I'll come with you," Cobra says.

"You said you wanted dibs on killing this one." Archer says, almost pouting.

"Yeah, well, I want to be with Jinx more," he says, wrapping an arm around my shoulder and escorting me out of the room. Each of the others gives me a kiss on the way through, and we head back up to the bedroom so I can get cleaned up, and rest.

Chapter Twenty Seven
Cobra

"You know I'm a lot like you, Little Mouse?" I tell Jinx on our way back to the bedroom.

"How so?"

"We're always on the run; never able to settle down and stay in one place for long. How do you plan to manage that once this is all over?"

"I'll figure it out, I guess. I just want to focus on my ascension until it's done. If I start getting too caught up in the 'what ifs' and the 'ever afters', I'll lose my shit. We can't afford for that to happen right now.

"What about you? What is there out there for Cobra after all of this is over?"

"Assuming Archer holds up his end of the deal? I'm not sure. I had some projects I was working on before he locked me up. Just some side gigs."

"Doing what?"

"Painting. Murals mostly."

"You're an artist?"

"Aren't all the crazy ones?" I say with a laugh.

"I don't think you're that crazy, though."

"Oh don't you? You know I could prove you wrong right now if I wanted, right?"

"But premeditated unhinged acts don't make you crazy. They just make you violent; reckless."

"It's not always premeditated. Like when I fucked you that first night? I was just going to torment you a little, but then I saw Archer, knot deep in that tight little cunt and I needed to be in there too."

We reach the bedroom and I open the door for her, allowing her to enter ahead of me. Once we're inside, I lock the door behind me.

She starts for the bathroom to wash the blood off of her, that the panther left behind, but I slip inside of her brain and make her stop in her tracks.

"What the fuck?" she whispers, trying to fight the control I have over her brain. She tries to push me out, but her mental shields are not strong enough for that.

"Let me go, Cobra."

"No," I say and force her to walk to the bed.

Once she's standing in front of it, I make her strip for me, real slow. She pulls her shirt up over her head, and slowly slides her pants down to her ankles revealing the beautiful ass to me.

"I'm not sure which hole I want to fuck more," I say casually as I sit on the bed in front of her. "I haven't been inside of you since the night we met, and I need to change that. Are you going to be a good girl and obey?"

"I think you prefer it when someone else is in control of you," she says. "Which, considering your abilities, is ironic."

"Is that what you need from me? To control me?" I *so* hope she says yes, but she doesn't strike me as a domme. If she is...

"I want to give you whatever *you* need, Cobra. The others demand submission from me. Even Camp to some degree even though he's completely submissive to Sully. But with you, I think you want to submit. So why don't you let me go, and let me give you what you need?"

I consider her offer. I force one last task out of her, first. She steps toward me and unbuttons my pants. I lift my hips so she can slide them down my legs and toss them to the floor. I pull my shirt over my head to even the playing field, then drop the control I have over her body.

"So what do you want me to do, mistress?" I ask, leaning back on my elbows.

"Rub your cock for me. I'll be right back."

She steps into the walk-in closet, and returns with a small trunk. It's Archer's pleasure chest. Everything in it is brand new. I assume he replaced all of the toys in it the second that Jinx showed up.

She pulls out a roll of leather and sets it on the nightstand, then pulls out a bottle of lube from the trunk. Inside of the roll of leather there are several different sized butt plugs.

"Straight to the kinky stuff, huh? I like it."

She sets the lube on the nightstand and pulls out some straps and cuffs.

"On your back and spread 'em."

Like a giddy school boy I do exactly as she says. I flop back on the bed and spread out like a starfish. She straps me, one limb at a time to the bedposts, then she returns to the lube and the plugs. She pulls out the largest plug and inspects it before nodding to herself like she made the perfect decision.

"The biggest?" I ask with a raised brow.

"Don't act like you can't take it. I've seen Archer fuck you–twice."

She pours lube over the silicone and then applies some to my asshole, swirling some inside of me. A small, embarrassing moan escapes me as her dainty finger enters me. Then she presses the tip of the plug to my ass and looks me in the eyes as she roughly shoves it in, making me cry out and arch my back off the bed.

She takes me in her hand and rubs long strokes up and down, and her silky hands, wet with lube, feel like pure bliss.

"I'll be right back. I'm going to go clean the blood off of my face," she says in a sultry voice, and steps off the bed.

"Wait!" I say. "Leave it."

"Are you forgetting who's in charge here?" she asks, crossing her arms over her chest.

"Please leave it. You look like a warrior goddess with it on, and I want you to fuck me like you just came back from war."

She crawls on the bed on her hands and knees, a flogger in her hand, and a sadistic look in her eye.

I need her to know what the rules are. "Just so we're clear, I won't always let you top me. Sometimes I'll need you to be my Little Mouse. But for tonight, I need you to be my ruler."

"Safeword," is her only response.

"I won't need one."

"Safe. Word." she demands, bringing the flogger down across my lower abdomen.

"Council," I say. "Nothing is more unsexy than that."

She rolls her eyes then sits back on her heels between my legs and takes me in her hand. She moves her hand slowly and with a featherlight touch up and down my shaft.

She spits on the tip and uses that as additional lubrication, working me up and down. She's taking her time, drawing it out. My balls ache with the need for release. Her hands feel like heaven, and I'm desperate for the oblivion her tight pussy would give me. Each time she feels me getting close, she stops. After the third time, I drop my head back on the bed and groan.

"Faster. Please." I beg, breathlessly.

"You want to come?" she asks with a devious smile.

I nod eagerly, but instead of giving into my demands, she stops all together. She climbs up my body until she's straddling my chest.

"Fuck me with your tongue, Cobra," she commands then she sits on my face, offering her pretty pink pussy for me to feast on.

I spear her with my tongue, and she gasps in pleasure. She could suffocate me right now, and I would consider it a beautiful and merciful death. I lap at her clit and her breathing increases. I wish I could touch her; slip my fingers inside of her, and make her see stars. But, fuck, if this isn't the sexiest thing a woman has ever done to me.

She rides my face and the softest moans escape her. "Fuck, Cobra, right there. That's such a good boy."

Her praise has my cock standing at full attention, weeping for her.

"Fuck, fuck, fuck," she whispers, before she cries out her release.

She shifts back my body, and straddles me, hovering just above the tip of my aching cock.

"I want to touch you so bad," I say with a groan.

She brings the flogger down across my chest. "No talking unless I ask you a question."

She lowers herself down so I'm barely notched at her entrance, then stops. Tiny pulsing movements of her hips have the tip of me slipping just past her tight hole over and over again.

"Fuck you *are* a goddess," I whisper in pure reverence.

The flogger hits my chest again. "What did I just say?" Then she stops, and pulls away, making me pout like a scolded child. She grabs her underwear, balls it up, and shoves it into my mouth. "I'm going to tease you over and over until you're begging for release, Ranger."

She moves back and takes me into her mouth, cleaning her own arousal off of me. I lift my head to watch her, and her eyes meet mine. Her tongue laps at the underside of my cock and the tip hits the back of her throat. She keeps me there for a second, and hums around me. My balls draw tight, as I walk the edge of oblivion, but then she pulls her mouth away. I drop my head back on the bed and close my eyes.

"You wouldn't want to come too soon and disappoint me, would you?" she asks, trailing the flogger over my abs, then down over my sensitive cock.

"Mm-mm," I say around the underwear, and shake my head.

A hard blow of the flogger makes me cry out. This one leaves beautiful red marks on my stomach and chest. She moves back up my body, and lowers herself down on my cock, then just sits there, not moving.

"I already came once. I can stay like this all night," she says. "Maybe I'll call Archer up here and let him please me and come inside of me, then leave you hard as a rock on the bed while we go have dinner."

She pulls the underwear out of my mouth. "How bad do you want to come, Ranger?"

"I don't just want to. I need to."

"And where do you want to come? In my mouth? In my hand? In my pussy?"

"There's only one place I ever want to come, and that's in your cunt."

"Then beg for it," she demands, hitting me with the leather strands of the flogger again.

My cock twitches inside of her as a result. "Please. Please fuck me, Jinx. I need it. I need to come inside of you. I need to coat your walls with my cum."

"Good boy," she purrs.

She moves up and down my length, almost pulling the whole way off then sliding all the way back down. The movements are slow and purposeful, squeezing me on the way up and sliding back down, then pausing at the bottom.

She reaches up and places one hand on my throat and the other on my chest to brace herself, and she squeezes, cutting off the air as she continues with her torturous movements.

"Come for me, Ranger," she whispers as she reaches the top and slams back down on me.

One more stroke of my cock with her soft walls, and I'm pouring myself inside of her, my eyes rolling back in my head.

She stays on top of me, and unstraps my hands. I sit up, keeping myself inside of her, and wrap her in my arms.

"Thank you," I whisper before I kiss her, and slip my hand up into her hair. I pull back and stare into her beautiful eyes. "That was possibly the best orgasm I've ever had. Even Archer doesn't edge that good."

"Archer was not a sex worker for over a decade," she says with a laugh.

"No, but sin is kinda his specialty," I say and kiss her again. "You're incredible."

She smiles, and kisses me again. "I could get used to you calling me a goddess."

"Good, cause I could get used to worshiping you."

Muffled voices in the hallway come right before the door opens, and the others stroll in, laughing. All of them are covered in blood except Archer who is suspiciously clean.

"What a beautiful sight," he says with a beaming grin. "My two loves tangled up together." He approaches and kisses first Jinx, then me.

"How did things with the suit go?" I ask, while Jinx slides off of me, and shuffles to the bathroom to clean up.

"He couldn't give us a ton of information. They have a couple of demons working for them as well, but lower level grunts," Archer says, laying on the bed and pulling me into his arms. "I'm not worried about that. Lanya is the strongest supe they have working for them. The invisible guy who shot you was apparently one of their more powerful men, too. They'll be pissed that you killed him."

"He shouldn't have shot me," I say with a shrug.

"Indeed," Archer says and inhales my scent before kissing the top of my head.

"We need to work on Jinx's ability to fight off mind control. I don't know if there's anyone else much like me out there, but I was able to walk right into that beautiful brain of hers and make her do exactly what I wanted."

"We'll start tomorrow. I'm sure you'll have plenty of fun training her until she can fight you off properly."

"I think with how little control they have right now, I could take over her *and* the pussy cat and make them fuck while I watch."

"Don't you dare," Colt warns.

"You're truly no fun at all," I say.

I pull away from Archer and join Jinx in the bathroom. She's sitting on the edge of the tub cleaning the blood off of her face, and the cum out from between her legs.

"Are you okay?" I ask, catching sight of the frown on her face.

"I'll be better once my ascension is done," she says. "I just want things to get back to normal."

My stomach drops. Normal for her didn't involve the five of us.

"Normal won't really exist anymore, Little Mouse. You'll have to adjust to a new normal. One that involves all of us."

She nods, checks her face in the mirror, and says, "I suppose you're right."

Then she leaves the bathroom without another word. I don't get the impression that she's all that excited about us all being together when this is done. One thing is for sure: I will not let her leave. Ever. Jinx is mine, and I will never let her go.

Chapter Twenty Eight

Jinx

A few days after we've returned to the mansion, we have a small celebration for our birthdays—much to Archer's dismay. He loves a big party and attempted to plan one, but we all agreed that with so many people gunning for us that we shouldn't invite anyone into the mansion.

Archer has agreed to leave his phone in his office and not look at it while we're having dinner and dessert. The guys have all agreed to not pick fights with each other, and Niall is allowed to join us until after we're done watching a movie.

I'm prowling around the kitchen waiting impatiently for the lasagna to be done and looking for a snack when Sully pops in.

"Hey Little Witch. I've been looking for you."

"Why?" I ask around a mouth full of chips.

"I have something for you, but I didn't want to give it to you in front of the others."

"Is it a sex toy? Because there's no reason to be weird about that." I put another chip in my mouth.

He snorts in amusement. "No, it's not a sex toy."

He pulls out a small velvet box, and my stomach drops making me stop mid chew and brush my hands off on my pants.

"Sully..." I warn.

"It's not what you think it is," he says with a laugh. "I mean. It is. But it isn't. Just open it."

I grasp the small box in my hands and give him one last pleading look before I open it. It's a black ring with a pink stone set in the middle of a rose shaped setting. There are thorns wrapping around the edges. It's beautiful, and also the only piece of jewelry anyone has ever gifted me.

He shoves his hands in his pockets and smiles awkwardly. "It's not an engagement ring, or something as silly as a promise ring. We're too old for that. It's just because it made me think of you. And I wanted to get you something nice for your birthday. I picked it out the day we went shopping for the new bed. If it doesn't fit, we'll get it resized. Also, I owe Archer for it because I can't use my fucking credit cards until Campbell and I get cleared after Murphy's death. But..."

"I love it, Sully. Thank you."

I slide it on the ring finger of my right hand. I step into him and place my hand on his cheek before kissing him softly. He toys with my hair, then strokes my cheek with his thumb.

"You're amazing, Jinx. Happy birthday, pretty girl."

The door to the kitchen opens again, and Cobra steps in. "Is the food ready, yet? I'm starving."

"Ten minutes," I tell him, and jerk my head toward the door hoping he'll get the hint and give us some privacy.

Instead he starts pull out plates and cups, crashing through the kitchen as he goes.

Once he starts humming a little tune, I snap, "Cobra!"

"What?" he whines. "I'm just getting stuff ready to take it to the dining room."

"Sully and I are trying to have a moment alone."

"Ugh fine." He grabs the plates and heads for the dining room. "Just bring the cups and stuff when you're done making out."

Once he's out the door, Sully sighs. "I guess we're going to have to come up with a schedule or something so that we all get some quality one on one time."

"We'll see. Maybe we can figure out a code word or something that tells the others to go the fuck away when we're trying to have a moment. But that's a problem for another day," I say and grab the oven mitts.

I pull the oven open and slide the lasagna out and put it on the stove. Tucking a trivet under my arm, I pick the lasagna back up and head through the door after Cobra.

After dinner we all sit down in the obnoxiously large in-home theater that Archer has in the basement. It feels weird being down here watching a movie while two walls over there are people being held prisoner for kidnapping me, or aiding in my kidnapping.

Sully and Cobra are sitting on either side of me. Campbell is on Sully's other side, and Archer is sitting next to Cobra. Colt is sitting on the floor in front of me, and I'm gently trailing my fingers through his hair, while he rubs small circles on the tops of my feet with his thumbs.

This feels comfortable and right. My mind keeps drifting away from the movie and to the future. The pitter patter of tiny feet on the floor of the mansion rings through my head. Images of a sweet little demon and a baby shifter playing together flit through my brain, and the thought brings a smile to my face.

I have never once in my life considered having children, but in this moment, I know that I could have a sweet little family with my guys. That is, until the doubt and anxiety creep in. What if one of the guys decides that they want to leave? What if I'm too much for one of them to handle?

"I need a few minutes on my own," I say and stand from my seat.

The deck is my safe space where I go when I'm feeling sad or overwhelmed, so without making a conscious decision, that's where my feet carry me. I step out into the cold October air, Sucking in a deep breath, I lean against the railing of the deck and sigh.

This happens every time I start to let myself feel comfortable and I'm tired of doubting the situation I'm in. Unfortunately it'll take at least several months, and probably many therapy sessions before I can get past my self-worth issues.

None of those issues are tied to my identity as a sex worker, but are wholly tied to my inability to maintain relationships. That and the fact that my parents couldn't get their shit together long enough to provide a proper home for me to grow up in. If they couldn't love me enough to protect me, why should anyone else.

Possessive hands slide around my waist, startling me out of my thoughts. I spin around to find Cobra, staring down at me curiously.

"What's wrong, Little Mouse?"

"All the same shit as usual," I say with a laugh. "I said I wanted to be alone for a minute."

"And we all agreed that we're not leaving you alone. I volunteered to come sit with you since I don't like talking too much about feelings, and would rather just fuck you until you stop stressing about whatever it is that you're stressing about."

"Unfortunately that won't work this time."

He takes a deep breath and tugs on my hand. "Come here."

He leads me over to the hot tub and pulls the cover off before turning it on. He pulls off his shirt and his shorts, then my shirt and pants, leaving us in our underwear.

"Get in," he instructs.

I step into the warm water and slip beneath the water until it covers my shoulders. Cobra follows me in and sits on one of the benches facing out toward the yard before pulling me into his lap.

"So are you going to talk about it, or am I going to have to get one of the others out here to nag you about it until you open up?"

"It's just the same thing as always. I'm too in my head, and I can't let myself be happy because if I do, that opens me up to get hurt."

"So what if you do?" he asks. "I mean, I'm not going anywhere. And neither are any of the others. You're stuck with all of us. But, so what if you get hurt at some point?"

"I...I just don't *want* to get hurt."

"But that's the thing about life, Little Mouse. It's painful. And if my memory is serving me correctly, you actually enjoy a little bit of pain. So I'm going to ask again...So what if you get a little hurt? As long as none of us leaves, we can work through any of it."

We sit in silence, and I stare at the stars, considering his words. How can I just push past twenty years of heartbreak and abandonment, and trust that not a single one of these guys is going anywhere?

"Why are you so convinced everyone is going to leave you that you feel the need to run?" he asks.

"Because not even my parents cared enough to stick around. I spent a lot of years thinking they died just to get away from me. I know that's ridiculous, now. But as a small child, it was a lot to process. So now I leave before I can be left behind."

He sits in silent contemplation, his arms wrapped tight around my stomach. Finally, he asks, "Did you know that my parents died when I was a kid, too?"

"No. I didn't," I say, pulling away and turning to face him. My face must give away how bad I feel for him.

"Don't pity me. I was the one that did it. And I'm glad I did. They were a couple of fucking assholes."

He says it as if it's a simple statement, but it's so loaded. To say I'm shocked would be an understatement. But there's no remorse or sadness in his eyes.

"What did they do to you?" I ask.

He scoffs. "What *didn't* they do? They sold me to the highest bidder at every opportunity. Eventually they sold me to a man who was convinced that he could *create* magic. And I guess technically he did. I wasn't born with these abilities.

"I was about seven when my parents realized that my intelligence was worth more than my appearance. A man my dad met in a bar told him that he was conducting some experiments to try to create supernatural abilities, and that he had succeeded in mice, but needed a human subject. My dad offered me."

"Cobra," I whisper.

"No, it's really fine. I mean, if he hadn't taken me, and pumped me full of drugs and electricity, I wouldn't have been able to take out my parents. And that was so satisfying, that it was worth it. I also wouldn't be here with you."

"You don't know that."

"I do, though. I only met Archer because he heard of my abilities and needed someone with a few screws loose to handle a situation for him that he couldn't do without causing an uproar."

"How did you do it?"

"Do what?"

"Kill your parents?"

"I tortured them first. I made my dad stick his hand in a blender. I made my mom get into a *hot* shower after I had turned the hot water heater thermostat up the whole way. It was an older model so it didn't have the safety features on it that the newer ones do. Did you know that the human body can only be under one hundred and fifty degree water for about three seconds before it suffers third degree burns?" He says, casually.

"I understand now why you felt so betrayed by Archer locking you in the asylum. That must have felt a lot like your parents abandoning you with the man who experimented on you."

"It was. Especially once they started sedating me. I could have never forgiven my parents for what they did to me. They stole every ounce of innocence I had, and then expected me to provide for them."

"I'm sorry you had to go through any of that."

He laughs. "I just told you how I tortured my parents and murdered them, and you feel bad for *me*?"

"I have a soft spot for orphans," I say with a smirk.

"Am I still an orphan if I'm the one that killed them?" he asks rhetorically. He pauses for a few moments, staring at the stars before finally asking, "I don't care about much, but I care about you and

Archer. As long as you stick by me, I'll be good to you. So tell me what you're most scared of, and let me tell you why you're wrong."

I inhale sharply and blurt out, "What if I'm not cut out for being in a relationship with this many people?"

"I think that any less people and you'd get restless and bored, but what do I know? I'm just a silly little psychopath whose own partner locked them up in an insane asylum."

"Are you ever going to let that go?" Archer asks, stepping out onto the deck. "You left the door open, Ranger."

"I knew the rest of you wouldn't stay away. Not on our Zodiac's birthday."

I can't help but notice that Cobra doesn't answer Archer's question. I'm not sure that he can ever let it go. My heart aches for him.

Archer and the others step out onto the patio.

"Do you want to come inside, or should we get in?" Colt asks.

"I'd like to stay out here a little longer," I say, leaning back against Cobra. I'm feeling protective of him, right now. I want to put a barrier between him and everyone else.

"Do you want to talk about it?" Sully asks.

"I don't think so. Cobra gave me a lot to think about. Let's just enjoy tonight, so tomorrow we can focus on planning for the mountains."

"Oh I plan to enjoy you all night long," Archer says and slides up next to me and Cobra.

The others all exchange looks then move in on me with predatory gazes. Tonight we'll unwind. Tomorrow, we'll prepare. The following day we'll leave for the mountains. And somewhere in the midst of all of that, I'll figure out how all of us fit together.

Chapter Twenty Nine

Jinx

It's a couple of weeks later when we head up to the mountains. The first snow has begun to fall, creating a scene that looks like a Kinkade painting. It gets cold in this part of New York, and the first snowfall tends to happen any time between Halloween and Thanksgiving. It came a little early this year.

It's a light snowfall that doesn't even stick to the road and it's absolutely beautiful. I sigh happily as I stare out the rear passenger side window of the SUV as we travel, as a family, to Archer's mountain home.

Living in the city, my experiences with snow were frequently limited to the grimy grey of snow that had seen the tires of dozens of vehicles. But on the rare occasion I was out and about during the wee hours of the morning when traffic was scarce and the snow was untainted by dirt.

"You like the snow?" Campbell asks, lacing his fingers with mine.

"I just never got to see it look this beautiful before. My entire life has been mostly contained to the city limits."

Archer makes eye contact through the rear-view mirror. "That'll change, Little Star. Just as soon as we get this ritual taken care of. I can show you the world."

"Did you just quote Aladdin at her?" Sully asks.

"How do you know Aladdin well enough to know if he did?" Colt teases.

"What's Aladdin?" Cobra asks.

"I don't know," Archer says.

My mouth hangs slightly agape at the conversation before I bark a laugh.

"I only want to see the world if it's with all of you. Nothing outside of this group matters once the ritual is done. Would I like to maybe go to the beach someday? sure. But Not if I can't enjoy it with all of you."

"I'll make you a deal," Archer says. "We can bring all these bozos with us as long as one weekend a year I get to take you somewhere, just the two of us."

"Yeah? And who's gonna watch the baby?"

Archer slams on the breaks and whips his head around. Thankfully there's no one directly behind us.

"What baby? Are you pregnant?"

I snort. "Not yet, but part of our deal was that I had to be...eventually."

There is a collective sigh of relief from the others.

"Don't scare us like that," Campbell grumbles.

"What? You guys don't want babies?"

"Oh I absolutely do. I told you that the first time we had sex. But this ritual is going to be dangerous and if you're pregnant...well let's just say it won't go well," Sully explains.

"It's going to be hard enough for us to stand by and let you do the ritual without intervening, as it is. It could kill you, Minxy. I just got you back. I can't bear to lose you," Colt says.

"I won't let that happen," Cobra says. "If it starts going south I'm pulling her out."

"You'll do no such thing," I tell him. "I want the world to survive. If that means I have to die, so be it. I've experienced enough love in the last month and a half to last me a lifetime, and that's enough. That's a life well lived. So you will not interrupt the ritual at any costs."

"The hell I won't!" Cobra shouts. "You're mine! You're all of ours. We're not losing you to this damn thing. The world can go down in flames for all I care. If you're not in it, I would rather watch it burn."

The rest of us sit in stunned, uncomfortable silence once Cobra is done talking. I knew he cared about me, and we'd had that conversation in Archer's hot tub, but he never alluded to feeling *this* intensely about me. He had mentioned that he might go out on his own again after the ritual was done. But thinking back, he has been acting weird since the hot tub talk.

"Cobra, this is my responsibility. I have to see it through. You can find someone—"

"There is no one but you, *Jinx*. You and Archer are it for me, and without you, it's incomplete."

"Then I guess we just need to make sure that I don't fail," I say.

He grinds his teeth in annoyance, but ends the conversation there. He's usually so upbeat and unconcerned with things that his behavior is catching me off guard. The remainder of the drive is quiet. I spend my time enjoying the views as we travel up the winding road.

The snow is coming down in earnest as Archer pulls off the main road. He has to put it in four wheel drive to make it the whole way up the snow covered slope. We crest the hill and a beautiful, massive, log cabin appears ahead of us. The snow clings to the trees, making the sight look like a ski brochure, or a Christmas card.

"Wow," I say in awe as Archer parks the car in the driveway. "This is beautiful, Arch. I love it here."

We climb out and he wraps an arm around my shoulder. "I'm glad you like it. Once this mess is over, we can come here as often as you like. I promise."

I grin up at him as he unlocks the door, and ushers me inside. It's chilly inside, but the atmosphere of the cabin is warm. It's homey and welcoming—a far cry from the stark white and marble combination of the mansion.

"Dude, why didn't you offer this as the safehouse?" Sully grumbles.

"Because it's my own personal oasis and I didn't want business being conducted here. But business turned to pleasure so here we all are. Don't look a gift horse in the mouth."

"We were only at the safehouse for two days, anyway," I say with a laugh. "And it wasn't exactly roughing it. That house was way bigger than my apartment."

Sully huffs in response as we start looking around the place. The kitchen here is about half the size of the one in his mansion, but still bigger than almost any other residential kitchen I've seen. There's a large deck that oversees the valley below with a hot tub and an outdoor, stone fireplace.

There is a loft with a king size bed, walk-in closet, and master bathroom. Then there are several smaller bedrooms around the downstairs. Archer goes around and turns on the heat and the water. He also brings in some firewood from the wood shed outside and starts a fire in the massive indoor fireplace.

The rest of the guys bring in the groceries and luggage from the car, and I begin putting things away. Once Archer has the fireplace lit, he walks up behind me and wraps his arms around me as I'm putting some boxes of pasta in the cupboard.

"You like it here?" He mumbles in my ear.

"I love it. So *so* much. It's so homey and warm and it smells like you. I would stay here forever if you let me."

"If I didn't have business to attend to in the city, I might. But maybe it's time for me to retire."

"Really?" I ask hopefully. Archer's business is important in the city, but being a part of the seedy underbelly has its downsides–including eating up all of his time. "Who would you pass the torch to?"

"I have an associate who has worked for me for years. I trust him implicitly. The last thing I want is for the city to fall into ruin because it's not being ruled properly. I may do some unsavory things but at the end of the day, my goal is to keep the city safer than if the younger generations took over. The crime is only beneficial if it doesn't ruin absolutely everything."

He dips his chin down and kisses me. It's slow and purposeful, as if he's trying to remember the way I smell and taste. His hand snakes up into my hair and I smile into the kiss as he gives it a playful tug.

He pulls back and stares at me. "I agree with Cobra. We're not losing you to this. You feel that you've experienced enough love to last a lifetime. You forget that I've been alive for dozens of lifetimes, and I've only had six weeks of you.

"I'm selfish. All the time in the world would never be enough. But if it comes down to you dying a month from now, or you surviving, and me getting to enjoy you for another couple of years…I'm choosing to save you.

"I love you, Little Star. I know that you don't feel comfortable with those words, and that's okay. You don't ever have to say it back as far as I'm concerned. But I know that I would sacrifice everything I've worked for, and all the wealth I've gained in all my centuries if it meant I got even minutes more with you."

He kisses me on the forehead and then walks away before I can respond.

Cobra seems to appear out of nowhere, startling me when he says, "You really did a number on him. On all of us. Archer has never once cared about anything enough to give up his empire. Not until you. So please don't tell me how you're willing to die for this shit. Because it'll kill us all if you do."

And then he follows after Archer, and I'm left stewing in my feelings.

A few hours later, I'm cooking with Colt in the kitchen. He's not very good at doing it himself, but he does make a good helper. Archer, with all his access to cooks and kitchen staff, has never bothered to learn how to cook.

Sully and Campbell were both living on bachelor cop diets of chinese take out and donuts before we moved into the safehouse. Cobra never cared enough to learn, and apparently Niall is the chef in Colt's family, but even still can only manage to make pasta and cheeseburgers.

"It feels a little unfair and sexist that all the cooking falls on my shoulders, so I'm teaching at least one of you how to make something simple like spaghetti."

Colt pins me to the counter from behind, and kisses the back of my neck while I'm chopping some peppers to make fajitas. "What's unfair, is me having to share you with all these other guys."

"Oh is that unfair?" I joke. "Well, suck it up, buttercup. We're all in this thing together."

"Watch that mouth of yours, or I'll make you eat your words later," he whispers into my ear.

I am instantly turned on. My attraction to this man makes me absolutely weak in the knees. He slips his hand down the front of my pants and touches me, groaning when he finds me wet for him.

"I need to finish making dinner," I say in a loud whisper.

"Not before I finish you," he says, sliding a finger inside of me.

"Colt, stop it," I warn.

"Or what?"

"Or you're not getting any later." It's an empty threat. I'll cave the second he looks at me with those beautiful eyes.

"I don't need to. I'll just rub one out in the shower thinking about this soaking wet pussy. I went twenty three years without having sex, Minxy. I bet I can hold out longer than you can."

He begins stroking my clit and my legs shake from the pleasure. How he's so good with his hands with his complete lack of experience is beyond me. I continue cutting the peppers and onions. The others are either unaware or pretending to be as they lounge just one room over.

"I bet I can make you come before you're done cutting those," Colt wagers. "If I do, you have to suck my cock as soon as dinner's over. If I don't, then you get to take charge in the bedroom tonight."

"I get to do anything I want?"

"Anything."

"Even peg you?" I say with a gasp.

"I'll up the ante. If you can hold out, *and* not make a sound, I'll let you peg me. But you have to believe that I have far more faith in my skills than you do. If you can't keep yourself from making any sound, then me and the others all get to take turns coming on your face."

I'm already close. But I'm stubborn, and I hate losing, but there's honestly no losing in this situation.

"You're on," I say, and begin chopping as carefully as I can in my current situation.

I gasp. His threats aren't threats. They're promises. And I hope he keeps them. I bite into my lip to try to remain quiet. I have one onion left to cut. I make the first slice and he increases pressure and pace. I cover my mouth with my knife-free hand to stifle a moan. But it's too late. He said not to make a sound.

"I guess no pegging tonight. Let's see who wins the other portion of our wager. What do you think? Do you want me to fuck your mouth while the others to watch? Do you want us to come all over you, and mark you as ours?"

His filthy mouth has me at the brink. I'm trying so hard to hold out as I furiously cut at the onion, trying to get it done. He grinds his erection against my ass, and a soft moan escapes him.

"I'm going to fuck this beautiful ass later, too. Just come for me baby, you know you want to. Just give in."

I cry out as his words tip me into oblivion. I drop the knife. It's suddenly difficult to stand, but Colt bears my weight as he slips his hand out of my pants.

"That's a good girl," he purrs.

I take a deep breath and regain the use of my legs. I go back to cutting the onion like nothing happened. Campbell walks in with a suspicious look on his face.

"Everything good in here?"

"Yep, just earning us a little treat later," Colt says and claps Campbell on the shoulder as he saunters out of the room.

I curse under my breath. Camp grabs a piece of bell pepper and eats it.

"You good, Buttercup?"

"Perfect," I say honestly.

"How are you feeling about things?" he asks, studying me carefully while he waits for a response.

"Which things?" I ask, hoping he's not going to try to talk about our emotional involvement again.

"Oh, the end of the world, the ritual, what'll happen if it fails, what'll happen if it succeeds...those things."

"It's still seven weeks away. I'm trying to not stress it too much."

"I get that, but I feel like there has to be something we can do to prepare, you know?"

"You all know more than I do. I'm just showing up when I'm told and doing the damn thing."

"I guess we'll figure it out as we go. Trix betraying us really threw a wrench into things since she was the one who knew about most of this stuff. I just don't understand why she turned on us. What was the point, you know?"

"I don't know. I didn't know her very well." But I do know why she turned. Because of Camp.

My words are clipped. I don't want to talk about Trixie. Trixie had slept with Campbell in the past, and she was the reason that Steve was able to get his filthy hands on me again. I'm cutting into the chicken with fury and rage. I'm not paying close enough attention and I slice into my finger. I hiss in pain as blood starts pouring from the wound.

"Fuck!" I shout and move to the sink to wash it before wrapping it in a paper towel.

I turn back around and Camp looks pale. Purple veins are showing around his eyes.

"Are you okay?" he asks.

"I'm not sure. Are you good?"

"Yeah, just...blood."

He steps forward and takes my hand in his. He slowly unwraps the paper towel which has already soaked through. He examines the cut, and brings my finger to his mouth and sucks on it gently. It's weirdly erotic.

"I know you're a blood mage, but I didn't realize that made you part vampire," I say with a laugh.

He doesn't pull my finger out of his mouth, instead he swirls his tongue around it. A weird tingling begins in my body and slowly turns into a mild buzz. Campbell stares me in the eye the entire time that he has my finger in his mouth, and finally slides it out.

I don't break eye contact with him as I grab his face and kiss him. That was one of the hottest things I've ever experienced and also the weirdest. He slides his tongue into my mouth and I taste the last of the metallic flavor of my blood. He lifts me and sets me on the counter without ever breaking the kiss.

He slowly slides a hand under my shirt and growls when he finds that I am not, in fact, wearing a bra. He pinches my nipple between his fingers and twists it gently, making me moan softly.

I pull away from the kiss, and look into his eyes. "I need to finish cooking dinner or we'll have a bunch of grumpy alpha males running around."

"So Colt is allowed to finger fuck you while you're cooking, but I can't get a little make out session?" he asks with a smirk.

"You heard that?" I ask with a wince.

"We all did."

"Colt didn't completely distract me from my task."

"Then he wasn't doing it right."

I smack him on the shoulder playfully. "He did it more than right."

"Fine, but I get you to myself for a little bit later."

"Okay," I agree. My brow furrows as I realize that my skin is still lightly buzzing.

"What's wrong?" he asks in concern. "If you don't want to spend the night in my room..."

"No! Of course I do. Just...my skin feels weird. Like it's humming. It happened when you tasted my blood at the safehouse, too."

"You don't always feel like that around me?"

"I didn't until you licked my blood off my—" My words fall short as I realize that the cut isn't there anymore.

"I healed it," he says, sensing my confusion. "So you never felt that buzz until I consumed your blood?"

I shake my head.

"Hey Archie!" Camp yells to the other room.

A few moments later, Archer enters with his cell phone pressed to his ear. "What?" he asks, holding the mouthpiece away from his face a bit.

"Is that call important? I have something to ask you."

"I'll call you back, shortly," he grumbles into the phone and hangs up. "What is it?"

"How much do you know about blood mages?" Camp asks. "My own knowledge is limited since I was adopted."

"You were adopted?" I ask with a frown. "Why didn't you ever tell me?"

"It never came up."

"I mean, any time we talked about the fact that I was a foster kid would have been a good time," I say.

"Can we talk about this later?" he asks with pleading eyes, and a sideways glance at Archer.

"Fine," I say with a pout.

I hop off the counter and set a skillet on the stove and heat up some butter to saute the vegetables.

"Admittedly, I don't know as much about blood mages as I do about other demon borns."

"Blood mages have demon blood?" I ask in surprise, and reach for my coffee.

Archer scowls at me. He hates that I drink coffee at all hours of the day regardless of how close to bed time it is.

"Yes. Usually not full blooded, and we're not afforded the same benefits as some of the other demon born folks." Camp says. "I know a little, but...mating rituals I'm unsure of."

I spit my coffee back into my cup. "*Mating* rituals?"

"As far as I know, blood mages require an exchange of blood, and intercourse within a few hours to complete a coupling. Almost all demons require sex of some sort, but some require extra steps. Blood mages also have fated mates, unlike archdemons and succubi."

"We weren't fated to each other?" I ask, feeling a little disappointed. It doesn't change how I feel about Archer, but it makes it feel less complete somehow.

"No, Little Star," he says, placing a large hand on my cheek. "At least not to my knowledge. It does seem odd that you were able to take my knot when others had never been able to, but I just chalked that up to your celestial gifts."

My eyes return to Campbell, and he gives me a soft smile.

"What's going on, Camp?"

He takes my hand in his. "If Archer is correct, I think you're fated to me."

Chapter Thirty
Campbell

"Excuse me?" Jinx asks, eyes nearly bulging out of her head.

"I'm not positive, but that hum you're describing, I've felt it from the first second we met. I thought it was just because of how powerful you were, but if you're feeling it now too...I think the mate bond is waiting to be completed.

"If you don't want to, I completely understand. You're already mated with Colt and Archer. And you're not even comfortable with long term relationships, so if you don't want to complete it..." The very last thing I want is to pressure her into a bond that she doesn't want. Archer bonded himself to her without her consent.

"I..." there's an uncomfortable pause as she contemplates how to finish that sentence.

"I'm gonna go finish my phone call," Archer says and awkwardly steps out of the kitchen, leaving me and Jinx staring at each other uncomfortably.

"It's fine. We don't have to complete it." I kiss her on the forehead and give her a smile. "Finish cooking dinner before your onions burn. I know you've gotta be starving."

I walk away from her and go stand on the deck overlooking the valley. The sun is setting, and the chill of the night time mountain air creeps through my sweater and settles into my bones as I lean against the railing.

Sully steps outside after me, sliding the large glass door shut behind him. "You okay?"

"Yeah," I lie. My heart is aching. The sting of rejection is radiating through me.

"Archer said you might need a shoulder, or an ear. What happened?"

I don't know how to answer that. I don't want to say it out loud. Jinx never actually said 'no', but it seemed pretty clear that she didn't want to mate with me. I don't blame her. We've only know each other for about six weeks. I decide not to bring up the bond.

"I'm not really sure. Jinx is just so hot and cold with me that I don't know how to handle her sometimes."

"I think she's just not convinced that we're here to stay. She's never had a constant in her life except for Linnie, and Linnie was bound to her soul. And now she's gone. Anyone who was ever important to her is gone.

"Once the ritual is over, and the impending doom of the world is over, she'll see that we're serious about her. She'll realize that we're not just spending time with her because we have to."

I nod, and we spend another ten or so minutes just standing in silence, watching the sun set. Eventually, Colt slides the door open.

"Jinx says dinner is ready," he says, and doesn't wait for a response before he goes back inside.

I sigh and follow him back in, with Sully in tow.

Jinx is placing plates at all of our seats, and she sets out multiple serving plates. One with warmed tortillas, one with chicken, one with beef, and one with the peppers and onions. There's also a bowl with sour cream and a bowl of lime wedges.

I take a seat at the large dining room table and wait until everyone else is sitting before I start building a fajita.

"What are the sleeping arrangements going to be here," Colt asks.

"Well, the bed is the same size as the one in the mansion, so we know we can all fit. But there are smaller rooms with doubles and queens throughout the downstairs. I'm not picky as long as I get some alone time with our girl," Archer says winking at Jinx.

"I'm good sharing with everyone if that's what everyone else wants," I say, trying to act casual about it. What I really want is a bed for just Jinx and I.

"You claimed alone time with me while we were in the kitchen," Jinx says, a hint of surprise in her voice.

"I did...I just...if that's what you want," I reply.

I've always struggled with relationships with women. They always expect me to be more aggressive and assertive than I am. As a cop I had all the confidence in the world, but as a boyfriend, a lover, I lack it. And it's not because I'm not good at it. It's just because I'm awkward. I always have been.

On more than one occasion I've been dumped by women who got frustrated with my inability to take control, and my indecisiveness. I wasn't what they expected or what they signed up for when they started dating a cop. They expected handcuffs and domination in the bedroom; not the tenderness that I brought to the table.

"Yes, that's what I want," she says, half in exasperation. "Why wouldn't I want that?"

"Okay," is the only word I can come up with.

Jinx stares at me, waiting for more, but I don't give it to her. I keep eating my dinner.

"This is really good," I say around a mouth full of food.

"Yeah, Little Witch, your food is amazing," Sully says.

"I'm glad you like it," Jinx says softly and takes a few more bites.

After about five minutes she quietly excuses herself and disappears into the bedroom she claimed for when she needed some alone time. Every other set of eyes at the table focuses on me.

"What's your deal?" Cobra asks before shoving his fourth fajita in his mouth and taking an obscenely large bite. The guy probably weighs a hundred and seventy five pounds soaking wet, but I feel like he eats more than any of us.

"What do you mean?"

"Jinx invited you to spend the night alone with her—after I won time with her, I should add—and you all but told her to fuck off," Colt says.

"No I didn't!" I protest. "I'm just trying to give her space. I want her to make her own decisions about things."

"You need to pursue her. At least a little," Sully says. "She needs you to go after her. If you keep acting lukewarm toward her, she's going to think that you don't want her."

I just stare at him blankly for a moment. My brain catches up to what Colt said.

"You 'won' time with her?"

"Yeah. A face fuck and a circle jerk," he says with a shrug. "I'll take a rain check, though. You should go talk to her."

I shake my head deciding not to question that any further.

"Go on, dude. Don't leave our girl hanging," Sully says, patting me on the back.

Everything in me wants to ask him to come with me so that I have him as back up, but it feels like it would cheapen the gesture somehow.

With a sigh I push myself back from the table, and walk down the hallway. I raise my hand to knock, but hesitate. I take a deep breath, steel my nerves, and just walk in.

I step inside and slam the door behind me causing Jinx to jump. She's laying on her stomach on the bed, playing with the tablet that Archer got her for her birthday. She's in a nightie, and she rolls on to her side to look at me.

"What are you—"

I pounce on the bed, and flip her onto her back, settling between her legs and pressing my mouth to hers. I grind myself against her, and she moans softly into my mouth. I pull back and look down into her eyes, and she smiles up at me, as she trails a hand absently down my chest. Then her smile fades.

"What are you doing, Camp?"

"Trying to prove to you that I care about you; just as much as the others, and just as much as you deserve. You need to stop doubting your worth. Everyone who has abandoned you over the years wasn't worth shit.

"You're perfect and wonderful and you deserve the world, Jinx. So stop running, and stop pushing us away."

I kiss her again, and slide my hand up her nightie and cup her breast. It's so soft in my hand. She takes my bottom lip in her teeth as I toy with her nipple.

I sit back on my heels and pull off my shirt. She bites her bottom lip and impatiently trails her hand down and slides it inside of her panties.

I smack her hand. "No. I will be the only one touching you, tonight. No one else. Not even you."

I slide her panties down in one swift movement and toss them to the floor. Then I unbutton my pants, freeing my already hard cock and stroking it languidly.

"Why do you get to touch yourself, but I don't get to touch myself," she pouts.

"Because I'm in charge," I say, removing my pocket knife from my jeans before tossing them to the floor.

A smile starts to form on her lips, but she schools her expression. "Are you playing bad cop tonight?" she asks in a sultry tone.

"Is that what you want?" I ask pinning her to the bed by her neck and teasing my tip against her clit. "Do you want me to take over? Take what I want without asking?"

I don't wait for a response. I just slam into her and her back arches off the bed. I fuck her hard, burying myself as deep as I can over and over, making small gasps and whimpers escape her. Those sounds are like a drug.

I reach for my knife with my free hand and flip it open before stilling inside of her. "If this is too much at any point, I need you to tell me to stop. I don't want this to go any further than you can handle. Do you understand me?"

She nods.

"Use your fucking words. Do you understand me, Buttercup?"

"Yes sir," she says.

"Such a good fucking girl. *My* good girl."

I press the tip of the blade to her stomach and look into her eyes, waiting for her to protest. She gives a slight nod of her head, encouraging me.

I slide the blade down her torso. She hisses in pain, but her pussy flutters around me as I watch as blood pools to the surface. I groan at the sight. I'm not a vampire; not in the traditional sense. But fuck if blood doesn't turn me on. I slide out of her and move down her body to lap up the red tainting her skin.

This is low stakes. I can heal her right now if I want. But I don't. I want to see how much she can handle. I pull back and look down as the line begins to turn red again. I place the blade an inch or two away from the first cut and slide it down her skin again, and I shove my fingers inside of her.

She moans softly as her eyes roll back in her head. I could come right now just watching her. With one hand I close the knife, and set it on the bed. I remove my fingers from her wet center, and place them in my mouth before replacing them with my cock once more.

Using both hands, I smear the blood around on her belly and delight in it as it paints her flesh. Her porcelain skin is the perfect canvas. This is something I've always wanted to do, but I've never had the right partner to do it with. The way she accepts my darkness makes me ache with the need to make her mine.

I grab my knife and in one quick movement I flip it open and slice open my hand. Her eyes go wide, and I pause just long enough for her to protest. I won't mate her against her will. Not tonight, anyway.

I place my palm on her mouth, and she refuses to open for me. I think for a second that she's refusing my mate bond, but then I see the playful challenge in her eyes. She wants me to take it. She wants me to prove my worth.

"Open for me Buttercup, or we're going to have problems."

She shakes her head defiantly. I pinch her nose shut and wait. When she doesn't give in and open her mouth, I worry that she might pass out so I change tactics. I thrust into her as hard as I can. She can't help the moan that escapes her, forcing her hand, her mouth opening for me.

I slide in and out of her, the delicious squeezing pressure of her wet center caressing me, begging me to pour myself inside of her. The buzz under my skin intensifies and I groan at the pulsing energy building between us.

"Fuck, I love you," I say as I'm fucking her into the mattress. This isn't the way I had planned to tell her, but it just falls out of my mouth.

She doesn't say it back.

A brief look of sadness crosses her face, but it's wiped away as her release builds inside of her, and crescendos with a scream, and her back arching off of the bed. The way she squeezes me has me grunting out my own release inside of her, coating her tight walls with my seed.

"As soon as Archer's baby is born, I'm putting my own in you. This pussy, this body, they're mine." I say.

I don't give her the opportunity to protest before my mouth crashes down on hers. The taste of her blood mixes with mine. I moan into her mouth and I pump in and out of her slowly, as my dick hardens inside of her once more.

Our intimacy turns from a desperate chase for release, to a passionate, and gentle love-making. Watching her, memorizing her, extending our pleasure. Within ten minutes, we're both coming again. I pull out and watch as my cum spills on the bed.

I lay down and face her as she stares at the ceiling.

"I'm sorry," she says, not looking at me.

"For what?"

"For not being able to say it back. I just...I don't know what the circumstances of you being adopted were, or what your adoptive parents were like, but I've never had someone actually care about me until very recently.

"It's hard for me to believe that anyone could really truly love me. I've been alone my whole life, Camp. Linnie was the only one who ever stuck around. And now..." A silent tear falls down her face, and she tries to wipe it away.

"Hey. You don't have to explain yourself to me. But I want you to know that I would *never* have done what we just did if I didn't really love you and care about you. I would never hitch myself to someone who I didn't want to be with for as long as we were both alive.

"You're it for me. And I know that you have the others, and I'm fine with that. I can see the way that they bring you joy. I see the way that they complete pieces of you that I never could," I say as I stroke her hair, and silently will her to look at me.

"I need you, Jinx. I need you as much as I need blood. Hell, I need you as much as I need air. I feel empty when you're not around."

She finally turns to face me. "Is that why you and Sully hooked up? To fill a void?"

"No. Well..."I hesitate, and think about it. "No," I say definitively. "It started off a little like that, but I think we both realized pretty quickly that we love each other as more than just partners, or friends. There has always been a touch of a romantic love between us. I felt it, but I didn't recognize what it was until the safehouse. Even then, I tried to ignore it—push it out of my head."

"Why?"

"Fear of rejection," I say with a shrug. "Sully never came across as being into me, and I just assumed that he would push me away."

"I could feel it between you that first day," she says. "There was more there than just the platonic love of good friends. The way he bossed you around, and you followed his orders, and the way he licked your cum out of my pussy...It was super hot, but also way more intimate than something 'just friends' would do."

"Yeah, I guess most guys wouldn't have done that," I say with a laugh.

I stand from the bed and go into the attached bathroom. I grab a washcloth and dampen it and bring it back to clean her up. "Do you want me to heal you?"

"I don't think so," she says. "I have my mark from Colt, and now I'll have these little scars from you. Proof of our mate bond."

"The proof is in how I feel for you," I say, wiping the last of the blood off of her.

"But this way, we'll have something tangible to show for it."

Something inside of me cracks a little at her need to have a physical representation of my feelings for her. I straddle her and look down into her eyes.

"I need you to understand something, so I need you to really listen to me. I am not going anywhere. The others are not going anywhere. We are in this for the long haul; with you and with each other. I like them. I care about them. I love *you*, and I care about you.

"I don't know what else I can do to prove that to you."

"That's the thing. You're going to have to choose me, every day, for a very long time for me to feel comfortable. And I may never feel one hundred percent settled with you and the others. There's always this nagging feeling in the back of my mind that I am unlovable.

"I am completely *likable*, sure. At least for a little while. I'm fun, and carefree, and I'm a great fuck. But no one ever sticks around long enough to know if they actually like who I *am*. I can count on one hand the number of relationships I've had in my life, and none of them lasted more than six months."

"And who ended those relationships?" I ask with a raised eyebrow.

She stares at me in quiet contemplation before she whispers, "I did."

"Mhmm. You're a wonderful person, and we're all lucky to have you. You've let us in, but you need to trust us to stay. And if any of those fuckers leaves, I'll kill them."

She smiles at me and nods, but doesn't say anything else. I lay down next to her, and she cuddles into my chest. Within a few minutes, her breathing has slowed and she's fast asleep.

Chapter Thirty One
Cobra

Campbell slips out of the bedroom a little after midnight. The rest of us are playing a board game at the dining room table. Archer, who has played all of these games a million times, is kicking our asses as usual. I know that he always wins, but Colt is not handling it so well.

"How'd it go?" Sully asks with a smirk.

"Good. She's good and thoroughly mine, now. You're up next." Campbell says, clapping Sully on the back, and kissing him on the forehead. "But I would give her a couple of days. She's a little worn out."

I stuff my jealousy deep inside. Mate bonds aren't something that people like me get. Both because of who I am as a person and because mutated freaks just don't have them. Each of the others being able to connect with her more deeply than I do is pissing me off.

"I'm going to bed." I say, and head for my room.

"I'll join you," Archer says standing from the table.

"No. I'd rather be alone for a bit."

I'm halfway down the hall when I hear Colt say, "Is he okay?"

And Archer replies with, "He's never okay."

At about four a.m. I wake to someone straddling me. Their weight on my crotch has me hard as steel already, and I just woke up.

"I'm not in the mood, Archer," I grumble and start to cover my head with my pillow. But then I realize that the person on top of me is too small to be Archer.

The sleep finally clears from my brain, and I can sense that the mental energy coming from the intruder is Jinx's. I rip the pillow off of my face and turn the light on. She grinds against me, and I reach my hands out and place them on her thick thighs, giving them a squeeze.

"You're not Archer," I say with a smile.

"Not even a little bit. And it seems like you're very much in the mood."

She slides my cock inside of her and begins riding me. Her hands move up to her tits and she starts playing with her nipples. "I had a dream about you," she says, bouncing up and down on my dick as I watch it slide in and out of her.

"What kind of dream?" I ask, placing my thumb on her clit, and rubbing small circles.

"One where you were sad, and there was nothing I could do to fix it."

She lets out a small moan. I start to wonder if *I'm* dreaming. How did we all get so damn lucky to have this girl?

"You would tell me if you were sad, right?" She asks with big puppy dog eyes, and places her hands on my chest to give her better leverage.

"Why would I be sad, Little Mouse?" I ask, my breathing getting heavier as I begin thrusting up to meet her hips with my own.

"I don't know. But you didn't answer my question," she says and she stops moving with me half inside of her. "Would you tell me if you were sad?"

I'm not going to lie to her, but I can't bring myself to tell her the truth either. She takes my silence as the answer that it is.

"I see," she says, and she tries to move off of me. Her eyes are full of hurt.

I grab her wrists and keep her on top of me. "I'm so broken, Jinx. You've seen bits and pieces of it, but I'm more broken than you could ever know. And those cracks, and dents in my soul...They make me act irrationally to things that I don't like. They make me act irrationally to things I *do* like. And it is taking everything in me not to punish you or the others just for being with each other."

"I thought you were okay with our arrangement?" She asks, her tone defensive.

"I am," I say, but then I correct myself. "Well, I would be if there was some way I could bind myself to you like the others have."

"You're not the only one not bound to me, Ranger."

Her voice is soft and loving. Her use of my real name makes a shiver run through me. Archer is the only one who calls me that. I have noticed that he doesn't call the rest by their real names. Just me.

"No, but I will be. Sully plans to mate you soon. and when he does, I'll be the odd man out. Just like I always am."

"Just because we don't have some spiritual binding to one another, doesn't mean that you don't have a place here."

"Doesn't it? If you try to leave any of them, you'll be physically and mentally unwell. The very fiber of your being will ache to be with them to the point that you'll have to come back. But with me? You can leave me if you want. And you will. Because No one can stand me for long. Even Archer got tired of me after a while and he went so far as to lock me up."

"He locked you up so that you wouldn't hurt me."

"Before he even *knew* you. He kicked me to the curb over some girl he had never met."

"Ranger—"

"I love you, Jinx. As much as I can love someone, I love you. But if you ever left me, I would kill you. And I would kill Archer for letting it happen. And probably the others just out of spite.

"I don't mean any of that figuratively. I mean I would slit your throat and watch you bleed out for breaking my heart. So instead, after the ritual is done, I'm leaving. I can't watch you with them knowing we'll never have the same thing."

If she's scared of me, she doesn't show it. Instead, all I see is sadness in her eyes. She slips her hands out of my grip and leaves my bed, grabs her nightie, and leaves me alone in my room. I don't bother trying to stop her.

I press my palms to my eyes and contemplate leaving the house tonight. Being here, being with them…It's too much. I'm thinking clearly now, but when my dark side comes out, I may not be able to stop it.

But I'm selfish. I want as much time with them as I can get. I just have to hope that by the time the ritual rolls around, I still have the same resolve that I have now.

I've just drifted off to sleep after jerking off, and cleaning up the subsequent mess when my door slams open and the overhead light flips on.

"What the fuck is wrong with you?" Archer growls. He's in his demon form and only wearing a pair of boxers.

He crosses the room, grabs me by the throat and holds me up in the air. I try to push through and gain control of him, but it's pointless. His mental shields are too strong for me to get through.

"Jinx is perfect for us; for *both* of us. And you're going to try to throw that away? You and I can finally be together in a nontoxic way. Is that what the problem is? That you can't pull your toxic bullshit if the girl that we're sharing cares about both of us?"

He throws me down onto the bed, and I let out a small cough, trying to recover from the grip he had on my throat.

"I will ruin everything, Archie. Just like I always do. It's better if I take my 'toxic bullshit' somewhere else so I can't hurt either of you."

His mouth pops open in surprise. For the first time in all of our years together, Archer is at a loss for words. I move to the dresser and start pulling on clothes, then I move to the door. Archer places his hand above my head and holds it shut.

"You can't leave. I won't allow it. I'll tie you up and stick you in the dungeon if I have to."

I spin to face him. I like that he's started dropping his human facade, more. His massive demon form is hot. I've always thought so, but he never believed me. I place my hand on his cheek and he leans into it. We don't ever have tender moments. We fuck and bicker, then fuck again. It's how it's always been.

"You wouldn't. Besides, we're not at the manor. You don't have a dungeon to lock me in."

"I have a dungeon in every single property I own. Just because you haven't seen it, doesn't mean it isn't there." He stares at me then sighs and lowers his voice. "If you leave her, you'll be reinforcing the idea that no one can love her enough to stick around."

My gaze drops to the floor. "I'll ruin her, Archie. If I catch even the slightest hint that she's losing interest, I will destroy her. It's better if I go now before that can happen."

"Why do you think she'll lose interest in you?"

"Because I can't be mated to her like you guys. She's stuck with you four. I'm just a spare."

He tips my chin up, forcing me to look at him. "We may be mated to her, but that makes you even more important than we are. Do you know why?"

I shake my head.

"Because if you leave her, it'll make her think that the only way someone can stay with her is if they've got supernatural forces pushing them toward her. Once Sully mates her, you'll be the only one who is here one hundred percent by choice. If you choose to leave, you'll be proving her right. Don't do that. Show her that she's worth fighting for."

"No pressure or anything," I say with the ghost of a smile.

"All the pressure, actually. Because if you try to leave, I'll kill you. And I imagine that I'm not the only one who feels that way. Jinx needs you just like she needs the rest of us. So stop doubting yourself and get back to being the crazy fucker that I know you are."

I nod, and try to go back toward the bed, but he turns me around to the door.

"No. You hurt her. Now you need to go fix it. She's up in the loft with Campbell."

I heave a sigh and shake away the last of my doubt. Jinx is mine. She's always been mine. Even if the stars didn't destine us to be together like they did with the others, that doesn't change how I feel about her. Or at least that's what I tell myself on the way up the stairs.

Holding my head high I go up to the loft and find Campbell and Jinx wrapped up with each other under the covers. Jinx's puffy red eyes find mine. Campbell turns and scowls at me.

"Can we talk?" I ask, hoping that Campbell will get the hint and leave.

"You've done enough for one day, snake. Get the fuck out of here."

"Camp," Jinx says softly, and places her hand on his chest. "I really don't want to talk about it anymore. You made your point."

"Then how about we just skip making up and fuck, then?" I ask with a smirk.

"Ranger," Archer's voice warns from downstairs. Having an open loft as the master bedroom is wildly inconvenient.

I roll my eyes. "Please just hear me out. Archer will have my head if you don't."

"Your balls, too," he adds and I shudder.

"Fine. You have five minutes," Jinx says.

Campbell slips out of the bed. "I'll be downstairs if you need me," he says to her before kissing her on the forehead. He shoulder checks me on the way through. "Don't fucking hurt her again."

"I won't," I say, then internally add 'emotionally'.

I crawl into the bed with her. She flinches away from me. I guess I deserve that. I want her to fear me a little bit, but not because she thinks I'll break her heart.

"I need you to swear to me that you'll never leave me," I say.

"You just tried to leave me after swearing to me in the hot tub at the mansion that you wouldn't. How is that fair?"

"I was trying to leave because I was scared. Things with Archer are good for the first time since we've met. And you...well you're perfect. You fit so well with not just me and Archer, but with the others, too.

"I'm scared to need you because there's nothing holding you here with me."

She sits up and faces me. She's back in her nightie and she looks so cute in it. I want to rip it off of her.

"The fact that I like you is enough to keep me here with you. And you and Archer are a package deal. I know that. And I want that. I want both of you."

"Do you love me, Jinx?" I shouldn't ask. She never tells anyone she loves them.

She crawls forward and climbs into my laps, straddling me. "I care about all five of you more than I've ever cared about anyone and I need that to be enough for you."

She takes my face in her hands and kisses me. My hands roam up under her nightie and rest on her stomach. She bites my bottom lip and I growl into her mouth.

It is enough. She is enough. And I think she understands just how serious I am when I say I will ruin her.

Her kiss is full of passion, and promises that she'll never say out loud. The way her body reacts to mine lets me know that she is mine, and that I was an idiot for ever thinking differently.

"You left me so frustrated earlier, Little Mouse. Do you know how irritating that was? I'm gonna need you to make up for it."

"Make me," she challenges.

"That's a dangerous game to play with me."

"I know what I signed up for."

"Do you?"

"Play nice Ranger!" Archer calls from downstairs. Then the voices of the rest of the guys clear out. I'm assuming they left to go to different rooms to give us some privacy.

I maneuver my way through the soft barriers that are shielding Jinx's mind. She's started learning how to block me out since the night of the executions, but she's not proficient at it yet. Once or twice a day I start to snake myself into her mind and see how far I can get before she notices. She's almost to a point where she can beat me. But I think a part of her wants this, so she's leaving herself more open to my suggestion.

"Lay down on the bed," I command.

I feel her resistance at first, but she can't hold back for long. She lays flat on her back and watches me, intrigue dancing in her eyes. I reach into the bedside drawer and pull out a bottle of lube, then I pull out a knife and cut down the front of her nightie and cut her underwear off of her. Then I pull my own clothes and toss them to the floor.

Climbing up her body, I straddle her stomach. I open the lube and pour it on her chest.

"You have the best tits I've ever seen, and I've seen a lot. I've wanted to fuck them since I saw them through the balcony window that first night." I snap the lube shut and grab a tit in each hand. "Open your mouth."

I slide my dick between her breasts and start thrusting gently; hitting her pretty mouth with each pulse of my hips.

"Touch yourself," I say. I honestly don't know if I need the mind control. She might just obey me without it, but I think that me making her obey is part of the fun for her.

She moves her hand down and begins fingering herself. I was going to punish her and just come on her face, but I want to fuck her properly. I wait until she's getting close and then I make her remove her hand. I pull back, and move off of her.

"On your hands and knees like the bitch that you are."

That earns me a scowl which I return with a smile. She complies because she has no choice. I pull a large vibrator out of the drawer and hand it to her.

"Turn it on, and put it in."

While she does that, I grab the bottle of lube and pour some on her tight little asshole, then rub some on my cock and press it to her back entrance. She likes it in the ass. I've seen the way she reacts when Archer's extra appendage slips in there during sex.

I push inside of her slowly, allowing her time to adjust and accommodate my size. I can feel the vibrations through the thin wall separating the toy from me. She gasps when I push in the last little bit.

"Fuck yourself with that toy, Little Mouse. I'm gonna fuck this tight little hole while you do," I say and thrust inside of her.

"Fuck, Cobra," she says with a whimper.

Her head drops to the bed, but I grab a fistful of her hair and pull, making her arch her back.

"You're mine, Little Mouse. You're mine as much as you're theirs and I will brand my fucking name into your skin so you never forget that. I will sear my memory into your body by fucking you in every single hole until you can't walk straight.

"And if you ever try to leave me, I will hunt you down like the rodent that you are, and devour you. Do you understand me?"

She tries to nod, but I pull on her hair. "I said 'do you understand me'?"

"Yes. Yes I understand," she cries.

"Good fucking girl," I praise and slap her ass. She cries out as she comes around me and the toy that is filling up her dripping pussy. I come inside of her with a growl.

I push her down onto the bed and lay my full weight on top of her. "I fucking meant every word. You got the sweet side of me, tonight. But I told you what was at stake. If you try to leave me, if you pull any shit at the ritual that could get you killed, I'm going to punish you so bad. The others won't even be able to protect you from my wrath."

"I'll never leave you, Ranger. I promise."

I expected her voice to be fearful, but there was resolve, and love in her voice. She may not be able to say it, but I know that in her own way, Jinx loves me. And in my own fucked up way, I love her.

Chapter Thirty Two

Jinx

We spend the next couple of weeks in the lodge getting to know one another, playing board games, and just in general enjoying ourselves. But despite our best efforts, there's the constant overwhelming sense of doom about the upcoming ritual, but we do our best to make the most of our time.

Archer has cut back on the number of people that he has working in his immediate circle. He doesn't trust anyone after Lanya and Trixie betrayed him, and I don't blame him one bit. He has two men who drive supplies up once a week, and other than that it's just been us.

As the ritual closes in, Archer brings the hostages from the compound to the lodge and stashes them in the dungeon in the basement. There are two new hostages who attempted to gain entry into the mansion after we left, but his men caught them. He's holding them for now, convinced that further torture will get them to admit who hired them. And whatever Trixie knows, she isn't saying.

The guys are losing their patience and even my presence and attempts to calm them down aren't working. We're about a week out from the ritual when Colt comes storming up the stairs with Sully and Campbell in tow.

"We'll figure it out, Colt. I know we will," Sully says.

Colt rounds on him and swings. For a moment I think he's about to hit Sully but his fist collides with the wall instead.

"I appreciate what you're trying to do, but I'm so fucking *sick* of your eternal optimism. If this ritual doesn't go well, Jinx could fucking die!"

I walk up behind him and place a gentle hand on his shoulder. He rounds on me, and is about to lash out on me, until he realizes who is touching him. His eyes are glowing, his panther pushing to be released.

"I'm going to be fine," I whisper.

"I didn't finally get you back just to lose you again Minxy. If anything were to happen to you…"

"You'll be there to protect me. I'll be fine. Why don't you guys let me try to talk to Trixie? Maybe she'll give me some answers."

"No. You're not talking to her," Campbell says. "I don't trust her even in the slightest and I'm worried that she'll somehow get to you."

"I could kick her ass. I'm not worried about it. Besides, Archer's got her magic locked down so tight. There's no concern of her being able to use it on me. Plus, I'm pretty sure that my magic is stronger. Especially with you all being mated to me."

"Sully and Cobra aren't," Campbell says as if Sully's bond could be the determining factor for keeping me safe against Trixie.

"We could go fix that right now, Little Witch. What do you say?" Sully says with a flirty smile as he pulls me flush against him.

I know he's not entirely joking. He's been hinting at mating with me since Campbell and I sealed ours. He's feeling left out, but after

Cobra's meltdown over me being mated to the others, I wanted to give it some time.

"I promise we will before my ascension. Just not right this second, okay?"

He frowns and nods his head. "I get it."

"I promise that it's not because I don't want to. I just want to be sensitive to Cobra's needs."

"I don't care about that, anymore," Cobra says coming out of one of the bedrooms. "I was upset about it for a second, but after we had our little heart to heart, I know you wouldn't try to leave me. You would be stupid to, really." He presses his chest to my back, pinning me between him and Sully, and bites down on my ear.

He's entirely back to his normal self. He and Campbell have been taking turns playing with knives in the bedroom. Sully enjoys slapping me around, and Colt is into just about anything that allows him to tie me up and use me.

Despite all of my years in sex work, I have never been so sated. They keep me happy, and our dynamic is perfect. Archer has Cobra, and Campbell has Sully. Any night that we aren't all tangled up in the king sized bed in the loft, Colt gets to sleep with me. It keeps his panther happy, but nobody feels lonely or left out.

"You wanna tag team her?" Cobra asks Sully.

"I'm standing right here," Campbell protests.

"Yeah, but it can be fun to change it up. You and Archer can spitroast her tonight."

I elbow Cobra in the ribs and he reaches around and grabs me by the throat and squeezes so hard I can't breathe.

"You wanna try that again? You know the fight turns me on," he says and presses his hard-on to my ass.

"Guys, we have work to do. We can fuck for the rest of our days after we get the information we need out of Trixie. So stop dicking around," Colt says.

He's obsessed with finding the best way to handle the ritual. He feels like it's his personal mission to make sure it goes smoothly. I get it, he's scared, but I honestly don't know how much more we can find out.

"Trixie said there was a chant, or something that needed to be done for the ascension," Sully says. "Do we know anything about that?"

"Just that it's been passed down for a couple of generations through some witches," Colt answers.

"I can try communing with my ancestors to see if any of them have an answer," I say. "Or I can try doing a discovery spell. I haven't done one in years, and it wasn't terribly successful. I actually used it to try to find you," I say to Colt with a laugh. "It was silly, really. I didn't have anything of yours. Just the memory of you. And the stars only guide me so far if they don't feel that it's important."

"When was that?"

"Probably about two years after I left. I just wanted to see if you had got out."

"It's probably for the best that you didn't find me. That was when I got involved with the gangs in the city. I eventually got out, obviously, but those were some really dark times."

"I'm sorry I couldn't find you and help. I would have taken you away from all of that."

"I didn't need you to save me, Minxy. Not then and not now."

I give him a sad smile. I still feel responsible for all that happened after I left them at Steve's house. I keep thinking about what life would have been like for us if we hadn't ended up with such tragic lives. I wish for a minute that my parents were around and healthy enough to help me through all this shit.

Wait.

"I wonder if the ritual chant was passed down through my family line..." I wonder out loud.

"Is there anyone left in your family that you could ask?"

I shake my head. "But like I said, I can commune with my ancestors. They might be able to help. ARCHER!" I yell down the hallway.

He bursts out of one of the spare rooms. "What's wrong?" he demands making a beeline for me.

"I need you to have your men bring a couple of weird items to the lodge next time they come so I can contact my great grandmother."

"Why her?" Campbell asks.

"Because she was the most gifted witch in the bloodline until I came along. My grandmother always talked about how good she was at spells and whatnot. I'm wondering if that wasn't because she received some sort of blessing from the stars. She would be my best bet to find anything out."

"What do you need?" Archer asks.

"You'll want to write this down," I say.

He pulls up the notepad app on his phone.

"Obsidian, bloodstone, mugwort, pine needles, and rose petals. Preferably organic for the plants, but if you can't find them, any will do. Most of my spells don't need supplies, but when it's something this intense, having something to pull energy from helps."

"Let me make some calls, and I'll have the guys up here tomorrow with it."

"In the meantime I would like to talk to Trixie. Alone."

"Absolutely fucking not," Archer says. "I'm not ever leaving you alone with anyone ever again. You either have one of us with you or you don't go."

I glare at him.

"Don't give me that look. Twice I've left you alone, and twice it ended up with you getting assaulted. It's never happening again. The bathroom is as far as you go without a chaperon and even that is pushing it."

"You're being overbearing and ridiculous," I say, crossing my arms over my chest.

"I'm being protective. I will not let you get hurt again. Never ever again. You're mine to love and hold and protect and worship and if anyone ever hurts you again—without your permission—I will turn them into dust."

"Fine. Can I talk to Trixie with Cobra present?"

"Why me?" Cobra whines. "I can't stand the sound of her voice."

"Because she knows you the least out of all of these guys. And you're the most intimidating."

"Hey!" the others all say in unison.

"It's true. It's the unhinged look he gets in his eye when something isn't going the way that he's planned. I know it scares the hell out of me sometimes."

"Awe. That's the nicest thing anyone has ever said to me," he says, placing his hand on his chest dramatically. "Just for that, I'll go with you."

"Okay. You two can go talk to Trixie. But if things even get a little bit weird, you're coming back upstairs. Do you hear me, Ranger? Anything at all weird and you make sure she gets back upstairs."

"What is Trixie going to do? Glare at me to death? I'll be fine. Stop worrying." I pat him on the shoulder and head down to the dungeon to confront the girl who got me kidnapped.

The dungeon is surprisingly high tech considering the rustic style of the cabin. It has glass doors and electronic hook ups to all of the cells with backup generators in case the power goes out. It's also sterile white save for the old rust colored stains on the floors of a couple of the cells.

Trixie looks up from where she's sitting on a cot and scowls at me. I give a condescending smile and a little wave of my fingers. I'm poking the bear, but she's a bitch and I don't care.

"We need to have a chat," I say, pulling up a chair and sitting in front of her cell.

"We have nothing to talk about. And you are going to fail because I'm the only one who knows what you need to do to complete your ascension."

"You know that I could have Cobra here make you peel your own skin off, right?"

"But you wouldn't because you need me."

"Need is a strong word. I would benefit from you sharing your information with me, but I have other ways of finding the truth. Once I do, you're dead anyway."

She has the wisdom to look a little fearful. "How could you possibly find out what only I know?"

"I'm a witch. I can find out just about anything with a little time and patience. Patience I have. Time, I'm lacking on. So what do you say? Will you give me the information I need in exchange for being released unharmed after my ascension?"

"That's an unbelievably fair deal considering she has five mates wanting to rip you into tiny pieces right now," Cobra says.

Trixie's head snaps in my direction. "You're mated to them? *All* of them?"

"It's only completed with three of them, but yes."

"Which three?" She asks, eyes narrowing.

I laugh realizing why she's being so hostile. "Does it really matter that much? Whatever you thought you had with Campbell was one-sided. He dropped you the second I showed up."

"Did...you...mate...him?" she says through clenched teeth.

I stare at her, considering how to play this. There's no point in lying. "I did. About three weeks ago."

She lets out a shriek of anger, and holds out her hands like she's trying to pull out her magic, but nothing happens.

"Last chance to accept my offer," I say with cool indifference. I'm almost positive I can get the information I need, but truthfully this would be way easier.

"Go fuck yourself," she spits back.

I stand and move closer to the glass. "By the time my ascension is done, you'll wish you had just told me." I start to walk away then pause and call over my shoulder, "And I don't need to fuck myself. I have Campbell to do that for me."

I stroll out of the dungeon like I don't have a care in the world with Cobra in tow. We make it to the top of the stairs and find that the others are just sitting around waiting for us to come back.

Colt jumps to his feet. "How did it go?"

"I'm surprised you all weren't watching on Archer's CCTV," Cobra says.

"His *what*?" Sully says.

"There are cameras in every single room in this cabin. I can't imagine that he left them out of the dungeon."

Colt, Campbell, Sully and I all look at Archer who is typing away on his cell phone.

He glances up and asks, "What? It's for our safety. They're deleted after twenty-four hours, too. Unless I choose to save them. Which sometimes I do. Like when Cobra and I had Jinx—"

"What the fuck Archer! You're making sex tapes of us?"

"They're for all of us to enjoy later," he says with a shrug.

"I think the more important thing is that we weren't watching while she was down there talking to Trixie," Sully says, crossing his arms over his chest.

"I was. On my phone."

"We're supposed to be a team, dude," Colt says.

"Did you just call a millenia old demon 'dude'?" Archer asks in annoyance.

Colt and Archer engage in a staring contest.

"Oooookay," I say and sit down at the kitchen island. "It went fine, to answer your original question. She won't give us the information, but I was able to confirm that her beef with me is entirely because of Campbell. Maybe he could go seduce the information out of her," I say with a laugh.

The guys all exchange looks like they're considering it.

"No. You're not touching her," I say definitively.

"I wouldn't have to *touch* her."

"I said no. I don't make many demands, but there is a hard line here. If it were anyone else, I wouldn't argue with you, but after what she did to me, I don't even want you pretending to be interested in her. I don't even want her to be able to look at you again."

"What did you say to her to try to convince her?"

"That we would let her go unharmed if she gave us the information we needed. I'll probably be able to get it, but it's going to take a lot out of me. Communing with my ancestors always does. And we only have about three weeks until the ritual."

"Why didn't we do this sooner?" Colt asks.

"Honestly, I didn't even think about it. My relationships with my family have always been crap, so I don't talk to my ancestors much. I also thought that Trixie would crack by now. But I can do it tomorrow night once the moon is out, and I should be able to get the information that we need. Or She should be able to at least point us in the right direction."

"It'll all work out," Sully says.

He really is eternally optimistic about everything and I'm grateful for that. Between Colts anger, Campbell's anxiety, and Cobra's intensity, I can't handle any more wild emotions about my ascension.

"Well, let's get some rest, and spend some quality time together before the guys get here with the supplies you need. If it's going to drain you, I want to enjoy you some tonight," Archer says before scooping me up into his arms and carrying me up to the loft with the rest of the guys following behind.

Chapter Thirty Three

Jinx

It's around noon when Archer's men show up with the supplies that I need. They were able to find it all so fast which shocks me. Fresh organic rose petals are hard to find in this area this time of year.

The guys spend the afternoon pampering me, and trying to distract me from my task. I think they can sense the anxiety I have about it. The last time I communed it was not the most pleasant experience. I tried to talk to my mom and she yelled at me and shut me out. Unfortunately, even if I'm trying to reach my great grandmother, it's not a guarantee about who I'm going to get on the other line.

At sunset, I take all of my supplies out to the deck. I'm only wearing a sweater, which Archer protests about.

"You're going to freeze. Please at least let me get you some blankets and a real coat."

"The amount of energy this requires expends a lot of heat. I will get overheated. I promise that it's better if I don't have anything else on."

"Fine, but if your lips start turning blue, I'm dragging you back inside."

I sit down and put the brass bowl on the deck. I write my great grandmother's name on a slip of paper and place it in the bowl and weigh it down with the obsidian. Then I top it with the pine needles, and rose petals. I light the mugwort on fire, and hold the bloodstone over the flame until it warms my fingers, then I put the stone in and the flaming mugwort into the bowl. Finally, I use my fire magic to ignite the rest of it.

I take a deep breath, then push out a small amount of each of my elemental magics searching for the rope that attaches me to my ancestral line. The ethereal rope loops itself around my waist, and I'm pulled into a vast darkness, surrounded by stars.

"I was wondering when you would call upon me, child," a deep female voice says from every direction. "You waited until the last possible second to find the answers you seek. Tell me, why did you wait so long?"

"Because I don't have a lot of attachment to my family. There didn't seem to be much point. But I'm here now. Can you help?"

"Your mother made mistakes; a lot of them. I'm sorry that she was not able to be the person you deserved. But I believe that it made you stronger."

"I didn't need to be stronger. I needed to be loved. But that's not why I'm here. I'm here because of the impending doom of the world. Can you help, or not?"

"You did need to be strong, though. You'll need all the strength you can muster to complete your trial."

I scoff in disgust. "Can you please tell me what I need to do?"

"Child, do you even know who you're talking to?" The disembodied voice chastises.

"Aren't you my great grandmother?"

A soft light in the distance grows closer and brighter, illuminating the vast darkness before me. It becomes blinding, and I shield my eyes from the burning light.

The brightness dims and I hesitantly lower my hand. Before me is an ethereal woman in a long flowing gown. Her skin looks as though it's made out of raw opal, and she glitters all on her own, like the light required to make her shine is coming from within.

"I am your patron. The star sign of Libra. And I have chosen you as my champion."

An assortment of emotions swim through me. There's anger that she's just now revealing herself to me, and awe that she's here at all. There's respect for the age old being in front of me, and bitterness that she left me to my own devices for this long.

"You are not pleased to be my champion," she observes. "And that is okay. The amount of responsibility that has been placed on your shoulders is immense. I know that this isn't what you would have chosen for yourself, but I believe you have what it takes.

"I poured every last bit of my power into you. You and the other chosen girls are all powerful and tenacious. You all have what it takes to save this planet for the beings that dwell here." She reaches out and places a rough crystalline hand on my cheek.

"Beautiful girl, I know you will do what it takes to accomplish that. Those men that you've surrounded yourself with, will provide you with anchors to this planet. Spilling their blood will provide you with everything you need to complete the ritual."

"Wait, like a sacrifice?" My chest tightens and my head swims. If this requires me to kill the guys, I won't be able to do it.

She lets out a laugh. "No. You don't need that much blood. Just a little bit will do. The most important thing is making sure that you trust yourself. You'll know what to do when the time is right.

"On the night of the solstice, you will travel to the highest point of the Restless Peaks. There will be a flat space at the top of that peak that will contain a large disk. That is where you need to perform the ritual. You can do this, Little Zodiac."

She kisses me on the forehead and I'm sucked back through the void and thrown back into my body.

"She's back!" one of the guys calls when I open my eyes.

In my current state, I can't discern who it is. I shake my head to clear away the fog, but it sticks around. Anxiety washes over me. I didn't want the guys to be right with me when I completed my ascension. I know what they all have said, and that makes me even more hesitant to have them there. But Libra said I needed them there. I just have to hope that none of them tries to put a stop to things if it gets a little sketchy.

"How did it go, Little Witch?" Sully asks, reaching for my hand. "You were gone for over an hour, so I hope you got what you needed."

He pulls me to my feet and brushes a sweaty strand of hair out of my face. He looks over my face, inspecting me. Then a large hand pulls me back against a wall of muscle. Archer.

"I was worried about you," he murmurs into my hair before placing a kiss on the top of my head.

I tip my head back to look at him. "I'm fine. It went okay. I was trying to connect with my great grandmother, but the wires got crossed. I ended up meeting with Libra, herself."

"And?" Archer urgest me on.

"She gave me the time and location and told me that I already had everything I needed to complete the ritual. I need to do a little research. We may need hiking gear."

I explain everything that Libra told me over some hot cocoa that Campbell had waiting for me when I was done with my spell. I tell them about the beautiful woman who imbued me with this power, and they listen, none of them saying a word.

"So you need our blood? Sign me up," Cobra says with a devilish grin.

"I know the mountain she was talking about. It's not too far from here, maybe a thirty minute drive to the base of it. And they're more like extremely large hills than mountains. I don't think we'll need much more than hiking boots and cold gear," Sully says.

"How do you know about them?" I ask. We're about four hours away from the city and I'm surprised.

"I hike a lot," he says with a shrug. "I'll take you once the weather is warmer if you'd like."

"I would like that very much."

We spend the evening formulating a plan, then once we feel that we have the details narrowed down, we all fall into bed together. But just to sleep.

The next few days pass with no incident, but Cobra is getting especially stir crazy in the cabin. The others are content to just eat, and play board games, and fuck. But Cobra has taken to pulling 'pranks' on us. The only problem is that his version of pranks are dangerous.

They started off harmless, with saran wrap on the toilet, and swapping the salt with sugar. Then they got kind of gross, like him ejaculating into Archer's coffee, and putting a jar of pee in the fridge in place of apple juice.

Then they turned violent. Like setting up Rube Goldberg Machines that end with knives swinging or fire starting. It's like living on the set of a Home Alone movie and no matter how many times we tell him that he can't keep doing that, he doesn't listen.

Colt got stabbed. Archer got his clothes set on fire. Thankfully he's a demon so he didn't burn, but it ruined his favorite button up shirt. Cobra was punished beautifully for that one, and I got to watch.

"You nearly decapitated Sully!" Campbell yells at Cobra.

"He has good reflexes! He was fine!"

"Cobra...You're not hurting my mates are you?"

"Technically no, because you still haven't taken Sully as your mate," he reminds me, making me feel guilty.

It's not that I don't want to make it official. It's that I just want him to be sure about it. I know that he pushed for me to commit to him that first weekend that we met, but a lot has changed since then.

But I guess we'll always be bound together since he's with Camp, and Camp and I around bound together. I sigh deeply.

"I guess I should talk to him about that."

"You could sound a little more excited about it," Sully says, stepping into the room. He's hurt.

"Looks like we've suddenly got somewhere else to be," Campbell says and ushers Cobra out of the room.

"But I wanna see!" Cobra protests.

"You're not sitting in on this conversation." Campbell is all but throwing Cobra over his shoulder and hauling him out of the room.

"No I wanna watch them fuck!" Cobra says, impatiently.

Campbell stops in his tracks. "You guys aren't gonna do it right now, are you?"

I give him a sarcastic look. "Even if we were, I've been allowed time to mate with each of you alone, so I plan to do that with Sully too. We don't need the added pressure of an audience."

"Fine," Campbell pouts. "But as soon as you're done...threesome."

"Or a sexsome!" Cobra calls as Campbell hauls him away.

"It's called an orgy, Dumbass," I hear Camp mumble as they're headed out of the room.

"Why don't you want to mate with me?" Sully asks. "I asked you weeks ago, and you've been coming up with excuses. I just need to know if there's something that I'm doing or *not* doing to make you hesitate."

"It's not you. It's the whole thing. With Archer and Colt it was so spontaneous, and then the whole thing with Camp and then Cobra having a fit over not being mated to me..."

"But you resolved all of that, and you've had plenty of time to get used to the idea of mating with me. So what is holding you back?"

"It feels more final," I admit. "It's like once I solidify our bond, then I'm truly attached to all of you, and that's scary for me."

"Not this again," he groans. "How many more ways can I show you that you have nothing to be afraid of? I *want* to be attached to you, Jinx. I want to spend the rest of my life with you. I've been wanting that since the second I laid eyes on you. And throughout the last couple of months, that hasn't changed.

"I just need you to tell me that you want that too. I can't keep doing this thing where I'm in limbo wondering if you're having second thoughts. But I also don't want to force you into something you're not ready for. So if you need me to back off, just tell me."

"I do want you, Sully. There's never been a question in my head about that. I think I'm ready. I just..."

He lets out a growl of frustration. He's losing patience which is saying a lot since he is typically the most level headed of the guys.

"I'm sorry," he says. "You take your time. I just think that we should consider getting it done before your ascension."

I take a deep breath and close my eyes. He's right, and I know he is. I also know somewhere deep down that he wouldn't abandon me.

"Let's do it," I blurt out before I can change my mind. I know, now that I said it, I can't take it back because if I do, I'll absolutely break his heart.

"Really?" he asks excitedly.

"Yes. I'm ready. I trust you. And if you break my heart I'll kill you," I add with a shrug. I honestly believe that I could. kill him. "So how do we do this?"

Chapter Thirty Four

Sully

I pull off my shirt, and Jinx's. "Can you create something to shield us from the weather?"

"Yeah, why?"

I pull down my pants and hers so that we're standing in nothing but our underwear. "Follow me," I say and lead her to the deck.

Archer is sitting on the couch, with his arm around Cobra, checking his phone. He glances up at us, and does a double take when he sees that we're hardly wearing any clothing.

"Where are you two going? The hot tub?"

"Nope, and you're not invited," I say with a pointed look at Cobra.

He's constantly trying to get us to swap male partners, and I'm not really interested in that right now. Things are so new with Campbell and I don't want to push it. Maybe I will in the future, but only after everything is more normalized.

"Fine," he says with a pout, and goes back to whatever he was doing.

I slide open the glass door, and pull Jinx out with me. She immediately begins to shiver. *Maybe this is a bad idea to do this up here.* I don't want it to be quick. I want to take my time with her, but I also don't want to wait and have her change her mind. But if I'm rushing it just to get it done, is it really worth it?

I pause and face her after I slide the door shut behind me. "It's freezing out here, and initially this is going to suck, but I promise you that it'll be worth it."

I take a step back from her and close my eyes, allowing my angelic blood to push to the surface and release my wings. Jinx lets out a soft gasp when they're at their full size. I'm not an exceptionally tall person, but my wingspan makes up for it in spades. I reach for her and she takes my hand. I pull her against me with one hand and with the other I reach behind me and pluck a feather from my wing.

"Hold on to this for me, would ya?" I say as I hand it to her.

She takes it and turns it over in her hand. The sun shining down on it shows off the pearlescent glow of the white feather. She beams up at me.

"It's beautiful," she says.

"I'm glad you like it." In any other circumstance, I would have spent more time deciding on which one to use, but she seems to like spontaneity so it'll work.

I grab her under her knees and lift her up so that her legs are wrapped around my waist. Her eyes go wide with understanding as she braces her hands on my shoulders. I leap into the air and begin beating my wings, flying in the direction of the forest. When I take off, Jinx lets out a squeal of surprise and glee.

She giggles nervously as we fly out of sight of the cabin. "This is beautiful, but a little scary."

"It'll get better and less scary, I promise," I say and come to a halt. "Can you put that shield up around us to protect us from the elements? It just needs to be big enough to surround us."

She holds out a hand and closes her eyes, and I watch as a sphere goes up around us. It looks just like a bubble—like it would pop if I poked it hard enough. It's instantly warmer, and her shivering settles down.

I do a little magic of my own, and make the rest of our clothing disappear. The added warmth, plus having her here in my arms, ready to take her as my mate, instantly makes me hard.

"I've been dying to do this, Jinx. I want you to be mine so fucking bad. If you have any other reservations about it, tell me now."

She shakes her head, biting her lip.

"Use your words, Little Witch," I remind her. I need her verbal confirmation that this is what she wants.

"I'm ready. I'm so ready."

"Feather?" I ask, and she hands it to me.

I place it in my teeth, then I line myself up at her entrance and thrust up inside of her. She cries out at the intrusion. I usually give her a little time to warm up before just shoving myself inside of her, but I can't wait. Not this time.

I begin fucking her hard and fast, her little gasps and moans encouraging me to take what I want from her. With both hands on her ass, I begin bouncing her up and down on my cock. She feels amazing around me.

When I can feel her getting close, I remove one hand from her, and pull the feather out of my mouth. "I fucking love you, Jinx."

I press the feather to her chest, right between her bouncing breasts as I continue driving myself inside of her. The feather binds to her flesh. She cries out at the searing pain that I knew it would cause before it disappears inside of her. Golden light spreads out from the spot where the feather melded to her skin; it blooms like cracking glass, glowing bright and warm.

Her bright eyes meet mine, her mouth falls open, and she cries out as she milks my cock, making me spill inside of her. Her head drops to my shoulder and she chuckles against my skin before placing a soft kiss to my collar bone.

"That was one hell of an experience," she says with a happy sigh. "I'll be chasing that high for a while. Why did I wait so long?"

"I've been asking myself that for weeks."

She kisses me hard, smiling against my mouth. She's sated, and happy, and it's all I wanted. It's a relief. I hoped that she would be happy once we completed our mating, but there was a part of me that worried that she would regret it.

I slip out of her, and my cum drips out of her, falling to the forest below. She tips her head to look down and cackles.

"I hope no animals were walking by, or else they just got a snow shower they didn't bargain for." Her gaze returns to mine, and she presses her forehead to mine. "I'm sorry I made you wait, but this was perfect."

"You know we technically didn't *have* to have sex in order for the ritual to take? I just knew the binding would be painful, so I figured I would use it to our advantage."

"You're brilliant," she says. "Can we head back? I'm tired, and my magic is struggling."

"Yeah. Let's go cuddle up with the others and watch a movie or something."

She drops the shield, and I take back off toward the cabin. A few minutes later we land on the deck and my wings fold back inside of me. I usher her back into the cabin. It's quiet, and the guys aren't where we left them. We weren't gone for long. Something smells like it's on fire, but I don't see any smoke.

"Something isn't right," Jinx whispers. "Let's go check the bedrooms," she suggests.

"Together though. Do not leave my side," I say.

She nods and we head toward her bedroom. The door is open and there's no one inside. She pulls on a pair of jeans and one of Colt's T-shirts. I put my own clothes back on. My phone is still on the dresser where I left it. I pick it up and dial Archer's number. The ringing is distant, and sounds like it's in the living room.

Jinx and I give each other a look. "Come with me," I whisper, and pull her through the bathroom she shares with me and Campbell. I open my sock drawer, and pull out my police issued weapon.

We creep through the halls and check the other bedrooms and bathrooms. They're all empty. Taking a deep breath, I lead her back to the living room where we heard Archer's phone. It's not out in plain sight, so I text it. It pings, giving away its location in the couch cushions. I pull it out from between the cushions and try to unlock it. He has a pin set on it, which I should have suspected.

"Fuck," I whisper.

"Give it here," Jinx says, and I hand it over. She immediately punches in the pin and it unlocks for her.

"How do you know his pin?" I ask.

"He gave it to me the day after we mated. He said that he wanted me to know what I had got myself into, and that he wanted me to be involved in his businesses."

"Businesses," I scoff. Nothing Archer does is above board. "Anything on it that can help us?"

Jinx goes white. "The last app he had open was the security app monitoring the downstairs. It looks like Trixie is gone."

Chapter Thirty Five

Jinx

"Where could she have gone? How did she get out?" I ask as we head downstairs to the basement.

The smell of sulfur and smoke assaults my senses. Archer only smells of sulfur when he's performing magic, and only for a second.

"Lesser demons," Sully answers my unasked question. "They can't mask their smell like the archdemons can."

"Could it be a succubus?" I ask my first thought being Lanya.

"No, succubi and incubi smell sweet to attract prey. I'm thinking maybe some imps or shadow demons. That's not to say that Lanya couldn't have hired them. They're easy for more powerful demons to influence."

We get the rest of the way down into the dungeon. There are scorch marks all over the floors. The bullet proof glass that was keeping Trixie in is now shattered, and her cell is empty. The rest of the council supporters are still in their cells though.

"Who did it?" I demand of the man in the first cell. I haven't bothered learning his name. He's going to be killed at some point anyway.

"Like I would tell you," he snaps.

"You're protecting someone who couldn't even be bothered to bust you out."

"All for the greater good," he says.

Growling in frustration, I storm out of the dungeon. My heart is pounding in my chest. My guys are gone.

"I'm going to kill that fucking pixie," I snarl.

Sully grabs my wrist and spins me around to face him. "We'll find them. It'll be okay."

"How the fuck did they get four men as powerful as the guys out of here? Why didn't they just kill them?"

"Because I wanted to watch you suffer," Lanya says from the loft.

I don't even think, I just lob a ball of ice at her face. It's not as strong as I would normally be able to cast thanks to using the shield spell earlier, but it'll do. The railing to the loft splinters and Lanya is knocked backwards. I'll deal with the destruction I'm causing later.

I use my air magic to propel me up to the loft. Lanya is trapped under the boulder sized ice ball. A menacing laugh tumbles out of my mouth.

"Where are my mates?" I demand.

She's struggling to breathe under the weight of the ice. Fire surfaces on my fingertips and I direct it at the ice to melt it enough that Lanya can breathe again.

"Don't make me ask a second time. I'm losing my patience."

Her succubus influence creeps over my skin, trying to draw me toward her. The place where Sully planted the feather turns hot, and deflects the spell she's trying to put me under just as Sully enters the loft.

"You're going to want to answer my mate before she gets really mad," Sully says with a smug look on his face.

Lanya's eyes go wild. "You mated both of them?!" she shrieks. "You selfish bitch!"

"If by 'both of them' you mean Sully, Colt, Archer, and Campbell, then yes. I did. Now where are my mates?"

Lanya mutters something under her breath and her hands go up in flames like torches. The ice melts enough that she's able to shove it off of her. She screams in frustration and jumps to her feet.

"I'm going to kill you. Archer was supposed to be mine!"

"And Campbell was supposed to be mine," Trixie says, materializing out of nowhere. Ropes of light emit from her hands, and begin to wind their way around me. Sully holds up his hands and sends a blast of radiant white energy toward Trixie, knocking her backwards.

"You were never more than a one night stand for him," Sully says with a laugh. "He was destined to be with both me and Jinx."

"No! He was meant to be mine. Our offspring will be powerful! I've seen visions of it!"

My mouth pops open in shock before blinding white rage takes over. The fact that she's even thought about having children with *my* mate makes me murderous.

I hold out my hand and begin chanting one of the old spells that Linnie taught me. A string of latin pours from my mouth, and Trixie screams in horrified pain. Blood starts dripping from her nose, and she drops to her knees.

"What are you doing to her?!" Lanya screams and she lunges for me, but Sully hits her with more of his angelic power.

Lanya's skin blisters like boiling hot water was poured over her entire body.

"Please stop!" Trixie screams between gasping breaths.

I press even more energy into my spell. Her screams cease as she explodes from a point within her, purple blood and body parts splattering across the entire loft and down into the living room.

Panting from the magical exertion I move toward Lanya whose skin is practically melting off of her body.

"Tell me where they are."

"I'll see you in hell, bitch." She growls as she passes out on the once white carpet.

Her body erupts into flames and I immediately douse them with water. I reach in her dress pocket and find her cell phone. Her fingerprints are too melted off to access the bio security on her phone.

I scream and chuck her phone at the wall then run my fingers through my hair which is coated in pixie blood.

"They can't have got far with them," Sully says, placing a gentle hand on my shoulder. "We'll find them. They're a part of you. Your soul won't rest until they're back with you, Jinx."

I gasp in realization, then sit cross-legged on the floor and close my eyes. Breathing deeply I push my powers out past myself seeking the small tendrils of energy that connect me to my mates. The place where the feather resides burns hot with Sully being so close, and at first it's distracting. I push past it, and slowly my mate mark from Colt warms, followed by my blood, and then my bones. Each of them tying me to one of my guys.

I stand and follow the trail out the front door. My bare feet hit the snow and steam rises up around me, my entire body might as well be on fire, but I can't feel it. To me it's just a pleasant warmth. I don't know how long I'm walking, but eventually the threads begin pulsing. Leading me to the mouth of a cave. I step inside and find them all coming to consciousness, bound by rope.

They each attempt to break their bindings. Archer attempts to shift, but the rope must have antimagic properties. I grab the rope on Colt's wrists, and a searing pain flashes through my palms.

"What the fuck?" I growl.

"Let me try," Sully says. He grabs the rope and he has the same reaction.

"It's demonic magic," Archer says. "You'll have to cancel it with a spell. The dark magic attached to it is reacting with your angelic blood."

"I'm not an angel though," I say with a furrowed brow.

"No, but you mated one. You have radiant energy in your system now."

My mind is racing with how that might complicate my relationship with Archer, but for now I need to figure out how to get my guys freed. I outstretch my hand and mutter a disintegration spell, aiming the power at Archer's rope first. The rope starts burning in the center and the flame travels out to the ends, turning the rope to ash.

Once his hands are free he's able to render the other ropes useless. The guys break free of their bindings and rush toward me, each of them touching me, and making sure I'm alright.

"I'm fine, guys. A little space, though, please."

"I'm going to kill—" Campbell says moving toward the mouth of the cave.

"We handled it," I say, placing a gentle hand on his shoulder. "Trixie and Lanya are both dead. We just have to hope that none of the other council members come looking for them."

My gaze shifts around to the four powerful men that Sully and I just saved. "How the hell did they get the jump on you, anyway?"

"Lanya had somehow managed to get inside of the house without triggering our security system. I'm still trying to figure out how. She knocked Ranger and me unconscious and then I'm guessing did the same to the other two. When we woke up we were here."

I laugh softly, and the guys give me a curious look.

"Something funny, Jinx?" Cobra asks with a menacing stare.

"Well, now you guys can't tell me I'm not allowed to be alone. If you can get kidnapped too, and I'm able to save you, then sometimes it's best if we're not all together."

"You're still not allowed alone," Colt says. "What if you had been at the house? She might have killed you."

"Oh she definitely would have. Or Trixie would have done it for her." I say with a snort. "They thought that I didn't deserve any of you."

Among all the other thoughts bouncing around in my brain, one stands out. I'm starting to feel as though I *do* deserve them. I saved them. maybe I can actually be enough for them.

"Let's get back to the cabin. I'm cold and hungry and exhausted." I start walking toward the cabin.

"Yeah, alright," Archer says and begins leading the way back to the cabin.

I move to follow him and Colt grabs my hand. "You do deserve us, Minxy. I don't care how long it takes to prove it to you, but you do." He slides his hand up to my jaw and pushes my chin up with his thumb. "You're amazing in every possible way." He gives me one intense, meaningful kiss.\

He takes a step back and asks, "Where are your shoes?"

"There wasn't any time for shoes. I needed to find you all."

Archer's head snaps in our direction and he runs back and scoops me up in his arms. "You're not walking back barefoot."

"The angelic bond isn't bothering you?"

"No. As long as you don't use any of its power on me, I'll be fine. And even if you did, It's going to take a little more than some heavenly ties to take me out. Even Sully wouldn't be able to take me down. It would take a full-blooded angel."

"And what about if I get pregnant?" I say, refusing to make eye contact.

"I'm not sure, but we'll cross that bridge when we come to it, Little Star. One task at a time."

I nod, my heart cracking a little. As my ascension draws near, I'm beginning to look forward to a normal life with my guys—whatever normal looks like with five men. I can only hope that I didn't complicate things.

Chapter Thirty Six

Jinx

A couple of weeks later, we're packing up our hiking gear into Archer's SUV and head toward the mountain. Archer had a clean-up team and a construction crew at the house within hours of the fight with Trixie and Lanya. No one asked a single question, and they had it cleaned up and rebuilt within two days.

The car is quiet except for the radio which is playing some K-pop song that Cobra insisted that we all listen to, and while I appreciate his excitement, I cannot understand the appeal. The drive to the mountain feels like it takes forever and not enough time all at once. Butterflies dance in my gut as we approach the trail head.

Archer puts the car in park and it's as if everyone in the car collectively inhales, and never breathes back out. The air is tense and I imagine it will be until we've accomplished what we've come here to do.

We all pull on our snow pants and mountain climbing boots and begin trudging up the trail together. The weather gets increasingly more harsh as we continue up the slope.

"Do you think this is really going to fix anything?" I ask Archer after about thirty minutes of unbearable silence.

"I don't know. But I do know that if we don't try, the world will end and so will our time together. I need you, Little Star. I need this entire group of misfits. So if you have any hope at all, hold on to it tight. I believe in you one hundred percent."

He pulls me in and kisses my head. "I love you. I know that I don't say it much, but I do. I've never had these feelings for anyone but Ranger before, and if I lose you, I don't know that I'll ever have a love like this again. Neither of you are allowed to leave me, got it?"

"Yes, sir," I say with a smirk.

"Let's get this thing done so that we can get back to the cabin and back into bed," Cobra says behind us.

"Is that all you think about?" Colt asks.

"Yes. It is. Isn't it all you think about? Putting your seed in that warm wet cunt."

"I know that you're just trying to lighten the mood, but it's not really working," Archer chastises him.

"That's not all I'm trying to do. I'm also reminding Jinx that the second this is over, she owes you a baby."

"Oh that's right," Campbell says. "So after the demon baby, do the rest of us get to take turns knocking you up?"

"Oh! I call second!" Cobra says.

"Woah! Let's enjoy our first hypothetical baby before we plan any others." I say, still anxious that I won't even be able to give Archer the baby I promised him. "Eventually, sure. But I'm not a broodmare."

"You could be though," Cobra says, and smacks my ass. The blow is dulled by the snow suit.

We continue our hike up the trail. The wind bites our cheeks as we trudge through the snow and ice to get to our destination. It should only be an hour hike, but considering the task that lays ahead, that's too much.

I'm in good shape from my time stripping, and the guys are all in great shape too, but hiking through the elements is an entirely different beast altogether.

We stop periodically for water; Archer insists that we stay well hydrated. On our third stop, I take a sip of water then slip the bottle into my bag. Colt pulls me into his arms and holds on tight.

"This is too real, now," he whispers. "We'll be right there with you, but I need you to stay safe. I need us to have a normal life together."

"What about our group is normal?" I ask with a laugh.

"You know what I mean. I need for us to be able to enjoy each other and the rest of these guys. I want for us to go on dates, and make out in the backs of movie theaters like a couple of kids. I want to take you to dinner. And someday—once you're done with school—I want to marry you.

"And I know you're going to get all weird about it, because commitment and you're not good enough and whatever else. But even if it's just a little ceremony, I want to show the world that you're mine. So just think about it, okay?"

"Yeah, okay," I agree.

Marriage is going to be weird with this many partners. Despite a lot of supes being polyamorous by nature, the human laws prevent the marriage of more than one partner. It's antiquated and frustrating.

"We've only got about another fifteen minutes to the top. Are you ready?" Archer asks.

"Not even a little bit," I answer honestly. "But I'll get it done."

He kisses me on the forehead and holds me to him. "We'll all be right there with you."

We pick up our trek and complete the climb. At the top of the mountain there's a flat circle that's covered in two feet of snow and likely ice under the snow. The weather is picking up and a blizzard blows up around us.

"I suspect that whatever we need for the ritual is below the ice," I say. "I can melt it, but that'll take a lot of energy."

"I've got it," Archer says. He crouches down to the ground and presses his hands into the snow.

The snow begins to sizzle around his hands, and the ground rumbles beneath our feet. The snow and ice begins to melt, revealing a large round slab of stone with carvings covering the entire surface.

The carvings are unfamiliar to me; they don't look like any symbols or languages that I've ever seen—not that I'm a linguist or anything. I inhale sharply and walk to the center. There's a strong magical aura about the slab of stone. It hums with power and pulls me to it.

"Does anyone recognize these symbols?" I ask.

"They're celestial," Sully says. "They're some sort of spell..."

"Can you type out what they say on your phone? I suspect I'll need to recite them during the ritual."

He pulls out his phone and sets to work deciphering the marks. I check the time. It's ten o'clock. My heart is hammering in my chest, and my stomach is twisting into knots. A million thoughts soar through my mind about the possibility of something going wrong.

"We have twenty-seven minutes to complete the ritual. I think I should start at about ten twenty-three just to be sure that we have the time to complete it."

I wrap my arms around myself and shiver. Even with the heavy gear that I'm wearing, now that we've stopped moving the chill of the mountain air is settling in. I consider putting up a shield to protect us from the elements, but I'm not sure how much of my magic I'll need to complete the ritual.

Archer wraps his arms around me. He's in his human form since it was easier for him to find snow gear for that form. I stare up at him through my protective goggles.

"This is going to go fine, Little Star. Remember—you owe me a baby. Nothing can happen to us until you hold up your end of the bargain."

He tips my chin up and kisses me. Even though it's icy up here on the mountain, his lips are warm and inviting.

"I wish we were warm and in bed. I hate the cold," I say once our lips part.

"Soon enough. As soon as this is done I'm not letting you leave bed for a week. Maybe more."

"Promise?" I tease.

"I promise," he whispers and kisses me softly.

His actions tell me that he's just as worried as I am. He's always caring, but he's never this soft with me. He's trying to reassure me which is just making me more anxious. I step away from him and curse under my breath. Why did something this important have to be placed on my shoulders? I'm just a nobody stripper. Then maybe my lack of family made me the perfect one to tie to this task.

The minutes tick by impossibly slow. The guys take turns holding me and trying to tell me it will all be okay, but something in my gut is warning me that this is going to go south.

Finally it's just a few minutes before the peak of the solstice. I stand in the center of the disk and take a deep breath. The guys—the relics—arrange themselves at four equal points around the disk. Sully stands to the side and watches over us.

Dropping to my knees, I pull off my gloves. The cold immediately stings my hands. The guys each follow suit. We each brought a pocket knife with us for letting blood. With a deep breath, I slide my blade across my palm and hold it over the center of the disk where the recess is.

The second my blood touches the disk, it illuminates with bright white energy. The power of it thrums through my body and I watch each of the guys cut their own palms and squeeze their blood into the divots at their points on the disk.

The light grows even brighter. I don't need Sully's translation. I can feel the spell in my bones. Against my will I begin chanting:

Divine Constellation, hear my plea
Four relics of Libra I bring to thee
To undo the selfish wonder,
That has torn the sky asunder,
I draw upon your divine magic,
I worship at your altar,
The wrongs are most tragic,
But still I do not falter
My heart is pure,
My soul complete,
Take all that I give,
So a new world we can meet.

Initially, nothing happens. I worry that we're too late.

The ground quakes beneath my boots. Frigid air blasts up around me and a star situated directly above me burns brighter than any star I've ever seen. For a moment I think it's falling to the earth, ready to collide with the mountain we occupy.

In the distance are the shouts of the guys. I want to look. I want to see what's happening, but I can't take my eyes off of that burning bright star. My soul feels like it's being pulled upward. The magical essence of my blood rushes to my heart and for the briefest of moments I feel as though it may explode.

I'm suddenly very aware of the thin magical lines—like strings—that link me to the guys; to my mates. I'm suspended, floating, as the power transfers from them to me, then to the sky. One final pulse of energy bursts out from my body and the star flares—then dies. A large black spot takes its place in the sky. Somewhere in my mind I hear the words 'well done'.

Then I'm falling. My stomach leaps toward my throat and a scream passes my lips. I call for my air magic, but it doesn't come to the surface. Something makes an impact with my side, and the wind is knocked from my lungs.

Chapter Thirty Seven
Colt

Jinx completes the spell, and her body levitates into the air. Her arms are out the side, and a bright light emanating from the ground, from her, and from the star above her make her look angelic—even in her mountain climbing attire.

There's a tug from deep within. Starting from my neck and working its way down my spine then out my limbs, I can feel the relic power pulling away like someone peeling tape from my bones. There's no visual representation of it, but with every piece of the power that leaves my body, Jinx burns brighter and brighter. It's as though she may erupt into radiant flames without warning.

I'm so distracted by her beauty that my animal instincts aren't tuned into the people climbing up the mountain around us. It isn't until the *POP* of a gun peals through the air on the mountain top that I realize anything is wrong.

The gunshot is followed by a roar of pain from Archer. It's unlikely that a gun would kill him even if he were shot in the heart, but it would hurt him, and possibly incapacitate him.

He drops to the ground before his body begins trembling from the shift into his demon form. Cobra rushes to Archer's side before another gunshot rings through the air. This time it was aimed at Jinx. It somehow misses her, and I scan the area for the source of the shots.

My eyes land on a man across the mountain top holding a handgun. I dash across the disk toward the man. He doesn't see me coming. I leap through the air and tackle him to the ground. We almost roll over the edge and down a steep cliff, but the stars must be watching over me, because we stop short.

I pin him beneath me and begin slamming his head against the ground over and over until crimson begins leaking out around him. Stupid fuck should have thought twice. Did they not see what we did at the farmhouse?

Another shot goes off, and I search for the other gunman, but I don't see him anywhere. Back on the disk, the other four are engaged in either hand to hand combat or magical combat with men wearing all black and ski masks.

Campbell is beating the shit out of one of the men, while Cobra has one of them lifted telekinetically off the ground. He lifts him impossibly high while causing the man's body to spin. His arms and legs splay out like a starfish, he looks like a fan rotating in the air.

Vomit begins raining from the man in the sky. It occurs to me that he probably vomited through his ski mask, and the mental visual makes me chuckle. Then he stops spinning. Then he stops levitating. Then he's falling back to earth from the equivalent of about twelve stories, gaining speed as he drops. His body hits the ground with a sickening thud.

Archer is crushing a man's skull between his hands until it smooshes like a grape. Sully is stripping off his shirt. I'm too busy trying to make sure everyone else is alright that I don't hear two men sneaking up behind me. They each grab one of my arms and slam me down to the ground.

A third man approaches and stands over me. "I had hoped for better from you," he says, and fires a gun into my thigh.

Agonized screams tear from my throat. My healing doesn't kick in. The bullet must be coated in something and made of silver. I thrash beneath the men who are holding me down. They're strong, but I manage to shrug them off. I attempt to shift, but my panther won't surface, so I push to my feet instead. I spin to face them, but they turn and amble away from me. I turn back to the last remaining threat.

My gaze shifts around the disk, searching for Jinx's other guys. Archer is now being held down by three men. Sully and Campbell are nowhere to be seen. Cobra seems to be holding his own, but who knows for how long.

I hop, dragging my injured leg behind me and swing for the man who shot me. He ducks out of the path of my fist with ease. I slip my hand in my pocket and firmly grasp the pocket knife, careful not to telegraph any of my movements.

"You're all a bunch of fools protecting that girl," he growls through his ski mask. "And now the lot of you will die, and this will have all been for nothing. My sacrifice will have been for *nothing!*"

He points the gun directly at my head. I make my move and whip my pocket knife at him. It finds its mark right between his eyes. His stunned gaze lingers on me as his body drops to the ground.

Limping as fast as I can, I approach and pull my knife from his skull. I pull the ski mask back. Bile rises in my throat when I find my brother beneath the mask. Realization falls over me—he's not my brother. He just looks like him. Or at least what I suspect he would look like in about twenty years.

My body is going into shock from the blood loss. With no small amount of effort I pull my belt from my pants, and slice into the fabric of my snowpants. I tear the material using every ounce of strength I have left. and slide my belt around my leg, cinching it tight above the wound. As I lie my head on the cold ground, my mind drifts to the man bleeding next to me on the ground.

A blinding white light flares, and a pulse of magic washes over me.

Then...there's nothing.

Chapter Thirty Eight

Archer

The first shot tears through the flesh of my shoulder. I can't hold back the roar of pain as my body shifts, trying to protect me from further harm. My clothing shreds and I'm left nearly naked on the top of a mountain in nearly below zero temperatures. Cobra rushes to my side.

"Get away from me!" I shout. "It'll be easier to pick us off if we're all in one spot. We need to split up to make it harder to kill all of us. As long as one of us is alive, Jinx is safe."

Ranger nods and darts away from me, taking control of one of the masked men as he does. Two men rush at me. My fist collides with the face of the first one, sending him back about ten feet. As he falls, his head connects with the stone surface below and he stops moving. He might be dead, he might be knocked unconscious, either way I don't care. They'll all be dead in a moment.

The second man leaps at me with a dagger in his fist. I reel back and kick him square in the chest sending him flying backward. Then I leap on top of him and begin pummeling him into the ground. He drops his dagger and I pick it up. The fucking thing is coated in holy oil and sears my hand, but I persist. I drive the dagger into his right eye and twist.

My victory is short-lived as two more men leap onto my back. Grabbing one of them with both hands, I flip him over my head and slam him on the ground before pulling the dagger out of the eye of the first man and plunging it into the new guy's chest.

The remaining one reaches around my face and claws at it relentlessly which only serves to piss me off. I grab his puny human arms and slam myself onto my back crushing him between my weight and the ground. Rolling off of him, I nimbly get to my feet. I take his head in my hands, lift him off the ground and begin to shatter the bone between my hands. The skull cracks and folds in on itself, brain matter and blood going everywhere.

Being the largest threat, the men keep coming for me. I'm watching Cobra manage two more men when a searing hot pain snakes its way around my throat–more bloody holy oil, and a silver chain. The men wielding the chain run around me, wrapping the length completely around my neck and squeezing to cut off the air.

Pushing through the pain I grab either end of the chain in my fists and hold on tight as I begin spinning. For three glorious seconds the men's feet lift off the ground, and they shriek in frustration as their hands slip off of the oil covered metal. I pull the chain off and throw it on the ground.

Another gunshot rings through the air, and I search for the source of the sound. Colt is on the ground, a man in a ski mask standing above him. He shakes off the men holding him to the ground.

"Ranger!" I shout. "Save the kitten!"

Ranger turns his attention to the men who were holding Colt, and takes control of their faculties. They walk, one foot in front of the other, right off the side of the mountain. I don't immediately see Sully and Campbell, but most of the men on the top of the mountain have been neutralized.

Colt is on his feet, and he takes out the last of the men that I have eyes on. Screams draw my attention away from him, and I rush to the side of the mountain where I find Campbell handling three more men. Sully is in the air, a lasso of radiant light wrapped around another one of the council's goons. He cinches it tight and bifurcates the fucker.

"Archer!" Ranger calls, in a panic.

He's standing over Colt. My footsteps thunder across the stone slab, and I land at Colt's side. The wound where Colt was shot is still bleeding. He should have healed by now, but it's pouring, coating the ground beneath him. He's unconscious, and the area around the entrance wound looks like it's already infected. Over my dead body will we lose him.

I scoop him up in my arms just as Sully and Campbell join us.

"I'm taking him back to the cabin. Campbell, and Cobra, you're with me! Sully, get our girl and get back. We'll get the car later! Hold on tight, fuckers!"

As soon as I feel their hands on me, I transport us to the summoning circle in the dungeon of the cabin. Cradling Colt in my arms, I kick open the door to the infirmary.

Chapter Thirty Nine

Sully

Jinx's body begins lifting into the air toward the bright star that looks like it's about to explode in the sky. She continues raising off the ground—fifteen, twenty, thirty, forty, fifty feet.

Seconds pass, and then minutes. We're all so enraptured with her that the gunshot startles us all as the bullet tears through Archer's flesh, splattering the enormous stone disk with his blood.

I waste no time stripping off my coat and shirt and taking to the sky to search for the threat. A couple dozen men are scaling the side of the mountain on top of the few that have already made it to the top.

"Camp!" I shout and swoop down to grab him just as another shot rings through the air, narrowly missing Jinx.

Colt is on top of the guy before he can even pull back the hammer on his gun and take a second shot. I take Campbell to the area with the largest concentration of guys, and summon my light blade.

"You ready?" I ask Campbell.

"Let's do this." He pulls two guns out of his waistband and checks both of them to make sure they're properly loaded and the safety is off.

I fly down to where four of them are congregated in one spot and spin in an enormous circle. I nearly behead one of them and cut the other three.

Bringing the blade back up to Camp, he takes the tip of the blade in his mouth and groans, his eyes turning black. He steps toward the three men, and holds out a hand, allowing his blood hunter magic to flow through him. The three men explode into pieces in unison. The onlookers hesitate. Two of them go running down the hill, but Camp shoots each of them in the back of the head. Their bodies tumble forward with the momentum, until they hit the base of the mountain.

"Go keep an eye on Jinx! I can handle the rest of these guys!" he calls.

There are only five of them. I have complete faith he can handle it. I take off toward the sky; toward Jinx. A bullet whizzes past me distracting me from my task. Two gunmen are on the other side of the mountain from where Campbell and I were fighting.

I fly down, now with two light blades in my hands. They each take shots at me, but miss every time. Once I'm within about fifteen feet of them, I realize that I made a mistake. One of them isn't a man at all, but a salamander in disguise.

A broad grin takes over his scaly face, and a stream of fire pours out of his mouth. I turn just in time to get my body out of the way, but his dragon breath catches my wings. I put away my blades and summon a spear instead. I chuck it at the guy next to the salamander, then summon my lasso.

The scaly son of a bitch doesn't have a chance as the radiant rope loops around his waist. He tries to destroy it with his fire, but fails. Nothing but demon magic can extinguish the light of my weapons. I lift him up, twenty feet off the ground, and using two hands I pull on the rope as hard as I can. It sears through his flesh, and cuts him in half, both pieces of him tumbling down the mountain.

Between Cobra and Archer, the top of the mountain is clear. A couple of men from their side turned tail and ran when they realized the mistake they made. Campbell has at least five more bodies he can claim laying around the ground in front of him.

I pick him up and bring him to where Archer and Cobra are. Archer has an incapacitated Colt in his arms. Archer yells for me to go get Jinx and bring her home. Just as they disappear, the top of the mountain goes dark, and Jinx is plummeting back to the earth. I fly up and grab her, and head toward the cabin.

Chapter Forty

Jinx

My stomach leaps toward my throat and a scream passes my lips. I call for my air magic, but it doesn't come to the surface. Something makes an impact with my side, and the wind is knocked from my lungs. It's Sully.

"Hey, Little Witch. Let's get you back to the cabin."

Sully is bare chested so that his wings are able to move freely.

"Aren't you freezing?!" I ask.

"A little, but it was more important that I get you to safety."

"What do you mean? It's done. The ritual is over."

Sully doesn't respond. The sick feeling returns to my stomach. He stays quiet the entire way back to the cabin. He takes me inside and I strip out of my cold gear and face him. It's only then that I see that his wings are singed.

"Where are the others?" I demand.

"We weren't alone on the mountain."

"What?" I say with a gasp. "Who else—"

"Jinx!" Cobra yells from the dungeon.

I shoot Sully one last horrified look then sprint toward the stairs. My cheeks and hands are chapped from the mountain air. My body hurts from expending so much magic. The links to my mates are there, but the one tying me to Colt is weak; like a neon light that's about to burn out.

Cobra takes my arm the second I'm in the dungeon and leads me through a door at the back. It leads to a small infirmary with an immense amount of medications, medical equipment, and jars with herbs and tinctures.

Colt is laying on a cot. He's pale and sickly. The others are standing around him arguing.

"What's wrong with him?" I demand.

"We don't know. Likely some sort of poison, but without knowing which one we can't treat it. He's fading fast, Jinx," Campbell says, lacing his fingers with mine.

"Can't you heal him?" I ask. It's not directed at anyone in particular, but I know that Sully and Campbell both have healing abilities.

"I tried, Buttercup, but there's something stopping it."

Sully moves to Colt's side and begins inspecting the wound before cursing under his breath.

"What's wrong?" I ask.

"It's some sort of venom. Either Naga or salamander judging by the color, and considering they had a salamander on their payroll..."

"How do we fix it?"

"We need the antidote. I don't suppose you have any here, do you Archer?"

"Give me a minute," Archer says and begins rifling through one of the cabinets.

I stand by Colt's side and take his hand in mine. I place a soft kiss on his lips as a tear rolls down my cheek and splashes on his face.

"I'm so sorry," I whisper against his cheek.

Archer returns with a small vial and a needle. He draws the bright green liquid into the needle and begins injecting it into the muscle surrounding the wound. Once the entire vial is gone, he grabs a large pair of tweezers and digs in the wound to retrieve the bullet.

"It seems like it came out in one piece," he says, inspecting the hunk of metal. "It's fucking silver, too. Sadistic fucks. That was all of the antivenom that I had for salamander toxin. If we had administered it immediately, I would feel a lot more confident about it working. As it is, we'll just have to wait and see."

A choked sob escapes me, and I press my ear to Colt's chest. His heartbeat is weak and unsteady. My big panther looks so weak and helpless on this bed.

"Please don't leave me, Colt. Please. I need you." In a whisper I add, "I love you."

"So we just have to be on our deathbeds for her to admit she loves us?" Cobra jokes behind me.

A grunt tells me that one of the other guys either elbowed him or punched him for the remark, and a smile briefly dances on my lips.

"Let's get him upstairs, Little Star. That way you can lay with him. Do you want me to call his brother?"

"Yes, please. Have one of your guys drive him up if possible."

He lifts Colt into his arms and we follow them up to the first floor. I grab some pajamas from my room on my way through, and join them in the loft.

"I'm going to shower really quick. Can someone stay with him while I do that?"

"Of course," Sully says and kisses me on the forehead.

Less than ten minutes later I'm stepping out of the bathroom with my hair in a towel, and my pajamas on. Sully is sitting on the edge of the bed with his head in his hands.

"Are you okay?" I ask, softly.

"Just exhausted," he says and he stands from the bed. "I'm going to shower. Lay with your mate. Get some rest."

I grab him by the wrist as he tries to step by me. "You're my mate, too," I remind him.

"I know. I wasn't saying that to be petty. I think that your presence is probably the best thing for him right now. It'll help him heal. So go. Lay with him."

He kisses me and steps into the bathroom and shuts the door.

I lay with Colt for hours. His breathing becomes stronger and more stable. His heartbeat returns to its regular state, but he doesn't wake up. Eventually I drift off, cuddled up next to him.

"Jinx," Archer's voice filters through my dreams. "Jinx!"

I bolt upright and glance around the room. Archer is standing next to the bed with a plate of food and a glass of water. Niall is with him.

"Hey, Niall," I whisper.

"Any change?" he asks. He looks tired; distant.

"His heartbeat sounds better than it did earlier," I say, taking the plate of food from Archer. It's just spaghetti, and some garlic bread, but I'm starving. "Thank you," I say before taking a bite.

I turn so I can watch Colt. His color is returning to normal. I pull back the sheet and am relieved to find the grotesque coloring around the wound is already disappearing.

"How did your ascension go?" Niall asks.

"Aside from Colt getting shot?" I ask, bitterly. It's not directed toward him. I'm just mad that they got the jump on us.

"I meant the actual ascension. Is it done?"

"Only time will tell if the other Zodiacs did their part, but yes. It's done."

"Good. At least this won't have been for nothing," Niall says, pulling his knees up and wrapping his arms around them. "I know things were rough with us in the beginning, but I'm glad it was you, Minxy. He never stopped caring about you."

I nod as I take a bite of my food. "It was always going to be us."

Archer takes my plate once I'm done with my food, and I step into the bathroom. I look like I've aged ten years in the last forty eight hours. Maybe I did. Sewing up the rift drained almost every ounce of energy out of me.

"Fuck!" I say, remembering the way that my magic refused to answer me when I was falling through the air.

"Everything okay?" Archer calls through the door.

I wrench the door open. "Are your powers still working?"

"Yes, why?"

I try to conjure my fire magic, but it doesn't surface.

"Sully's was still working, and yours is still working. Niall, can you still shift?"

"I haven't tried, but I can feel my panther, so I assume so."

"Maybe the ritual just depleted your stores," Archer suggests.

"I'm worried that the actual magic is gone. Your magic comes from your bloodline. So does Niall's and Sully's."

"What about Cobra?" Niall asks.

"He's a mutant," Archer says dismissively. "Let me make some calls. I'll see if it's just you or if there are others who are suffering from it as well." Archer leaves Niall and I alone in the loft with Colt.

"A mutant?" Niall asks about Cobra.

"Yeah. He doesn't talk about it much," I say.

"And Campbell?"

"Apparently he's part demon," I say. "Some of my magic is natural ability, but the rest I had to learn. No matter which type I'm using, I have to pull from the elements. I'm worried that sewing up the rift removed the magic. Or at least it removed mine."

Niall reaches over and grabs my hand. "Either way, you'll be fine. You've got your guys, and me."

"Get off my girl, fucker," Colt says. His voice is raspy and his eyes are half closed.

"Yeah, and what are you going to do about it if I don't?" Niall challenges, playfully.

"As soon as the room stops spinning, I'll fucking kill you."

Niall snorts in response. "I'll leave you two alone, but I'll be right downstairs if either of you needs me."

"Thank you," I say, squeezing his hand.

"What happened?" Colt asks once Niall is out of the room.

I move up the bed so I'm sitting next to his side. "You were shot. There was venom on the bullet. You almost died. You know, the usual shit. How do you feel?"

"Like I got shot with a bullet coated in venom and almost died. Did the ritual work?"

"Time will tell. I'm so glad you're alive. I lo—"

"Don't say it right now. Wait until I'm healthy and you're not about to lose me. Okay?"

"Okay," I say and kiss him softly on the lips.

"Come here," he whispers and pulls me into him.

I nuzzle into his side, and rest my hand on his chest. "I'm glad you're okay."

A soft purr rumbles in his chest. "I'm glad *you're* okay. I was so worried about you. I'm just glad all that fuckery is over and we can just...exist."

"Me too."

There's a long silence, and for a second I think he's fallen back asleep. When he finally speaks, it startles me.

"I killed my dad," he says.

I sit up to look at him. "I thought he died when you were a baby, how on earth—"

"He was on the mountain," he whispers. "He abandoned me and Niall when we were babies, and we were working for opposite sides of this conflict. He was the one who shot me. He was going to kill you. So I put a knife between his eyes."

"Colt..." I don't know what to say. I wrack my brain for an appropriate response but it never comes.

He tucks his hand behind his head and looks at me. "I would kill every single person on this planet to keep you safe. Even Niall. The man I killed on the mountain may have provided part of my DNA, but he wasn't my family. He was one of the ones who was at the farmhouse. He helped Steve assault you. And my only regret is that he's dead and I didn't have the chance to dismember him while he was still breathing.

"I love you, Minxy. I love you more than anything. And stars help anyone who tries to hurt you."

"Did you talk to him at the farmhouse?"

He shakes his head. "I didn't even see him. Cobra told me. He was looking out for me. And I appreciate it. Even with the heads up, it still caught me off guard. I thought he was Niall at first."

"I'm sorry you had to do that."

"I'm not. It's his fault that we were in foster care all our lives."

I tip my head up and kiss him. He hums into my mouth, then pulls away.

"I wish my body weren't so fucked up. Nothing would make me feel better than to be inside of you."

"You need to rest. We both do. There will be plenty of time for that later."

We fall asleep together, and after a while I wake up to all the other guys cuddled up with us. I stifle a laugh when I find Cobra spooning Colt. Shifting just enough that I can see behind me, I find Camp pressed against my back.

"You okay?" he whispers, his voice raspy with sleep.

"I'm great," I say and kiss him. "I can't wait to get back home."

"Mmmm home. I guess that's what the mansion is now, isn't it?"

"Can you two keep it down? I need my beauty sleep," Cobra grumbles.

I snort. "Sure thing, princess."

He sits up rapidly, and stares at me over Colt. "Next time you take over in the bedroom, I'm gonna need you to call me that again. Dammit. Now I have a boner."

"Keep it away from me," Colt grumbles.

"You smell like death. I want nothing to do with you. Archer," Cobra whines, shaking Archer awake.

"Go back to sleep Ranger."

"But Archer!"

"*Now!*" Archer growls.

Cobra lays back on the bed and starts rubbing his cock.

"Ranger!" Archer yells.

"I can't sleep with a boner. And you're not helping, so I have to do it myself,"

"In the bed with the rest of us?" Sully asks, indignantly.

"I'll be quick."

"Take your time. From the smell of it, our little witch is turned on," Colt mumbles into my neck as he snuggles me tighter to him.

The others turn their attention to me, and descend on me like a meal they want to devour. While being mindful of everyone's injuries, we spend the rest of the early morning hours, enjoying the fact that we all made it out of the ritual alive.

Epilogue

Jinx

"I'm just glad that it's not just me. I'm sorry other people don't have access to their magic, but I was going to be pissed if I sacrificed all of my magic to sew up a rift that I didn't cause," I say before shoving a fork full of chicken salad into my mouth.

It's been two weeks since my ascension, and occasionally my magic flickers but it won't fully surface. There have been reports across the globe of people losing their powers.

The majority of the council have gone into hiding because supes started picking them off one by one after the truth was revealed about the prophecies.

None of that matters to me though. What matters is that I'm here, with my guys, enjoying our time together.

"Any news on whether that angel bond will fuck with her ability to carry our baby?" Cobra asks Archer.

"*My* baby. And from what I've been able to determine, it shouldn't cause a problem. There have been a couple of cases of angels actually mating with demons. The only thing that may happen is that the demonic properties may neutralize the angelic properties and the child may come out human."

"I'm sorry," I say, dropping my gaze to the table. "If you don't want to go through with it, I understand."

"What the fuck are you talking about?" Archer asks with an incredulous laugh.

"The whole reason you wanted to mate with me was so that I would produce a powerful heir for you. If I can't give you even a witch, there's not much point."

"How is it that you're still convinced that the only thing you bring to the table is your abilities. I love you, you silly girl. I want you to have my baby because I *want* a baby with you. So next time you're in heat, I'm knocking you up."

"Dude, how many times do we have to explain that it's not called a 'heat' when we're talking about a human?" Colt asks, slapping his hand to his forehead.

"I don't know. How many times do I have to tell you not to call me 'dude'?" Archer retorts, going back to answering emails on his phone.

Cobra leans in and says, "Just for the record, it is going to be *our* baby because I will not force you to bear my spawn. You don't need that burden on your shoulders."

"You don't want to walk around knowing that you put a baby in me?" I tease.

"Nothing terrifies me more than providing half a blueprint to a whole ass human. Nah, you can have Archer's baby, and I'll help raise it."

"I feel like you watching the baby is more terrifying than you contributing to a kid's genetics."

"Hmm, fair," he muses.

"I still don't think it's fair that he gets first dibs on having a baby with you. I've known you the longest," Colt protests.

"I'm the oldest, though."

"So because you're old enough to be her great great great grandfather, you get to knock her up first?"

"Don't make it weird," I scold Colt.

"Too late!" Niall calls from the next room before joining us with a carafe of fresh coffee.

"When do you move out again?" I snark.

"You didn't tell them?" Archer asks Niall.

"Tell us what?" Colt asks.

"I offered him a job in security for me in exchange for living here. And for a reasonable salary of course. He's taken a liking to one of my guards daughters and so he wants to stick around."

"Good for you," I say, earnestly. "What's her name?"

"Alex," Niall says, blushing brilliantly. "She's a wolf shifter."

Campbell and Sully finally make their way into the kitchen and plop down in front of their salads. I do not envy Archer's new cook. Not only does he have to provide food for all of the staff, but it's important that we all have our food made the way that we like it. I would probably have quit by now if I were him.

"I have news for you two!" Archer declares as they step into the room. "I pulled some strings and the investigation against you is being dropped at the station. I explained the situation, leaving out certain details of course, and you're no longer wanted men."

"Me too?" I ask.

"Yes, of course."

"Oh thank god. I can go back to work."

The room goes silent and every pair of eyes lands on me.

"That was a joke, right?" Colt asks.

"Not even a little," I say before taking a sip of my coffee. "I've been stuck either in the safe house, in this mansion, or in the cabin for almost four months. I need to get out of here. I need to do *something* with my time even if it's not escorting."

"What if I made you a deal?" Archer asks.

"I already owe you my first born. What more could you possibly want?"

"Not that kind of deal. I just mean, I'll accept you going back to stripping as long as you do it for private parties only, let me set the prices, and let me provide security. Niall here can be your bodyguard."

"No!" Niall and I say, simultaneously.

"Ew," Niall says, pretending to gag.

"Yeah, no thanks," I say with a laugh. "It would be like stripping for my brother...if I had one."

"Fine, I'll find someone else. Do those terms work for you?"

I mull it over for a few seconds. "Fine. I'll agree to it. But I get to work as much as I want."

"You also have to stop once you get pregnant."

"Fine," I grumble.

"Now give me your birth control," Archer demands, holding his hand out.

"Right now?"

"Right now. It's been two weeks since your ascension, you're in therapy, I'm allowing you to keep working. Give me the pills."

Several weeks pass, and truthfully, I should have been stripping for private parties a long time ago. The income is much better, and I have regulars who hire me a couple of times a month. Archer lets me keep all of the money I make so that I can feel as though I'm making my own way, but I know that if I quit right now, he would fully support me.

Sully and Campbell have found private security jobs. Archer has tried to tell all the guys that they don't need to work, but they're in the same boat I'm in. They've been working their whole lives and want to continue providing for themselves.

I'm sitting in the bedroom on our new bed registering for classes when the door slams open, and Archer and Cobra come inside and lock the door.

"I'm busy," I say, and go back to choosing my classes.

"You're fertile," Archer growls. "And I'm locking you in here until you're not anymore so that the fucking panther can't impregnate you."

"Really?" I ask. My stomach lurches, at the same time that heat coils inside of me. I knew it was coming, but I didn't realize it would be this soon. "What about school? I already had it delayed a semester."

"We'll work through it. Now take your fucking clothes off."

Archer and Cobra start stripping. Archer helps Cobra out of his shirt, and rips his pants down.

Cobra places his hand on Archer's chest and says, "Easy big guy. Deep breaths."

The feral look in Archer's eyes registers in my brain. He's barely hanging on by a thread. I shift onto my knees, and his eyes snap in my direction. In three huge strides he crosses the room and chucks my laptop across the floor, ripping the charging cable from the wall.

"Why are you still clothed?" he snarls, crawling onto the bed, and grabbing me by the throat. "I told you to get naked. You're so disobedient sometimes."

He slams me back on the bed and rips my sundress off of me. He grumbles in appreciation at my nearly naked form. He slips his own pants off, leaving his belt on the bed, and pulls my underwear down. Cobra comes and sits at the head of the bed. A roar tears through Archer's throat, directed at Cobra.

"I'm just here to make sure things don't get out of hand," Cobra insists, holding his hands up in front of him.

That seems to appease Archer who buries his face in my pussy, and inhales deeply. "That is the sweetest thing I've ever smelled in my life," he says, and shoves his long forked tongue inside of me.

"Fuck!" I cry out as he twirls his tongue inside of me.

Cobra strokes my hair. It's so gentle and sweet, and is such a stark difference from the way Archer is behaving. It takes no time at all before I'm coming around Archer's tongue, holding onto his horns and grinding my core against his face.

He pulls away and flips me over onto my stomach, before lifting my hips into the air and slamming inside of me. I grasp the sheet in my fists and scream as he fucks me, like he's daring my body not to accept the gift he's giving me.

He grabs a fist full of my hair and wrenches my head back. "Look at Cobra. Watch him while you come for me, Little Star. Then I'm going to knot you and fill you up, and we're going to stay locked in here for the next three days to make sure that none of the others can give you their seed."

Cobra gives me an apologetic look, and casually strokes himself. Archer's tail slips around to my front and presses to my clit as his tentacle probes my ass. Cobra comes all over his stomach. I clamp down around Archer as he shoves his knot inside of me, and roars.

It's terrifying, and painful, and so fucking hot.

Archer wraps his arms around me and maneuvers us so we're laying on our sides.

Cobra lays down in front of us and smiles. "I feel good about this. I think it'll take. And then we'll have a sweet little bundle of joy to cuddle and love." He kisses me softly on the lips, and Archer nibbles on my neck.

Frantic pounding at the door followed by Colt's shouts of annoyance filter through our post sex haze.

"Go away!" Archer yells.

"Let me in!" Colt shouts.

"You can have her in nine months!" Cobra yells back. "Bring us some snacks!"

Cursing followed by stomping footsteps tell me he's going to do just that. Because even if he's not getting his way, he still wants to make sure we're taken care of.

Two weeks later we're all asleep in the bed together after a night of group sex and watching movies. Archer has been extremely possessive of me since our mating, so he claims spooning me every night after sex.

A strange magical disturbance causes me to sit up in bed. It's as if a magical zip tie has been cut off of me. Archer sits up as well.

"It took. You're pregnant."

"What?" I ask in shock. "How could you possibly know that?"

"You fulfilled your end of the bargain. The deal is complete and our contractual binding is dissolved."

"We're still mated though, right?" I ask, panic washing through me.

"Yes, of course, silly girl," he says and kisses me. "Even if we weren't you'll always be mine."

I sigh in relief and place a hand on my belly.

"What's going on?" Colt grumbles next to me, rubbing the sleep from his eyes.

"Jinx is pregnant," Archer says with a bright smile. "We're having a baby."

Dawn of the Zodiacs Series

Capricorn Blessed by Rachelle Bonifay
Pisces Blessed by Remy Cavilich
Aquarius Blessed by Georgina Stancer
Cancer Blessed by Aisling Elizabeth
Leo Blessed by S Lucas
Virgo Blessed by Ella J. Smyth
Libra Blessed by KD Fraser
Scorpio Blessed by Mia Davis
Sagittarius Blessed by Charli Rahe
Aries Blessed by Kat Blak
Gemini Blessed by Nova Blake
Taurus Blessed by Mia Davis

Feed the Author

One of the easiest (and free-est?) ways that you can help out any author that you love is by leaving a review. Reviews are not for the author, but for other readers to know what to expect, and what you loved about the book. Please, if you enjoyed Libra Blessed (or even if you didn't), please **share your thoughts** for others to see.

If you would like to know what I'm up to, and what I have planned next, you can always join my **Facebook Group**. I post new ARC opportunities there, along with polls, and information about merch.

I am my most ridiculous authentic self on **TikTok**. Follow me there for lives, random videos, and updates on new ARCs and future releases.

If you have a couple of dollars to spare, and enjoy exclusive content such as early access, or bonus chapters please consider joining my **Patreon**.

Also by

Bound By Chance is book one of the Fate Bound Saga. It's a dark, why choose, fantasy romance with 5+ mates, and one plus sized, thirty something FMC.

There is MM intimacy within the harem, and bullying from one of the guys along with some dubious consent. The series will be completed by the end of 2024

Blurb:
Secrets are being kept, but does the truth really set you free?
Until my early twenties, my life had been one tragic event after another. Which is why I was content with the mundane life I had with my fiancé, Todd.
That is until two insanely hot strangers showed up, and told me he had been lying to me for the last ten years.
Oh. They also kidnapped me and whisked me away to a different realm as payback for past sins of my soon-to-be ex.
Now I'm a prisoner in a world full of magic I didn't know existed with five (no, make that six) gorgeous guys following me around and growling at anyone who tries to talk to me. Meanwhile the fae of this kingdom keep getting abducted, and I may be the key to saving them.
Lucky me.

***

Once Upon a Krampus is a sweet and spicy monster novella featuring Krampus unlike you've ever seen him.

Blurb:
I was alone in the world, and alone in my house in the woods. My husband had passed, leaving me to tend to our dream home by myself.

Then one day he showed up. The tales were real. Krampus was real. And he was in my home, sharing my meals, and my bed.

***

Frosted Nightmares is a dark, why choose, monster novella. It's short and spicy. A perfect filler between major series.

Blurb:

My boyfriend Doug and I just broke up, and I was looking forward to focusing on graduation. Then an old friend showed up and stole me away and held me hostage until a mutual friend of ours agreed to help him. Can I convince them to put their differences aside and work together for the greater good?

***

Nocturnal Valentines is a dark, stalker, shifter, why choose romance.

Blurb:

My two best friends and I are more like brothers. We're also con men. As shifters, we've always found it easy to pull one over on the humans, so that's how we survive. Every week we do the same things, and every week it goes the same way. Until one night, it doesn't.

Eloise thinks she's home safe in her bed, but her quaint little ranch style home cannot keep her safe from me--not once I decide that she belongs to me.

NOTE: This is an MMMF shifter romance with instalove and MM elements (though no on page intimacy between the MMCs). It is a fast paced novella that takes place over the course of a few very short, very intense days. If instalove is not your thing, I suggest skipping this one.

Made in the USA
Columbia, SC
13 October 2024